FOR
Love
OF
FAMILY

In *For Love of Family*, Terri Neunaber Bentley offers readers a rich, immersive setting with well developed, lovable characters.

Greta Picklesimer

Author of the *Love in the Kentucky Hills* series

TERRI NEUNABER BENTLEY

FOR
Love
OF
FAMILY

IN A LAND SO STRANGE   BOOK ONE

AMBASSADOR INTERNATIONAL
GREENVILLE, SOUTH CAROLINA & BELFAST, NORTHERN IRELAND

www.ambassador-international.com

For *Love* of Family

Paperback ISBN: 978-1-64960-380-7

eISBN: 978-1-64960-384-5

Cover design by Hannah Linder Designs

Interior Typesetting by Dentelle Design

Edited by Martin Wiles

Scripture taken from The Holy Bible, English Standard Version. ESV® Text Edition: 2016. Copyright © 2001 by Crossway Bibles, a publishing ministry of Good News Publishers.

AMBASSADOR INTERNATIONAL

Emerald House

411 University Ridge, Suite B14

Greenville, SC 29601

United States

www.ambassador-international.com

AMBASSADOR BOOKS

The Mount

2 Woodstock Link

Belfast, BT6 8DD

Northern Ireland, United Kingdom

www.ambassadormedia.co.uk

The colophon is a trademark of Ambassador, a Christian publishing company.

To my husband Dale,

who never tired of my sending him out to work on his car so I could write.

Dear Reader,

In the decade leading up to the American Civil War, over two million European immigrants flooded to America for a better life. The land of opportunity was not what many of them expected. The alarming practice of slavery and hard times away from family and the familiar awaited them. In this story, slavery is part of the backdrop of the immigrants' reality when coming to America. The plight of the abolitionist's moral duty to right the wrongs of the slave trade are also addressed. I hope that it inspires you to right the wrongs you encounter in your world as well and to treat all people with love and respect.

Prologue

erman Neubauer had ached to leave his homeland more than the rest of his family. He read the volumes of American ideologies that his brother Martin hauled home from the library. Reading James Fenimore Cooper's trilogy of *Bravo, The Heidemauer,* and *The Headsman* began Herman's serious dreaming about America. He quoted passages about the adventures outside his small town. He insisted the American way of living gave the ordinary person far more freedom than the European aristocracy. Other works by Cooper held less ideological adages but examined the American wilderness like *The Last of the Mohicans* and *The Pioneers.* Herman devoured these books and taught his younger brother Thomas about the American Indians. Eventually, Thomas pretended to hunt like the Mohican, and every conversation centered around Herman going to America.

But Herman did not have his eyes set on an adventure on his own. He convinced Katarina Neufeldt to accompany him on this great adventure. Everyone knew Katarina was smitten with Herman. For months, she batted her eyes at him whenever she saw him at church or in town. Herman finally got the hint and began courting her. Of course, Katarina's papa insisted they marry before he would allow his only daughter to go away with Herman.

The whole family contributed to the wedding preparations. Sister Heidi redesigned Katarina's pink, floral dress, adding strips of flowery Guipure lace her father had imported from Italy. The whimsical lace fluttered in the breeze as she floated toward her groom. The added layers of the skirt flounced beneath the hemline with each step.

Sister Eva baked them a delicious white cake, dotted with dainty, jeweled Edelweiss petals cascading over it. Young Thomas, who loved to hunt, supplied the venison for the feast, and Momma roasted it to savory perfection. During the ceremony, his youngest sister Maria perfectly sang Martin Luther's hymn "Our Father, Who From Heaven Above." And his sister Lena busied herself by helping Katarina with anything she needed.

As soon as the wedding was over, Herman and Katarina left for their new life in America. Several months after setting foot on American soil, they wrote home to their families that they had become parents and that they had purchased farmland in southern Illinois, where other Germans were settled.

Herman wrote that other German Lutherans had traveled from Bremen together, and they had found fertile lands up the Mississippi River near a flowing stream. The next letter, which arrived several more months later, said that he, Katarina, and little Hans were happy—and a new baby was on the way.

But as much as Herman and Katarina wrote about their love for their new home and their growing family, eventually Herman sent home a letter with disturbing news.

Momma and Papa,

The farm is producing more corn and wheat than you ever saw in Germany. And Americans eat corn as much as their animals, so profits are excellent with this crop.

But I must send distressing news. My darling Katarina died while birthing our daughter, Hannah. Little Hans and the new baby are well, but I need help. I cannot run the demands of the expanding farm and tend to two babes in diapers. Frau Greta Stolz, the butcher's wife, helps me as much as she can, but I cannot expect her to raise my children indefinitely.

I want you to send Lena to me. She has always been good with the little ones. I will pay for her passage and look after her here in America. Your last letter indicated you had no marriage match for her yet, even though she will be eighteen soon. If Lena is free to come to my aid, I think she will like our German community here in America. I seldom need to know English in the village circles of trade, and the church services are German, too.

I am enclosing all the information she will need to find me in America.

Please send her soon.

Your Loving Son,
Herman

CHAPTER 1

Cast Upon the Waters

"Cast your bread upon the waters, for you will find it after many days.
Give a portion to seven, or even to eight, for you know not what
disaster may happen on earth."

Ecclesiastes 11:1-2

1857

OLBERS IMMIGRANT SHIP
CROSSING THE ATLANTIC FROM GERMANY TO THE U.S.

"Thomas! Thomas!" A distressed father dashed away from his young family in search of his wayward son. The escaped child weaved through steerage passengers like a skilled athlete through an obstacle course. The scamp, no longer visible in the dark recesses of the ship's hull, sent a frantic father's volume reverberating off the ship's low rafters. Heads turned, and tongues wagged at the intrusion. Since the *Olbers* originated in Bremen, most passengers and deckhands spoke German.

"Can't control the kinder."

"Can't we have some quiet down here?"

"Quit all the ruckus."

I roused from the berth where I lay reading my morning Scripture. Ironically, "Be still and know that I am God"[1] leaped from the open pages in my lap. *Still?* The ship fought another turbulent wave as I grasped my Bible tighter before it flew to the floor.

You cannot be serious, Lord! This ocean voyage is anything but still.

I looked upon the congregating souls in homespun dresses and ill-fitting jackets holding nearby beams to keep their balance as the shipped bounced. All talked over one another.

"You hear they have a Know Nothing party that do not like us immigrants coming to America?"

"Don't worry. Many others have come here before us."

"There is a new president, too."

"Ja, Buchannan," another added. "If we don't settle in the cities, they shouldn't bother us."

"We have family in America. We'll be fine."

The sought-after child, presumably young Thomas, appeared at my feet as I swung my toes over to touch the floor. He retrieved his red-and-blue-painted wooden top from beneath my bed-rumpled skirts. Blond curls curtained his big, blue eyes staring up at me.

"*Guten tag,*" I greeted him. He clasped his prize toy tighter to his chest without a word. "Are you Thomas? I hear someone looking for you." An almost imperceptible nod escaped him. "Is that your papa looking for you?" Without waiting for his acknowledgment, I asked, "Can I walk you back to your family, so they don't worry?"

The lad glanced across the cavernous living quarters that accommodated about 150 travelers. Most adults were up stretching their legs in the daytime and visiting with fellow shipmates of

---

1   Psalm 46:10

this two-month voyage. Although most appeared friendly, I had stayed to myself up to this point, too cowardly to mingle outside my corner of the ship. Young Thomas was my first visitor in the weeks I had hibernated away from the others. My voice was almost unrecognizable to me as I spoke to him. He stepped back from this strange woman as I cleared my throat.

Young Thomas' family bunked several stalls away from mine. I had noticed them across the way. However, Thomas' statue held no vantage point for him to see them since, at his height, he stared into a man's waistband. Panic clouded his eyes as he realized he had chased his spinning toy top far away from his family. How could he return to them on his own when one berth resembled another in this sea of people? The surrounding ocean of legs blocked his path back to his family. He looked up at me and squeaked a timid, *"Bitte."*

I took the lad's hand and squeezed it gently before bumping through the gossiping crowds as the wood planks swayed under us. I grasped a nearby beam to steady us as another wave shifted our footing, but no one parted for us as I towed the frightened child behind me. Caught up in their own impatient, unsteady idleness, their irritable voices barked at each other over minor inconveniences in the confined space.

Many of the children, cooped up for too long on a rough sea, were sick. The smell of vomit reeked below deck, and fresh sea air above beckoned folks upward whenever the sea did not threaten to make them fish bait or the sailors did not insist that the passengers impeded their work. No one below knew a top sail from a main sail or what should be done with either of them during a storm.

As we approached Thomas' family, a sweating, disheveled father rose and nearly yanked the young man from my grasp. "Where did you go? Don't you know how sick your *bruder* is? I can't go chasing after you."

A smaller version of Thomas was perspiring beneath the covers on the bunk where his momma dabbed his cherub face with a damp cloth while two other tots cowered in the corner of the berth. A boy nearer to Thomas' age sat sucking his thumb, and a baby girl crawled near him in a sagging diaper.

Their father shifted his attention to me. "Sorry for your trouble."

His hand still on the boy's arm, he drew Thomas to his mother's side. The distraught woman briefly acknowledged Thomas as her sleep-deprived eyes rose to meet him; then, without a word, she returned her concern to her feverish son on the cot.

The cowering, healthy tots on the bed moved to get a better look at me and asked, "Is Tom in trubba?" The thumb-sucker tried to mimic his father's words about the *trouble* his older brother was causing.

Their mother snapped, "Do ya see a switching shed here? Do you? Sit quietly so Otto can get better. How can he rest with you *kindern* making such a fuss? Now quiet!"

The harried woman went back to dabbing the sick boy's face with a soiled, damp cloth; he was so pale. He only groaned during her efforts to comfort him.

"How about I take the *kindern* off your hands for a while, so you can attend to young Otto? I can see you need to devote all your attention to him right now. Little ones have such a hard time staying still when they are young." I nodded to the sweet imps still huddled on the bed.

Thomas' father shifted his feet and puzzled over my offer.

"I don't mean to be so forward. I should introduce myself first—Magdalena Neubauer." I thrust my hand out to shake the father's hand. "I have five younger siblings, and I have been watching little ones my whole life. I can take them to my berth. I have stories I can read to them. I brought a copy of *Grimms' Fairy Tales* with me. I love reading to children, and I'm missing my family anyway."

The father hesitantly extended his hand to reach mine as he sized me up and down. "Krueger. The name is Krueger. It is so kind of you to offer to help, Fraulein Neubauer."

He sought his wife's permission with his eyes on allowing me to whisk away her children, although there was no place to take the children away from the ship if I even had a mind to do so. I prayed they would allow me to keep the children for a little while. Growing up surrounded by family, I missed them. My mind wandered to such worrisome places when left alone without a task to keep it busy. Although Peter says to "[cast] all your anxieties on him, because he cares for you,"[2] I cannot help myself on such a long journey. *They do not know me, Lord. Help me explain myself.*

"Everyone calls me Lena. I am meeting my brother in America. I am sure the good Lord directed young Thomas to me to help relieve some of my homesickness. I am happy to help you."

"I suppose that will be fine." Krueger glanced at his children, looking curiously at the woman who had returned their big brother. "If they get to be too much, bring them back over here. You have no idea how much this means."

Both husband and wife took deep breaths of resignation. Young Otto stirred again, and the worried parents returned their focus to their failing son. Herr Krueger scooted his healthy tots to the edge of the bed to release them into my care.

"I am honored to help." I nudged the children toward me. "Thomas, you can bring your toy top if you want. And who is this?"

The thumb-sucking brother grabbed Thomas' hand and cowered into his gingham-checked shirt. His little suspenders hung loosely on his shoulders, and his father straightened them for him as he slid from the bed to the shifting wood floor.

"This is Tobias and my sister Stella."

Thomas became emboldened around his family and took on the role of the dutiful big brother. Father Krueger lifted baby Stella and gently placed her in my arms. She clung to her father's shirt sleeve, twisting her dusty rose pinafore in a knot as she reached for her papa and teared up. The embroidered daisies on her little dress must have indicated how happy her momma was to give birth to a girl amongst her brood of boys. The doll-face girl buried her golden locks into her father's work shirt.

"It's all right, Stella. Auntie Lena has you now. We are going to go have fun on my bed over there. Do you have a dolly?" Taking her from her father's arms, I gave her a little squeeze and tried to point out our destination across the open passage.

I jostled the child to lighten her mood, and at the mention of a doll, Krueger produced one from behind the blankets. "There you are."

Stella grabbed the rag doll with yellow yarn hair similar to her own and large, blue button eyes. The lovable doll wore a dress like Stella's and was likely made from the remnants of her frock. She squeezed the doll tightly, straining the stitching of her fearless companion.

"She calls it Dotty. I think she is trying to say Dolly but can't say her L's yet." Krueger shrugged. "We really do appreciate your generosity . . . eh, Lena."

He tried the informal address for me when proper etiquette dictated a more formal greeting with a new acquaintance. I smiled at the acceptance of his trust and children as I repositioned little Stella on my hip.

Thomas clasped Tobias' hand and stood straighter as if to await marching orders from a commanding general. Then, ready to battle the forest of legs between his family and my berth, he braced himself. He confidently guided his younger brother through the moving jungle of legs as I maneuvered our small band ahead.

Babe in arms and two young boys in tow, I bumbled through the still-standing masses to my corner. "Excuse me. Excuse me." I apologized every couple of steps to open a path for our party of four to pass.

The repositioning of the gossiping trees did not part easily in the confines of the *Olbers'* hull. The movement did not disturb their chatter in the least.

"Where are you taking that brood?"

"No room for them to play over here, fraulein."

Although others hurled random comments our way, I smiled and kept walking until reaching my destination. There, I could sit little Stella down and help her brothers onto my bed.

I pulled out my copy of *Grimms' Fairy Tales.* "Do you know any of these stories?"

I held the book out so Thomas could leaf through the pages. Not sure if Thomas was old enough to read, I waited to see if he could tell me about any titles in the Table of Contents. He flipped through more pages as Tobias leaned in to capture a look. The block print pictures caught his attention, and he wanted to see them better. Stella watched her brothers monopolize the book as she happily held Dolly.

"Oh, I want the 'Frog King.'" Thomas pointed at the title in the Table of Contents after Tobias relented his hold on a page with a picture of a girl with long hair in a tower.

"It looks like you can read. What a smart boy! Gather in. 'Frog King' it is." The boys settled in between me and the wall in anticipation of the story, and Stella snuggled under my arm, holding Dolly with one hand and firmly affixing a thumb between her pursed lips.

Eyes wide with excitement, the boys searched the book as I began the story. "Once upon a time, long before the prince and princess rode away in the carriage . . . "

First, Stella fell sound asleep, sucking away. Soon after, the lulling of the ship rocked us all to sleep.

I awoke to three children nestled around me as I was tucked aboard the *Olbers* and bound for New Orleans. Rows of bunks lined the hull of the ship. Families had no partitions for privacy. One group blended into the next. These little waifs surrounding me reminded me of the loved ones I had left behind.

My sister Heidi was a talented seamstress. Everything she touched blossomed into a masterpiece of fashion. I now regretted declining her offer to help me complete my amateurish sewing. I was older, after all. It did not seem right to have my younger sister correct my sewing mistakes. To swallow my pride was difficult. As the oldest sister, I should be better at things than my siblings back home. I know the apostle Peter said to clothe ourselves in humility,[3] and my lack of talents certainly did that! What a fool I was. Now, I was shipped a world away and likely would never see her again. I should have cherished our time together more.

---

3   Colossians 3:12

Everyone in my family was blessed with more God-given talents than I. It was probably easier for my parents to send me away and keep the talented children at home. I was not the most attractive either. My mousy brown hair lay incongruent with my three sisters' long, blonde locks; and my cloudy blue-gray eyes did not shine like their bright sky-blue orbs. I could neither dance nor sing with any grace either.

No wonder no suitor was pounding on my papa's door, asking to court me. My sisters would be of age soon, and I was sure the boys would chase them around the schoolyard before long. Papa need not worry about finding me a match, since I would be far away. He could see to the fortunes of the rest of his children. Not that I had done anything to disgrace my family. I merely possessed no special talent to brag about like the others.

My brother Martin was a young scholar, destined for the university. He completed his chores in a cursory fashion before pawing through his beckoning textbooks of history, biology, and mathematics. He began reading at age four, and books became his closest friends. Martin hid in the loft with a book under his nose and a blanket over his head, escaping family scrutiny as often as possible.

Sister Eva could bake the most delicious strudel by the time she was old enough to reach the kitchen counters. She delighted in wearing a flour-caked apron and mixing savory and sweet concoctions that filled the house with the most delicious aromas. Whenever an occasion called for a special dessert, Eva volunteered to supply the kuchen. I remember the smudge of flour on her face under those sparkling blue eyes and her blonde braids swinging down her back as she danced through her kitchen ministrations.

My younger brother Thomas had established himself as a successful hunter by age ten. He often supplied the table with meat from the nearby Saxon forests. Because of his skill, the Neubauer table did not go without when many other tables in our area suffered. We often shared our table's bounty because of Thomas' and Eva's skills. Their contributions to family and friends far outweighed my own.

Even my youngest sibling, Maria, sang better than the mountain birds. Many churchgoers sat near our family pew to listen to her voice. "Maria, the little angel," they would say. Of course, at home, we knew she was not always an angel. The little trickster would hide Eva's baking supplies or Martin's books just to aggravate them. She never meant real harm to anyone, and she repented of her deeds with a quick "God bless" and a handful of field flowers as soon as someone discovered her misdeeds. Her dimples alone melted hearts, so no one minded her mischief too much.

If only I did not miss them all so much. Momma and Papa took such good care of us all. I could have stayed there forever. Only my older brother Herman was anxious to leave our idyllic Saxon home. Tall and strong-willed, he complained of too many people in our small house. "You can't take a step around here without stepping on someone." He slept in the loft with Martin and Thomas, which cramped his long frame. "I need some space for myself."

We four girls shared the other room. With nighttime secrets and giggles, we slept more content with the closeness. Maria jumped in beside whomever suited her fancy each night and snuggled under the quilt of any available sister.

A familiar warmth accompanied the companionship of the loft. The comforters spread over the sisterly bond that kept us warm. If a wayward foot kicked us in our slumber or a pillow dislodged to a drooling sister, the whispered familiarity of secrets and sisterhood refreshed our sense of contentment with the world each day.

Herman had taken his lovely Katarina and boarded the *Olbers* in Bremen almost three years ago, and he had never returned. He had paid fifty dollars for his forty acres and worked day and night for months before leaving home to earn enough money for their passage and the grubstake. Katarina had held fast to Herman and glowed as they departed our little town, but I wondered if her happiness had lasted into her new life in America. However, her world was Herman, and it had not mattered where they lived as long as she lived with him.

Why had I been shipped off to another country at my brother's request? Just because I had no marriage prospects and worked well with children? Oh, poor Katarina. I felt she would have rather stayed in Germany herself if my brother had not been so headstrong about America. Now, two babies needed someone to care for them. Maria was old enough for school now, so Momma did not need me as much at home with Heidi and the others to help her. It made sense for me to go help my brother in a new land. The Lord had given me the talent to watch after little ones, and here was His call for me to use my gift again. I sighed with the weight of the life planned for me as the three waifs sleeping in my berth began to stir.

And then, across the way, I heard weeping. I held them each tighter as I realized that their brother, little Otto, had died.

CHAPTER 2

Stranger in a Strange Land

"How shall we sing the Lord's song in a foreign land?"

Psalm 137:4

Weeks had gone by since we had buried the little one at sea. The days stretched on with no end in sight, and many more had fallen sick in the damp, drafty conditions.

One morning, before the sun had even risen, I was awakened by Thomas' shouts. "Lena, Lena!" He and his remaining siblings visited my berth daily for more stories but never as the sun was rising.

"Oh goodness, Thomas. What is all the fuss about?"

He grabbed my hand and tugged me to my feet from my bunk. I shook the fuzzy dreams of Herman and Katarina from my head and focused on the scene before me. All the steerage travelers were organizing their belongings. Folded blankets were placed in sacks with precious clothing. Cases latched around beloved books and heirlooms.

"We're here, Lena!"

"Here?"

"Ja, 'Merica."

Thomas jumped up and down with all the enthusiasm of a pent-up monkey. Sixty-four days aboard the *Olbers*, and everyone itched to stretch their legs off the swaying temporary home. The children squealed at the new sights and smells of a sprawling city before them on the shoreline. The relentless October seas had cost six children their lives on the voyage. No parent begrudged the overexcited ones they still held close. The blessing everyone had prayed for on those long, sleepless nights aboard the tossing waves had finally arrived as their feet yearned to touch solid ground again.

I slipped into line with all the other departing travelers and hauled my meager belongings on deck. Our sister ship, *Ernestine*, traveled from Bremen alongside the *Olbers*. We had sighted her several times on the high seas, but she was now docked nearby, alongside many barges, steamships, and passenger liners that waited for their next destination away from the New Orleans Bay.

The ocean-going vessels like the *Olbers* dodged the Mississippi River paddle wheelers, merchant ships, and fishing boats as they vied for the same passageways. Their system to keep from crashing into one another baffled me. A passing barge nearly swallowed a small fishing boat near the mouth of the river. The shouting from the fishermen was drowned out by the horn blasts of the larger vessel.

"I have no idea how they do not end up in one big heap at the mouth of the river," I whispered as I shook my head.

Thomas had scampered off to sound the alarm of our impending escape from the confines of our sea home, so no one responded. The docks themselves swirled with more activity than those in Bremen. Burly black men guided overloaded carts of freight of every size and shape. Receiving dock workers unloaded the wares onto the pier at a steady rhythmic pace. The grimy men sweated under their burdens, placing cargo ashore and reloading ships for future voyages.

In Germany, I never realized such a mix of people existed together in one place. Unaware the Lord created people in so many colors, my imagination had failed to conjure up this cacophony of Spanish, African, Caribbean, Native American, French, or other European cultures together in one place from any books I had read. In fact, the whole city radiated with a swirl of vibrant colors, languages, and odd dress. Some traditional European attire blended into the mosaic of life ashore, while some women wore colorful blouses that draped past their shoulders and barely covered their bosoms. Their loose skirts swirled around their bare feet as they sold bright delicacies in a nearby fruit market.

Many men worked shirtless, exposing broad chests and strong arms as they strained to move cargo. I glanced away. Was it right to gawk at such a view? My brothers always wore their shirts when they labored with heavy chores, whether it was warm or not. How could these workers dress so immodestly? The season was late autumn, but the air was warm and damp. My own clothing chafed as the morning sun rose overhead, but I would never strip down to reveal so much of myself in public as the sleeveless women on the docks did.

I had practiced some English before arriving in America, but my rudimentary schooling resulted in poor language skills. Beyond hello, I could only count in English and recite a few colors and directions. I had tried to listen to the sailors on our ship to improve my skills on the voyage, but many of them spoke German to the passengers or used other European languages. Most of the sailors did not hail from America or England, so listening to them did not improve my English.

However, the language I heard on the docks did not sound like the English I had studied at home. Did I land in the right country?

This was not what I thought America would be like at all. Herman had written nothing about such a fascinating but confusing place. In fact, his letter reported that he lived near a German-speaking village.

A deckhand passed me while I gaped at the scene unfolding on the docks. "Sir, vat language is dat?" I asked in my best English.

"Creole, Miss." He tossed the answer over his shoulder as he prepared the ship for the passengers to disembark.

Creole? I had never heard of Creole. Was that a country? How could anyone navigate here when there were so many new and strange ways? What was Creole, anyway? I thought people spoke English in America.

The sailor glanced back at my puzzled expression and chuckled. "No worries, Miss. It's a mixed language of all the breeds down there. Most of us cain't follow it our own selves. It's a little French, Haitian, Spanish, and who-knows-what-else. If you don't stay in this area, you won't need to worry yourself about learnin' it." He grabbed his coil of rope and moved farther down the deck.

Alarmed at his response, I decided it might be wise to stick with those I could understand. Though, would those who disembark with me be more aware than I was? What had Papa said about the blind leading the blind? I thought I had better trust Herman's instructions and follow them the best I could without trusting any lost shipmates.

Lord, please help me arrive at Herman's door safely.

The skiff ferried passengers to shore a dozen at a time. Once deposited on the dock, the ship's captain relinquished the passenger list to the U.S. officials, who had to account for all immigrants.

Luckily, I was young and healthy and possessed the proper papers—the sort of newcomer they wanted in this country—nevertheless, I still feared something could go wrong. What if my documents were not in order? What if I answered a question wrong because I did not understand? What if . . . what if?

Lord, take my "what if" away and help me.

From the crowd, a plump, kind-looking woman approached me. She was dressed smartly in German peasant browns and flashed twinkling blue eyes behind wise wrinkles and generous girth. This graying, matronly woman bounced the wood planks as she approached in her determined gait. She walked up to me, and I towered over her at least six inches.

"Mädchen?"

"Ja?" I did not expect to have someone speaking German approach me in America.

"Young miss, are you traveling alone?" The businesslike woman held a small journal and jotted occasional notes as she spoke. She sported a welcoming smile that stirred an immediate kinship to the German newcomers.

I did not hesitate to answer. "I am by myself, but I am to meet my *bruder* up the big river, Miss-i-ssip-i."

I struggled with the odd English word Herman had written in his instructions. I searched for his letter among my papers to show this kind woman what I was trying to tell her.

"Oh, dear girl, I am Olga Oldendorf from the *Deutsche Gesellschaft* here in New Orleans. I can help you get to your brother. Many Germans travel up the Mississippi to settle in the plains. I am here to help German immigrants as they arrive. Your name, lass?"

"Magdalena Neubauer. Everyone calls me Lena. Do I need all these papers now?"

Nervously, I juggled my folded documents from my satchel while trying to hold my bulging carpet bag.

Frau Oldendorf took my paper bundle and sorted out the necessities for port authorities. I had no idea there would be a welcoming party of sorts. I instantly felt at ease with this woman. She was a real-life answer to prayer. The Lord had sent me an angel to personally accompany me through the immigration process and translate any uncertain questions. She also told me how to answer some of the more obscure ones, so I moved along quicker than the young families and single men.

Handing back my approved papers, Frau Oldendorf said, "You get all your documents organized, and I will check the steamboat schedules for you, my dear." Frau Oldendorf disappeared for a few moments while I watched the Krueger family go through the immigration process across the auditorium. They had to explain the death of Otto for the change in family numbers, and it broke my heart to see Frau Krueger relive her grief.

"The steamer, the *Diana,* will be leaving in two days for upriver. I booked your passage on it. So, you should see your *bruder* next week. How does that sound?"

Startled by Frau Oldendorf's sudden return from behind me as I watched the Kruegers, I saw her holding a ticket for me. Tears welled up in my eyes before I impulsively hugged this woman who had been a stranger only hours before.

"*Danke,* Frau Oldendorf. I am so happy you found me. I would be so lost here. You are my angel."

"Oh, no angel, dear. I just know how hard it is to be a stranger in a new place. It is my pleasure, young fraulein. Now, grab your things and follow me. We will make sure you have a proper place to stay until you board the steamer the day after tomorrow."

The world of opportunists waited for the new arrivals on the docks. Men waved bold-typed flyers in arrivals' faces, offering to help them find a place to live and work, as well as a place to buy most anything at inflated prices. The loud, barking advertisements in many languages assaulted my ears. One waved a flyer in my face offering a place to stay. Another grabbed my elbow and tried to turn me to his establishment for "young ladies." I realized I would have been at their mercy if not for the assistance of Frau Oldendorf and the German Society. She led me through the throng with ease until we erupted beyond them. Indeed, the German Society answered the newcomer's prayers for assistance.

As I gawked at the busy New Orleans street life all around me, I escaped the chaos of the docks for more chaos of the city. A smartly dressed man in an evening coat and top hat careened through the middle of the street on an ornate enclosed carriage. The glass enclosure housed two men who looked like they would be comfortable in a board room or a government state room. Their necks were draped in silk cravats and their beaver hats reflected a sheen of a fresh brushing. The driver flipped his horse whip high over his head to strike a black man pushing a freight cart for not moving out of his way fast enough on the street.

Watching the scene before me, I lost my own footing and almost tumbled off the boardwalk into the street, where the rapid carriage approached. Dropping my bundle, I squeaked a gasp as I realized I was being lifted off my feet and placed back on the walkway next to my new German shepherdess. I had narrowly missed the whip's backswing after it struck the man in the street squarely on his back. Frau Oldendorf grabbed my arm to steady me as I recovered from the ordeal. I straightened myself and smoothed my skirt, curious about the strong arms that had moved me out of harm's way. A flash of a green jacket vanished around the corner before I could get a thorough look at him.

The carriage had sped out of sight in the other direction without a backward glance. The black man simply lowered his head and continued working the docks as if he had not been struck by a horse whip. Nor did he attend to the red welt rising on his bare back.

Frau Oldendorf motioned me closer to her. "Stay close, dear. The streets can be dangerous down here."

She continued her hurried pace as if this was to be expected. My senses stirred at the scenes before me. How could anyone treat another person that way? The area teemed with people; yet no one aided the injured man, nor did they chastise the carriage-driving assaulter. On the other hand, who was the young man who had kept me from harm? Was he so hurried that he could not wait to be thanked or make an acquaintance? Was this how people in America lived? In what kind of place had I landed?

We veered away from the docks and traveled a block or two farther into the city, where a mass of people engulfed us. Men shouted numbers to a yet-unseen platform. Frau Oldendorf took my hand to navigate us through the crowd. We rounded the corner and saw the commotion was a slave auction. I had accompanied Papa to livestock auctions before, but I had never seen an auction like this.

A muscular, black man of about twenty stood on the platform, wearing only an undergarment. Chains that bound his hands hung loosely in front of him. He held his chin high in a defiant stance, looking above the crowd, although everything about his circumstances screamed humiliation. The beak-nosed auctioneer strode over to him and pulled his lips back to show the crowd his teeth, as if he were horseflesh. The victim kept his teeth clinched as long as possible until he was struck to open his mouth wider by a handler who stood behind him. The auctioneer turned him around so everyone could see the muscular strength in his arms, legs, and back.

Nothing in my life had prepared me for such a scene. Shouts of "one hundred" and "125" came from the crowd.

The auctioneer, disappointed in their meager bidding, encouraged them. "C'mon, men. This is a buck in his prime. Think of the field work you will get outta him."

"Looks lak he might be trouble," one voice from the crowd shouted.

"Nothin' a good whippin' won't cure," replied the auctioneer.

"Two hundred!"

"That's better. Who'll make it 250?"

Frau Oldendorf tugged harder on my hand. "Fraulein, you simply must keep walking. You don't want to watch those men and that nasty business."

To the right of the platform, more black men and women waited their turn for auction. A few small children hid in their mother's skirts, trying to escape the shouts of the white men nearby.

"They sell children, too?" I asked my shepherdess.

"Yes. And they split up families. The mothers do not always get sold with the children. Most never know the papas either."

"What kind of country is this?"

"Oh, it is as good a country as you can find, but you will want to stay away from that ugliness, my dear." Frau Oldendorf tugged harder, but I planted myself where I stood, taking in the horrifying scene.

A determined man hopped upon a nearby soapbox and shouted for the crowd's attention. "You should be ashamed. God created man in His image. No one should be a slave to another. Set these people free!"

He said no more because three burly men immediately pulled him down and dragged him behind the platform and out of my sight. In those fleeting seconds, I realized this had been the green jacket of the man who had pulled me to safety moments earlier. Sounds of scuffling and groans ensured he was taking a beating.

"Who is that?"

"Not everyone agrees with the practice of slavery, my dear. As long as there is a profit from it, I don't think anyone will be able to stop it. Most Southern farmers say they cannot run their plantations without slaves. I think it is an ugly way to treat people myself."

"Have you seen that man before? The one in the green jacket who was yelling before he was attacked?"

"I think I've seen him talking to some men at the German Society before. So many new people coming in these days. It is hard to say."

"What was he doing? One person could not stop that auction—so many people."

"They are called abolitionists because they are set on abolishing the slave trade. I say there is nothing they can do. I don't know why they stir up so much trouble, no matter how noble the cause."

"But . . ."

Frau Oldendorf turned away and led me past the crowded auction square to a quieter street. The discussion about the slaves and the foolish, young man who had brought harm to himself ended. Not wanting to disrespect this kindly woman, I kept my questions to myself. I did not know how stopping such a grievous treatment of God's people could be wrong. I thought the young man must be braver than foolish for at least trying—a David against a Goliath. Maybe God would give him victory over tremendous odds, too.

Eventually, Frau Oldendorf guided me to the boarding house. After a meal of brats and fresh vegetables, I tucked myself into a comfortable room for the night. After two months at sea, it seemed strange for my bed not to sway back and forth; but the visions of the New Orleans cruelty would make for a fitful night of sleep as images of the inhumane treatment on the docks haunted my dreams.

I woke with a start, thinking the whip had hit me squarely on the head. I thanked God I was safe, and mulled over how I should thank that young man who had pulled me back from that whip. I supposed I would never have a chance to do that. I would pray for those who were not living safely here in this purported land of freedom.

CHAPTER 3

A City of Refuge

"In you, O Lord, do I take refuge; let me never be put to shame;
in your righteousness deliver me."

Psalm 31:1

With my passage on the *Diana* a day away, I wanted to experience more of this strange city. Both compelled and revolted by the sights and sounds of the day before, I sat at a table in the dining area—a familiar place after dining at the same table for dinner the previous evening— with no idea how to proceed. Should I find a guide among the kind people at the *Deutsche Gesellschaft*? I feared getting lost and not being able to find my way back to my lodgings with so many people speaking that strange language. When Frau Oldendorf had led me to the German hostel, my mind had been elsewhere, and I had not noted landmarks as I should have.

What would Papa think of me, losing my head when I was scarcely off the boat in America? He would tell me I was a silly girl and needed to pay attention to my surroundings, or I may never arrive at Herman's farm.

As we had been walking the day before, Frau Oldendorf had told me that New Orleans was the wealthiest city in America. I wondered what else lay beyond the docks, the slave auction, and my current lodgings. I possessed no money to shop or language to barter, but I wanted to look at the wonders of this new world. I had only one day to explore before leaving the city.

I doubted I could master this Creole language spattered about on the docks. So much of the culture had seemed more French than English. I thought America had been liberated from the British and spoke English, but maybe my history was insufficient. After all, Herman had written that he spoke German to his neighbors.

This country baffled me. I wish I had paid more attention to languages in school. My brother Martin always had his nose in books—reading, researching, and learning. We girls were not encouraged to attend to such things. We tended to the household, occupying our days without all the deep, masculine thinking of the boys. I knew no more French than I did English.

I felt safe among the German-speaking folk who had welcomed us at the ship. I dared not try to venture out on my own and be subject to more abuse by charlatans with flyers or other ne'er-do-wells who may lie in wait for unchaperoned ladies.

Frau Oldendorf appeared from a small kitchen to the side of the dining area. I stared at the apple and cheese she delivered to me on a glass plate.

She read my hesitation as refusing her offer of breakfast and gently scolded me in our native tongue. "Eat, girl. You are practically skin and bones."

The appetizing food churned my stomach as I folded my hands and tried to smile at her.

"*Vas ist los?*" she asked.

How could I tell her what was wrong? Most of my journey was behind me. I was well on my way to my brother. Nothing should be wrong now.

"I hoped to tour a little of the city before I leave again tomorrow. But how can I do that without getting lost? Can you help me?" I asked, relieved to communicate in my native tongue still.

"I think most of the new arrivals are resting up from their time on the ship before heading on the way again. I will ask if anyone is going out. Maybe you can help them with some errands, and then you can see more of the city without getting lost."

"*Danke.* That is kind of you. I want to stretch my legs while I am here after being shut up on the ship for so long. I am happy to help someone with errands."

Frau Oldendorf returned to the kitchen and asked several other volunteers about their plans for the day and whether I could tag along. A white-haired gentleman, donning his plaid cap for outdoors, soon agreed to take me with him on his errands.

He strode over to the table, removed his hat again, and began to speak in German. "*Guten morgen.* I am Bernhardt Schiller. I understand you would like to take in more of our city today. I would be happy to have you accompany me on my errands around the parish."

"*Danke.* I am so grateful. I leave tomorrow and this may be the only time I will be in this city. It is all so strange to me." I rose from my chair and extended my hand.

"Nothing like it anywhere else, fraulein. There is a mix of many cultures and influences. I am glad you are interested in seeing some of it while you are here." He donned his cap and began to steer me toward the door as I pulled my shawl over my shoulders. Looking down at my unfinished breakfast, he added, "Take that with you. You can eat it on the way."

I gathered the sampling of food in my kerchief. As I followed him toward the door, I asked, "Have you lived here long?"

"I arrived about the time of the German coast uprising in 1811."

"There is a German coast here in America?"

He chuckled. "You are not the first German to land in America, my dear. My family came when I was only a boy. We got here just as a large slave revolt broke out. Many black slaves were killed, and the plantation owners stuck the heads on pikes to warn other slaves not to try the same thing."

"How horrible!" I placed my kerchief over my mouth as the bile rose in my throat.

"Yes, sorry. Not the best story to tell a lass like yourself, I suppose. Remember, I was only a boy myself, but I will never forget seeing dose faces, even when my parents tried to keep the sight from us children." Herr Schiller shifted his cap back to reveal more of his blue-gray eyes and nodded at my distress. "Sorry, didn't mean to upset you. That was a long time ago. The *Deutsche Kueste* is upriver a ways. That is where I grew up. My brother inherited the farm, and I came to the city. I found I was a handy watchmaker, and it has served me well."

Happy that he steered the conversation to a different topic, I turned my attention to the shops. We walked and talked for many blocks. He let me gawk in the windows of small shops: tattoo parlors, fancy French-inspired clothing stores, and spicy food restaurants. The shop aromas beckoned customers to stop, but the exotic scents pierced my plain, German, meat-and-potatoes nose.

We drifted along with the aromas until I saw brightly colored candies in a shop window and paused. The neglected apple and cheese in my kerchief did not make my mouth water like these tempting treats. Herr Schiller strode two paces ahead of me before he realized he had lost his charge. He smiled at my distraction and returned to my side.

"These sweets are all made from the sugar grown on local plantations. Come along. I will take you to something you will like up ahead."

We arrived at bustling Rampart Street. It was the hub of business activity for New Orleans. Vendors hawked their wares among crowds of people milling about in the midmorning haze from the nearby bay.

"Pralines! Fine cheese! Fresh pastries!"

"*Wunderbar!*" Herr Schiller added a skip to his step as he zeroed in on one of the vendors. "Eula is here today."

"Eula?"

"*Ja.* She is a Marchand in the parish. We have become friends over the years. You will like her."

Eula's dress was far finer than any I owned—or any I had seen. The shimmering, ivory, satin skirt flared away from her tiny waist and draped over an ample hoop skirt. Accents of roses and blue ribbons laced expertly across her bosom. Her bonnet reflected the newest fashion I had seen displayed in the store windows a few blocks back. The brim fanned out to shade her face smartly with the same ribbon accent matching her skirt and bodice tucked behind her ear.

I turned to Herr Schiller and whispered, "She's black."

He laughed. "Why, yes, she is, dear. The colored population probably outnumbers the whites three to one in New Orleans. Have you not noticed?"

"But she doesn't look like a slave at all." I turned away from her to prevent Eula from hearing my private query to Herr Schiller. "The other black people I've seen are laborers or slaves. She looks like the Southern ladies I've seen riding in fancy carriages."

"Many free people of color live here in New Orleans. The French call them *gens de cauleaur*. Eula is one. She is also a *placée*."

"Pla-say? What is that?"

"It means a white plantation owner keeps her, like a mistress. Eula stays in the city when her man is on the plantation with his white family. He takes care of her and the children's needs here. Home, food, clothes, and so on. She doesn't need to work, but she gets bored when he is gone, and she sells some of her goods on the street when he is away. She is a good businesswoman, that Miss Eula."

Moving close enough for this woman to hear our conversation, Herr Schiller almost shouted his final statement about her businesswoman skills as we approached to be sure she heard him. He took her hand, gently squeezed it, and greeted her with a deep bow and a kiss on the back of her hand.

"*Met Bernhardt. Mwen zanmi.*" She greeted him in the same language I had not understood at the docks. She then turned to me and asked, "*Kiyès nou genyen isit la?*"

I did not know how to respond, so Herr Schiller responded instead. "This is Fraulein Magdalena. She is here for only the day and wanted to see some of our fine city. She heads upriver tomorrow."

"One day is not enough, mademoiselle."

Even though she tried to address me in English, my limited command of the language and her thick Haitian accent dissolved the words into a swamp of vowels I could not untangle.

"Pardon. My English . . . not so *gut*."

I shook my head and pleaded for Her Schiller to rescue the situation with a shrug and upturned hands.

"I am showing her what I can, Eula. We have walked by a number of the shops on the way here, and I showed her Our Lady of Guadalupe Chapel. The cemetery is up the block there."

"No, no. A young one must listen to the music and sample the sweets." She dropped a sugary glob wrapped in brown paper into my hand. "Praline," she called it. "You will lak."

Mixed in the tan sugar confection were nuts. The sweetness danced on my tongue as I let the sugar dissolve into the recesses of my mouth. "Umm."

I closed my eyes and all sounds wafted away as I enjoyed this tantalizing magic. I opened my eyes and thought I saw the green-jacket stranger from the slave auction dash across the crowded Rampart Street.

I blinked. The euphoria in my mouth shuddered down my body in exquisite waves. I must be associating the pleasure in my mouth with the young stranger and somehow conjuring him up. I swallowed the savory sweetness and regained focus on the world of vendors and shoppers. The vision vanished. What a silly girl I was.

To Eula, I sputtered, "*Danke*—uh, tank you."

I must learn to practice my English as much as possible. While visiting with German-speaking Bernhardt Schiller all morning, I almost forgot I was in an English-speaking country. This contradictory city was far from my simple village with its strange customs and odd language.

We said our goodbyes to Eula, and Herr Schiller replaced his cemetery tour with the temptations of French Quarter streets. The soulful brass sounds greeted us as they seeped into our beings. I involuntarily swayed a bit to the rhythm when I heard a woman's voice moan to the melody beyond the open glass doors.

Herr Schiller allowed for the disruption in his errands for as long as he could before we returned to the familiarity of the German Society boarding house.

I did not want to leave the kind treatment of Frau Oldendorf, Bernhardt Schiller, and others in the New Orleans German Society. They were a touch of home in a foreign land, and I feared more American surprises awaited me on my journey upriver. They were such a blessing and filled my head with more travel advice for the remainder of my trip.

The next morning, I gathered my things in my carpetbag and stood by the door of the German Society boarding house waiting for transport to the paddle wheeler. Frau Oldendorf took my hands and squeezed them tightly, squinted her blue eyes, and warned me, "Stay clear of the scoundrels that travel the steamships, mind you."

I nodded and smiled at her motherly concern. She leaned in for a goodbye hug, and I held her as if she were my mother. Finally breaking apart, I noticed Herr Schiller standing at the ready beside us.

Frau Oldendorf handed me a tied checkered cloth filled with cheese, fruit, and sweets from the kitchen. "We will send you with your own food, so you will not be swindled by those upriver."

I tucked it under my arm. "Oh, you've done so much for me already. I don't know how I would have managed without your help."

Herr Schiller prevented another hug by interrupting. "We need to go, ladies. These steamships run on a schedule; you know."

He hoisted my carpetbag onto the cart, and I climbed on the wagon seat beside him. I turned to give Frau Oldendorf a final wave as we pulled away.

Herr Schiller recounted his travel wisdom as we wound our way through the still-crowded New Orleans streets. "Don't remain at the steamship railings while on board. The captains are often reckless, and passengers sometimes end up in the river. Do not get off at St. Louis, where most of the travelers will likely exit. The next stop on the Illinois side of the river is Alton. You'll want to exit there because that will be closer to your *bruder*."

"Ja, dat is what Herman wrote me. Get off the riverboat in Alton, Illinois." I took a deep breath. "I know a nice German welcoming party won't greet me in Alton like here in New Orleans. You and Frau Oldendorf were such a welcome surprise."

"Many Germans in that area will be willing to help you. Immigrants are farming all along the Mississippi and will be familiar with your trip, so I think you will be fine." He turned to me and winked in his fatherly way.

I touched Herman's instructions in my satchel. It bolstered my confidence that Herr Schiller confirmed its contents. God had seen me safely to America, and the journey would be over soon. Although I could not expect God to send a Frau Oldendorf or Herr Schiller to my rescue at every turn, I knew He would not abandon me either.

Rescue? The stranger God had sent to save me from tumbling into the street had been an unexpected miracle. *Oh, Lena, get your head out of the clouds and back on getting yourself to Herman and his kinder.*

CHAPTER 4

The Race Is On

"Let us run with endurance the race that is set before us."

Hebrews 12:1

"Oh, Herr Schiller. You have been such a drink of cool water on this long journey. I will never be able to repay you."

I pulled him in for a big hug before the mass of humanity waiting to board the *Diana* engulfed me.

"Take care, young lady, and get safely to your *bruder*. That is all the thanks I need."

He straightened his beret I had left askew from the hug and pretended to smooth the wrinkles from his shirt to detract from any unmanly emotions. I gathered my carpetbag of meager belongings and found a place in line behind other like-minded passengers and their luggage—careful not to trip on any bags and trunks scattered about the dock. Everyone ahead of me lumbered single-file up the ramp with their possessions, slowing the progress.

I set my bag down in front of me as I waited my turn and gave one last backward glance at the New Orleans skyline. The spire of the St. Louis Cathedral jetted above the other buildings, and I remembered

Herr Schiller's kind tour of that area near Rampart Street. After only two days in New Orleans, I was sure this was not the place for a country girl like me. The busy streets, the odd customs, and the social practices left me uneasy and ready to return to more open spaces, even with the haunting music and friendly people I had met.

I had read about a new American writer, Thoreau, who thought too many people in one place bred corruption. That must be what I had witnessed in New Orleans with the disregard for human dignity and the slave auctions that destroyed families. I was sure Herman did not live in a place such as this. He had never said so in his letters, at least. Thankfully, getting on the steamship meant seeing him soon.

Lord, make it fast, please.

I turned to examine the *Diana*, wanting to assess this new conveyance that would carry me a matter of days to my brother. My eyes caught a familiar frame on the gangplank. Boarding the same vessel was the brave—or foolish—young man from my arrival, standing proud in his green jacket. He paused at the pinnacle of the ramp, surveying his surroundings as if assessing his domain. His bruised cheeks and chin, visible under the shadow of his peasant cap, boasted a defiant glint. Although he had surely lost the fight against the gang that had pulled him down, he bounded off the gangplank onto the vessel with ease. A moment later, he was swallowed by the crowd of boarding passengers.

I smiled. I had not met him, but our lives had become intertwined somehow. From the dock to the slave auction, to my city tour, and now this? Destined to meet, I looked forward to that moment. Doing so might help pass the time before finding Herman and settling down to a quiet farm life with my brother and his children. His children? No, not just his. They were *my* niece and nephew; these darlings would be my responsibility.

Deep in my thoughts, I hardly heard the young shouts of "Lena, Lena" coming from behind me in line. It was young Thomas. The *Deutsche Gesellschaft* must have booked his family passage on the same steamship to travel upriver. Delighted to be together again, I opened my arms. Soon, the two Krueger brothers filled them by leaping in for precious hugs.

"Well, *guten tag*, Thomas and Tobias." I was happy to be speaking in our shared language. "It looks as if we will be passengers together again."

"Momma said this is a short trip."

"Much shorter than the ocean voyage, for sure. Only a few days this time."

I gently patted Thomas' head and gave them both another squeeze. Frau Krueger held her daughter in her arms and nodded to me over Stella's head. Their mother sighed with relief at the realization that I would be on the *Diana* with them. I nodded in silent agreement that I would help care for the boys, who had latched onto me the last couple of months aboard the *Olbers*. The children were once again a welcome distraction.

While reuniting with the Krueger family, a loud shout erupted between two men on the dock. Everyone strained to see what was causing the ruckus, but the masses of people waiting to board made it difficult to see much further up the pier.

A bit taller than those around me, I caught glimpses of each man through the crowd. One wore a ship captain's uniform and had a disheveled headful of dark, wavy hair escaping from his cap and his equally dark mustache turned up at the corners of his mouth in its own smile. The other captain's darkened complexion from too much Southern sun was no match to his unkempt, light red hair that was flying about with no hat at all. Both muscular men appeared to be in their thirties or forties and postured themselves in aggressive stances and spewed angry retorts so extreme, I was happy my English skills kept me from understanding their meaning. Some men in the surrounding crowd urged them to strike each other for their own entertainment, but the shouting sufficed for each man.

Thomas and Tobias clung a little closer to me. "What is it?"

"I don't know, Thomas. But I don't think we need to worry." It was likely another example of the harshness of the city that we would be away from soon. I redirected my young charges. "We will be on the boat soon. Look at the big wheel on the back of it."

The line moved forward again, and we gathered our belongings for the next trek of our journey in America. Once all were aboard, the massive paddle wheel strained to propel the steamship away from the New Orleans harbor with labored turns. The fascinating cascade of water lapped over and around the gigantic wheel, and Thomas and Tobias gaped at the mechanism. We kept our distance, mindful to keep the boys far from it. Herr Krueger herded his young family inside, me included, as the ship glided into the river's rhythm.

I recalled the advice about staying clear of the railing, but the warning appeared silly now. The ship slid smoothly through the calm waters. The riverbanks stretched far from the gentle, rhythmic beat of the wheel, and the farmlands and wilderness areas slid past without incident. The Mississippi was far more magnificent than the rivers in Saxony—many of which a person could jump over in a single bound.

This nautical ride felt stable and relaxing compared to the Atlantic Ocean waves knocking everyone about. A nap beckoned me as the peaceful rhythm of the paddles strummed us forward along the gentle river. The children tucked themselves around their mother and dozed to the hypnotizing repetition. I stepped outside, where the Southern sun warmed me as I basked in the midday glow on deck. An open bench welcomed me, and I relaxed into a peaceful slumber.

I jolted from my dozing posture as I slipped off the deck bench. My arms flailed about as I tried to catch myself before I fell unceremoniously onto the wood plank flooring.

"Careful now."

A masculine vise grip around my arm elevated me until I stood upright and came face to face with the young man in the green coat.

"These steamboat captains are known to swerve around any ol' thing in the river with no warning," he said to me in German. "If you want to nap, you may want to go inside, Miss." He released his grip on my arm but kept close enough to steady me if the river captain swerved again.

I gazed into his stare and said, "You keep coming to my rescue."

I tried to back a step away because his body heat radiated from his towering six-foot frame, making it difficult to focus on polite conversation. The sun held high over his head, casting an imagined halo behind him.

His puzzled, steel-blue eyes crinkled as he tilted his head to examine me closer. "I'm sorry. I think I would remember a pretty maiden like you. Are you sure we have met?"

"No, we have never met. The last time you pulled me from harm's way, you ran off so fast, I could not thank you." I steadied my feet and gently shook off his assisting hand.

"I'm afraid you still have me at a disadvantage. But let me introduce myself now. I am Karl Muller, at your service."

In a sweeping bow, he swept his hat off his unruly, tumbling curls.

"Glad to meet you, Herr Muller. I am Lena Neubauer. The last time you kept me from falling into the street and getting struck by a horse whip on the shipping docks. Then, you ran around the corner, where you tried to speak out against a slave auction in progress."

"Please call me Karl. Herr Muller is my father. And, you saw that, did you?" Shamefaced, he stroked his bruised chin. "I do remember steadying someone on my way, I think. Sorry I wasn't more social, but I knew the auction was starting, and I intended to be there to stop it if I could. A foolish thought, I guess."

"You thought you could stop the auction?"

"I'm sure that sounds ridiculous, but I had to try." He stroked the bruise across his cheek this time. "Those people need a champion. Not sure it will be me, though."

"But that was a dangerous thing to do. You could have been seriously hurt."

"I'm certainly not welcome there, that's for sure." He hesitated. "You saw them. They need someone to help. It is barbaric how some people are treated."

He hesitated and examined me more closely. I am sure he noticed my lack of social status, my youth, and my lack of a companion before asking his next question.

"Why were you at the docks?"

"I had just arrived on the *Olbers*. A woman from the German Society was taking me to a place to stay until my passage up the Miss-i-ssip-pi." I stammered over the odd word.

He gazed a moment too long, making me uncomfortable, so I started to turn away. "Welcome to America, Fraulein Neubauer." He stuck his hand out to shake mine—an odd gesture, since he had touched me far more intimately moments before when he rescued me from my fall off the bench.

"Call me Lena. Everybody does. I must say, I find this America more disturbing than I thought."

"You mean, that business on the docks?"

"Yes. And I met another black woman selling pralines on the street yesterday who was not downtrodden at all. But my guide, Herr Schiller, told me it was because she was a mistress to a white plantation owner who had a whole other family somewhere else. This strange custom is not like home at all."

"It is not like this everywhere in America either. There are slave states and free states here. I work with people who want them all to be free states. That is why I was foolish enough to jump into the middle of that slave auction. Rather dumb, now that I think on it."

"The Lord put it on your heart to help those in need. He often works against insurmountable odds. Don't give up hope." I needed to refocus away from this intense young man with a heart for those in need. "I am sure they need you."

I was beginning to think I needed him, too, but that was ridiculous. We had just met, and our plans did not travel the same life journey.

"I'll have to change strategies, though. Maybe God can help me with that since I was told to leave town or be thrown in jail." Karl paused and stroked his stubbled, injured jaw again, shadowing his fresh bruises. "So, here we are." He glanced around the ship and back to me. "And where are you heading?"

I did not know him well enough to tell him my plans. After all, he had just told me that he was on this steamship only to avoid jail. Who knew where he was going? It was not wise to invite him to travel with me.

"I am traveling with another family from Germany. They are helping me get to my *bruder.*"

I did not think the Krueger family would mind if I made myself a part of their party. The mutually beneficial arrangement worked for both of us—I did not appear to be traveling alone, and they received a temporary nanny of sorts.

"St. Louis?"

"Right."

I intended to disembark at Alton, Illinois, twenty-five miles upriver from St. Louis. That was close enough to the truth. I was unsure where Thomas and his family planned to get off the steamship, but it would be a few days before I needed to worry about those details.

"I'd better go find my friends. Thanks again for your help."

"My pleasure."

Before he could say more, I slipped inside. Although he was handsome, I needed to stay away from him. He was impulsive and wild. Herman would not like me speaking with a man who was so full of abolitionist ideals. Besides, my mission was to get to Herman's farm and help him.

Even on such a smaller vessel, I managed to avoid Karl's company for a couple of days. The steamship chugged and turned less peacefully than I had first envisioned, and again, we weary travelers longed for our destinations.

I was walking the deck with young Thomas Krueger, his younger siblings, and his parents—giving all of us a much-needed outing—when suddenly, the paddle-wheeler engines strained loudly, pulling the wheel into a faster frenzy. The riverboat jerked from the effort to increase speed, causing us to stumble on the wood planking.

As seemed to be his habit, Karl appeared from nowhere when the unsteady toddler Tobias began to stumble toward the Mississippi River. Karl grabbed Tobias by the back of his denim jacket and swung him over the railing into the arms of his waiting mother. She smothered her son with kisses and a gentle scolding about never letting go of her hand again. I marveled at how God always placed this knight wherever a rescue was warranted. His timing was impeccable.

I remembered my manners and introduced Karl to the Kruegers. "This is Karl Muller. We met briefly in New Orleans."

I turned to Karl. "You always show up in a time of need, Herr Muller. God must have you on His angel assignment duty."

"I don't think God has anything to do with it. I try to help when I can."

He smiled at me with little regard for the Krueger family's gratitude.

The ship lurched again, accompanied by mechanical clanking. A high-pitched hissing emitted from the boiler room, and the paddles spun around faster than before. Conversation was impossible without yelling.

"What's happening?" I shouted.

"It's a race, I believe." Karl pointed to another steamship nearby on the river. Although downriver from us, it appeared to be catching up. "Our Captain McGregor does not like to lose."

"Lose what?" I leaned closer and spoke louder so he could hear me over the surrounding din of engines, paddles, and splashing water.

"A race. A bet, maybe. You must have seen him argue with Captain Stewart before we left New Orleans?"

I only nodded since trying to answer over the noise was pointless.

"Let's find somewhere safer in case that boiler blows." Karl shouted his instructions and guided the Kruegers and me back inside, where the noise diminished to a level of a roaring train chugging down uneven tracks.

The scared children hung tightly to their parents. The baby squalled from disrupted sleep and the incessant clanging and crashing of the ship's mechanisms. Frau Krueger tried covering the child's ears to protect them from the invading sounds but had no luck diminishing the noise.

"Can I tell you a story?"

Thomas nodded, so the ever-helpful Karl came to the rescue again. He crouched near the frightened boys and commanded their attention.

Although Thomas was clinging to his mother's skirts, he tried to appear brave in front of little Tobias, who sucked his thumb and looked wide-eyed at this stranger who had kept him from a morning swim in the Mississippi.

"I can tell a story about a monster along the Mississippi River."

Frau Krueger glared a warning at Karl that said, "Don't scare my children anymore, thank you very much."

Karl caught the menacing look from the protective mother. "I promise a happy ending," he declared as he flashed his most disarming smile her way.

"There was a monster who roamed the Mississippi. It had horns on its head like a deer." Karl propped his fingers on his head to demonstrate. He deepened his voice for a sinister effect and continued. "It had horrible red eyes and a beard like a tiger. His body was covered in scales, but his wings were feathers. His tail was so long, it could wrap around his whole body, and it had a fishy point at the end of it."

The children tucked themselves deeper into the folds of their mother's dress, and Frau Krueger's furrowed brow deepened as she listened to Karl's distressing tale. Karl discarded his deep voice for a more congenial timbre to lighten the story's mood.

"He was a colorful monster. He was green and red and black. Do you have a favorite color?"

Mesmerized, young Thomas erupted with "Blue." Tobias tried to imitate him by squeaking out a "bu" himself.

"Blue is a great color. However, I'm rather partial to green, as you can tell by my jacket." The children leaned closer to him, and Karl continued. "This monster's name was Piasa. Can you say that? Pee-ah-sa." Karl drew out each syllable so the children could try it out for themselves.

"Piasa is a Native American word, meaning, 'the bird that devours.'"

The children shrunk back a bit with this revelation but were still intent on listening to Karl's story. "Piasa would eat the people, and they were scared of it."

I could tell Karl knew he was on thin ice with their Frau Krueger, but he hurried on. "But they had a warrior chief among their people who had a plan to kill this horrible monster. Chief Ouatoga and his twenty warriors could not let this monster attack their people anymore, so you know what they did?"

Both boys shook their heads, eyes wide.

"They decided to use Chief Ouatoga as bait—like when you go fishing and use a worm to catch the fish."

"My papa showed me that," volunteered Thomas.

"Right. So, if it worked for fish, the natives decided it would work for a monster. Chief Ouatoga offered himself to Piasa. The monster did not know that twenty warriors were waiting for him with poison arrows. And when Piasa swooped down to attack Ouatoga, the twenty warriors ambushed the monster with all their poisoned arrows, killing him."

Karl swooped in and flew young Tobias in the air as the story climaxed. Tobias squealed in delight. "And the people were saved!"

Both boys cheered, much to Frau Krueger's relief.

I leaned toward Karl. "You are quite the storyteller."

"I admit, I left out some of the gorier details. Sometimes, I will need to tell you about the cave of bones, where Piasa stored his kills." He winked at me.

"I appreciate your discretion, Karl." I shifted in my seat and looked around. Did anyone else notice his flirting ways?

The ship noticeably slowed, and the accompanying noise subsided. "The race must be over."

"Wonder who won?"

I tried to search beyond the sea of travelers to the approaching shore outside. Others noticed the slowing ship and began to gather their items. Moments later, a messenger announced, "St. Louis. All passengers for St. Louis, prepare to depart!"

"Your stop, Miss Lena?"

"Not yet," I answered sheepishly, knowing I had lied to him earlier. "I will get off in Alton. I understand it is not far from here."

"How fortuitous. That is my stop, too."

Karl gave me a sideways smile that left me wondering how truthful he was.

Lord, I had not asked him before where he was heading. Now, I can't discern if that was his plan all along or not. Lord, help me get to my brother. This sweet-talking, storytelling Karl is possibly trouble for me.

CHAPTER 5

Delivered

"Because he holds fast to me in love, I will deliver him;
I will protect him, because he knows my name."

Psalm 91:14

Most *Diana* passengers gathered their bags and family members to disembark as we approached St. Louis. Captain McGregor squeezed the steamship between dozens of similar vessels with towering paddle wheels. Apparently, every steamship on the Mississippi stopped at St. Louis. There must have been two dozen or more lined up along the riverbank with people milling around each one. The paddles ceased their loud, rhythmic sloshing, and the din of shouting dockworkers rose below us.

Like New Orleans, grunting men kept busy loading and unloading cargo, while passengers bumped their way through masses heading in various directions. New arrivals looked for familiar landmarks or friendly faces in the crowd. Others waited to board steamboats departing the nearby docks. I delighted in watching the ensuing chaos below, rather than being a part of it by staying aboard the ship for a few more miles.

Young Thomas broke loose from his gathered family and ran into my arms for a last farewell.

Hugging him tightly, I said, "Thomas, you be good for your momma and papa now. Grow up to be a good man. Okay?" His doe eyes welled up with tears. "Don't cry, Thomas. Help with your brother and sister. Momma and Papa need your help."

"I don't want to say bye," he sobbed into my collar.

"I have to go to my own home, Thomas. I can't go with you this time." I pushed him away from me and looked deeply into his eyes. "But we will always be special friends. Maybe your momma can help you write a letter about your new home when you get settled. I told your momma where I'll be."

"Okay," he whispered as he wiped his eyes with his sleeve.

Little Tobias joined his big brother and grabbed his hand. The whole time Tobias' attention held fast to Karl, who stood sentinel, watching the painful farewells. He hoisted young Tobias to his towering shoulders, much to the tot's delight.

"We need to get you two back to your family, so you can go to your new home." Karl bridged the gap between the Kruegers and us in a couple of long strides.

"Remember, stay close to your folks. Don't want anyone getting lost with all those people running around."

Tobias slipped from Karl's shoulders to the ground as I handed Thomas back to his parents.

Waving frantically, the youngsters shuffled their way off the steamship with their family, disappearing into the masses on shore. The muddy streets led to many brick and stone buildings not far from the docks. I could see the growing city boasted a courthouse, a school, a church, and more that could be seen from the river.

"So many stone buildings," I marveled aloud.

"They had a fire here a while back and made an ordinance that all buildings must be brick or stone."

Karl startled me with his impromptu explanation. Not that I had forgotten he stood beside me. How could I? His tall frame, musky smell, nearby warmth filled the early November coolness. The sun no longer kissed our cheeks with a daytime glow like in Louisiana but nipped us in a chill that tightened shawls and jackets against the colder North. Being so near Karl's warmth, I almost forgot my shawl draped loosely across my shoulders. I peered up at him in response to his mini history lesson.

"You know a lot about this area—monsters and all."

"My parents came over in '35 with other German immigrants. I was only a kid. No bigger than little Tobias, I think. That is pretty much all I know," he said, gesturing across the horizon.

"Oh, so you are a true American. Do you even remember Germany?"

I stood too near him. The heat rose in my cheeks, and I stepped away.

"Not really. What I learned of the Fatherland is what my parents brought with them. Language, traditions, and all. My parents still speak German at home."

Most of the departing passengers gathered their belongings ashore now. Karl stayed steadfast on the ship with me.

"Why are you going to Alton?" I asked.

"That is my home, and I have friends there who help with the Underground Railroad."

His voice lowered to a mere whisper when speaking of the railroad. My puzzled expression urged further explanation.

"Missouri is a slave state like New Orleans, but Illinois is a free state. Even though the Mississippi River is wide here, slaves sometimes escape across the river, and we help them when we can."

"But what is the Underground Railroad?"

My visions of massive tunnels for locomotives running through the countryside conjured an impractical escape system.

"Depending on the desires of the ones escaping, sometimes we help them go all the way to Canada. We have an elaborate system of safe houses across the North. We can't let their masters get wind of this. That's why we call it an underground movement, or railroad."

"Isn't that dangerous?"

I pretended to notice the people milling around on the riverbank as the ship readied to depart. Would Karl volunteer the secrets of his business to me? It might be best if I did not learn too much about him, though.

Karl continued, "St. Louis is such a growing city and so near access to freedom along the Mississippi that many petitions for freedom suits are drawn up in Alton. Some slaves legally declare freedom from their masters once they are away from them. I help the legal teams prepare their cases." Sensing I wondered about the danger, he added, "We try to stay out of trouble if we can."

"You are a lawyer, then?"

He did not act like a lawyer. Not that I had encountered many lawyers in my life, but the ones who'd visited my father sported pouchy stomachs and smudged spectacles and impatiently checked pocket watches as though being kept from more important business—much like train porters or accountants. They certainly did not sport wavy, blond locks and steel-blue eyes and wear a smirk on their faces that good-naturedly said, "I am watching you, so don't try anything."

"I don't try the cases, but I am part of the legal team." He appraised my underwhelmed reaction to this news. "By the way you are reacting, I gather you are not a fan of lawyers."

"It's not that." Then, I blurted out an apology. "You don't look like the lawyers back home."

My cheeks burned again. He must have thought I was so forward. I tried to steer the conversation elsewhere. "Were you in New Orleans to write—what did you call them—freedom suits? It seems you were jumping into something much more physical."

"That was different. I was sent to New Orleans on legal business, not to stop a slave auction." He rubbed his healing chin. "But I could not stand by and watch them sell those poor people without trying to do something. Most things worth doing involve risk, don't they?"

He leaned forward, and I stepped back, sure he was no longer speaking about slavery or lawyers anymore. His piercing scrutiny distracted me as I caught my foot on a loose floorboard. I reached out for the railing to catch myself, but I found my hand wrapped around his wrist instead.

"I'm so sorry," I stammered as I pulled away from his touch.

"I'm not," he answered in a low, masculine growl. "I am always happy to rescue you, Lena."

Diana's whistle blew, causing me to jump and break up the increasingly intimate moment. The noisy paddle-wheeler forced its way away from the St. Louis skyline. I steadied myself without Karl's assistance this time and prepared to go below.

"Lena? When we land in Alton, I'd be happy to show you around." He kept in step with me and followed me inside.

"Actually, I won't be staying in Alton. That's only where I get off."

Drawn to this man and his charm, I was unsure I should reveal my plans. The last thing I needed was for Herman to scold me about being with some wild lawyer. Herman respected men who worked with their hands more than those who studied books. Maybe all those years of finding Martin's books poking him in his back while trying to sleep in a cramped loft had tainted his perspective.

Herman did read but only as a pastime, not a career. Reading had prompted him to seek his fortune in America, but Herman thought men who learned physical trades and got their hands dirty earned their manhood. Spending too much time indoors revealed a weak man to Herman.

Not that I pictured Karl sitting at a desk. He walked as if the world awakened to his command and the elements bent to his will. However, a rugged fellow may not help my cause with Herman, no matter his profession, if Herman found his unchaperoned sister being too friendly with him. No need to gauge Herman's reaction to any man when my virtue might be questioned.

With all the many reasons not to become involved with Karl, I must stay clear of him, even if he did champion himself as my on-call rescuer. I came to America to help my brother, not find a beau. Those babes still needed me, and Karl would have to find someone else to rescue. My responsibilities did not include Karl, and he might be difficult to shake.

"Where are you headed?" Karl asked. "I have many connections in Alton. I can help you on your way."

Now what? I appreciated help, since surely no Frau Oldendorf would meet me in Alton. Although Herman had sent me instructions and the German Society had assured me that many German-speaking folks lived in the area, I preferred not to navigate this new place alone.

I noticed him waiting patiently for my decision, sure that he had read my thoughts. His friendly, protective demeanor prompted my involuntary response. "Is Bethel far?"

"Only a few miles down the road from Alton. Is that where you'll find your brother?"

"He farms nearby. I am supposed to stop at the butcher shop. They will take me to him, since Frau Greta Stolz, the butcher's wife, has been helping with his children."

"His children?" Karl raised an eyebrow.

I had remained so guarded during the trip that I had not told him why I had come to America or traveled alone. He must wonder why I did not disembark with the Krueger family if we had journeyed together from Germany. If I accepted his charity, I might as well tell him the rest of the story.

"Yes. My *bruder* requested I come to America to help raise his babes, since his wife died in childbirth. So, my *bruder's* family needs me. That's why I'm here."

"Does he know when to expect you?"

"Well, not exactly."

Not sure why that would matter to him, I obviously had not read his mind as well as he had mine.

"Then I have time to show you around a little, and I will be sure to deliver you to Frau Stolz in a short time."

The agenda for the day settled between us, although I wasn't sure I had a say in the matter. If I wanted to keep my guide, I felt I had to agree with this arrangement, but his high-handed way of making decisions for me only because he was a native of the area presumed too much. Both relieved and cautious, I gave him permission to lead our little expedition when the *Diana* arrived in Alton in less than an hour.

Lord, surely You will walk with me on this journey and keep me safe.

The *Diana* docked in Alton with less fanfare than St. Louis, but it still was not the only ship there. Above the waterway, large prison walls loomed like sentinels in the hills to the north, overlooking the Mississippi River. Guard towers accented the corners of the stone walls, where men with rifles impeded all threats. The unexpected view alarmed me as it came into sight. Karl followed my eyes upward.

"That is the state penitentiary. No worries. Everything is quite secure."

"I wasn't worried, only a little surprised. I realize more and more my brother wrote so little about this country. Look at all those steam mills, for instance." I gestured at another large structure near the water's edge in the other direction.

"Alton is an important town on the Mississippi. Three rivers converge north of here, which makes it an up-and-coming port for trade."

He gathered our belongings and carried them for both of us as we left the *Diana* to paddle farther upriver.

"You make a terrific guide. I doubt if Herman explored the area this well before settling down with Katarina."

"I am sure he was busy with his farm and not out sightseeing. Do you know about the Lewis and Clark Expedition about fifty years ago? They explored the way west to the Pacific Ocean."

"I am not certain. Why?"

Not the sort of news or history we followed at school in Frohn. I yearned to absorb much more about this new country now that I would live here.

"They prepared for their trip up the river a little farther." Karl pointed north beyond the prison. "I must say it is a point of contention to the locals that St. Louis always gets the credit for their beginning. They started on the Illinois side." He smiled. "It is not Europe, but we have some history here."

"Why does it make any difference where they started, though?" When Karl stiffened, I added, "Well, I guess there is a sense of pride for it."

"Yes, Lewis and Clark left before the Louisiana Purchase. That means Missouri was not even a part of the United States yet. An expedition that momentous needed to begin in the U.S. to be an American triumph. Illinois should be the one to make that claim."

I enjoyed listening to Karl. He would make a great teacher. His knowledge bubbled from him as he relished teaching this newcomer all about the area. He stopped mid-story about some of the area natives and apologized.

"I'm sorry. You didn't ask for a history lesson, did you?"

I giggled. "I like your enthusiasm. It sure doesn't hurt me to know about this area, since I plan to stay."

"I'm glad to hear that."

He leaned down and hesitated a moment. His head and mouth were uncomfortably close to mine. Unsure of his intentions, I stepped back. He bent farther and grabbed my meager belongings from the ground, and we headed up the hillside that constituted the town proper. His expert tour-guiding continued as the day sped forward.

Karl walked me back toward the massive river and pointed to a small inlet. "That is where I got my first introduction to the horrors of slavery."

"What do you mean?"

"I was only about fourteen. I had spent a summer day fishing along the river, and I caught a few catfish. Mother enjoyed cooking them for dinner. That day, I had about five dangling over my shoulder. Not a bad catch. It was a good day. No chores. No responsibilities for a kid. I hurried to make it home before dinner when I heard someone crying. I followed the sound to the riverbank and saw a black woman, all wet and doubled over, stifling her cries with her hands over her face. When I approached her, she screamed at me, 'No, don't take him!'

"I didn't know what she was shouting about. Then I looked past her to the ground, and it was a child. A dead child. He must have drowned because he was soaked and his face blue and swollen. He couldn't have been more than four. I promised the lady I wouldn't take the boy away from her, but I offered to help. She told me she had run away from her master because they were going to sell her away from her son. They had sold her other children, and she would not let them do that again.

"So earlier that morning, before work, she had taken the child and jumped into the Mississippi with him. She thought the small log she clung to would keep them afloat until they reached the Illinois side. With both clinging to the same small branch, it submerged. The little boy panicked and started to scream. She had to stop him, or the master would hear where they were. She kept saying, 'No baby, no baby' until he was quiet."

He turned away from me and breathed deeply to abate whatever tears threatened to ambush him.

"No . . . " I did not want Karl to finish his story. "She didn't."

"Yes. I don't think she knew she was drowning him at all. She only knew she had to keep him quiet. We buried him under that tree."

"And the mother?"

"I don't think she ever recovered from the ordeal. I was just a kid, remember? I got her in touch with like-minded adults and never saw her again."

"How horrible."

For a moment, Karl mentally relived his fourteen-year-old past that shaped the man standing before me. Finally, he shook off the memory, and we turned back to town.

Before dinnertime, Karl bought tickets on the Alton-Terre Haute train and boarded it with me for Bethel.

"You don't need to escort me to the butcher. I can manage from here."

He neglected to answer the protest and followed me aboard anyway for the short ride on the rails to the next town.

New buildings dotted the main street of Bethel. Miller's brickyard and the sawmill appeared to be thriving businesses. Building materials were stacked in the yards with destination documents attached to each bundle. Tyron's General Store's windows advertised every needful household item a town needed. Shiny, new farm tools stood near tables of smaller essentials of razors and women's toiletries. Nearby was a table of bolted calico fabrics and heavier shirting, shelved like books and ready for customers to purchase. A blacksmith shop and the new Carroll Hotel continued side by side until we reached Stolz's Butcher Shop. The freshness of the town appealed to me, and I imagined Herman liked beginning his new life here.

As we approached the butcher's entrance, I turned to dismiss Karl in my kindest terms. "Thank you so much for everything. I appreciate you sharing so much with me."

I wanted us to part on happy terms. Hopefully, my hint to leave would become apparent as I held out my hand to shake his.

"You don't want me to go in?" He arched his eyebrow in a questioning challenge.

"No need. You must return to your home and business. You can't miss the last train back to Alton. Besides, these fine people will surely deliver me to Herman, as he said." I fidgeted with the handle of my bag and kept glancing at the butcher shop. "You have been so nice, and I appreciate your kindness, but . . ."

"But you don't want me to meet your brother?"

Karl and his mind-reading again. How did he guess that?

"No, it's not that. Herman would not understand me showing up with a man I just met—with no chaperone or anything." I struggled to say the right thing without offending him. "He holds to strict, old German ways of doing things, and I don't want any trouble. After all, I haven't seen him in a long time. We don't need any distractions."

I glanced away. Karl was more of a distraction than he possibly knew, especially with his mind-reading abilities.

"I understand. But don't think this is goodbye. I will definitely meet you again, Miss Lena. You can count on it."

Karl dramatically brought my still-extended hand to his lips and kissed it, sending a quiver through my whole being. He then turned abruptly and strode off before my wits gathered enough to say anything. I had no idea what to say to this generous and gorgeous man, who had delivered me safely to my brother's town. He was not even out of my sight, and I wanted him to return.

Oh, Lord, I don't think that is a prayer I should be praying, is it? I can't want him, can I?

CHAPTER 6

The Reunion

"If anyone loves me, he will keep my word, and my Father will love him,
and we will come to him and make our home with him."

John 14:23

I slowly cracked open the door to the butcher shop, taking in the surroundings. A hearty man with more forehead than hair busied himself behind a counter. Although neat and clean, the shop was small, with enough space for only a few customers to wait on orders or conduct business. Not noticing my stealthy entrance, he continued packaging a plump roast in brown paper. I stood there waiting for him to look up.

"Excuse me," I ventured after my long-ignored presence drug on.

Still reeling from Karl's goodbye, my voice was not strong, and I feared it sounded more like a squeak than a request for recognition. The man evidently never heard my first attempt, so I offered a more confident summons to the meat-cutter.

"Excuse me, Herr Stolz?"

Startled, he snapped to attention. "Oh, my! *Guten tag.*" His gray mustache fluttered as he spoke in German. "Sorry, I did not hear

70

you come in." He briefly scanned the rest of the shop. No other customers wandered in during his preoccupation with the meat counter. "How can I help you?"

He saw my bag, and his eyes narrowed. He tilted his head toward the carpetbag sitting on the wood floor next to me.

"I am Lena Neubauer. My *bruder*, Herman, is expecting me. He sent me word to come here, since Frau Greta has been helping him with the *kindern*?" I wish I sounded more confident, but he had not confirmed he was, indeed, Herr Stolz. "Am I in the right place?"

As I spoke, his face lit up. "Ja, ja."

He rushed around the counter, took my hand, and pumped it vigorously. "We were hoping you would be here soon. Frau Greta will be home from Herman's in only a few minutes, and we will take you there. I have been saving a nice roast to celebrate your arrival." He embraced me in a fatherly hug. "He will be so happy that you are here. My name is Helmut."

After his introduction, a woman I assumed was Frau Greta slipped through the door. She could have easily doubled for Frau Oldendorf's sister. Her small stature, the happy wrinkles around her eyes, and the graying hair pulled back from her face replicated those of the New Orleans woman.

"Greta, this is Herman's Lena!"

He gestured excitedly toward me, like the woman celebrating the discovery of her lost coin in Jesus' parable. Upon hearing her husband's proclamation, Greta opened her arms to me as Helmut stepped back, allowing her to give me a motherly hug.

"Oh, my dear. Your brother will be so happy you are here." She looked down at my bag and the wrinkled clothes I wore. "You must be tired from your trip, so we must not keep you from your brother one minute longer. The cart is ready, since Helmut has not yet had a chance to mind it from my drive back. We can take you there now."

She smiled at her husband in the knowing way that long-time couples share. There was an acknowledgment in a secret look I could not discern. "It is time to close the shop for the day, anyway. We will take you to Herman's straight away."

The small woman and her husband flitted around, and soon, a closed sign propped in the window. Helmut hung his butcher's apron on a peg and grabbed the promised roast, while Greta gathered other food for the intended feast ahead. In only a few moments, we all settled on the cart that doubled as a meat wagon for the Stolzs' butcher shop. A quick flip of the reigns, and the horses trotted over a well-worn dirt road to Herman's farm.

At the crossroads on the edge of town rested a small, white church. The freshly painted spire above it reached to the heavens to declare its otherwise diminutive presence. An equally small cemetery grew a few stone monuments in the adjacent yard, surrounded by a low picket fence.

"That is where we go to Sunday services," Greta volunteered. "We hope to see you this Sunday with Herman and the *kindern*."

I realized I had said almost nothing to these people since arriving. Frau Greta prattled on most of the way, pointing out landmarks and mentioning farm owners or people she assured me I would want to meet once I settled. None of the names registered because I had no context for them yet, and she did not seem to have the teaching ability of Karl—jumping from one subject to the other without proper transitions. I hardly knew what subject she was on or whom she was telling me about at any given moment.

Maybe Karl was my problem. I needed to quit thinking about him and focus on Frau Greta's dissertation. Helmut generally only grunted acknowledgments without much personal commenting on Greta's introduction to Madison County. Her incessant talking allowed the time to pass quickly, and we approached Herman's farmhouse in short order.

The horse drew our wagon over a gentle ridge, and a well-built farmhouse appeared before us on the other side. The two-story home towered over the young oak trees planted nearby for summer shade. Now, in November, they stood leafless and bare, quivering in the breeze of an impending evening storm, like naked sentinels for Herman's home.

A large, red barn hovered nearby—more lavish than those usually seen in Germany. Herman must be doing well here. A few cows grazed in a fenced pasture, and a chicken house graced a nearby enclosure. I could tell Herman busied himself to provide for his family. The farm appeared prosperous, a testament to my brother's hard work. A sense of pride rose in me, and I began to understand why he emphasized the farm so heavily in his letters home.

The yellow and blue gingham curtains lining the windows showed a woman's touch. A few empty flowerpots sat by the porch, now devoid of blooms. The sturdy oak door promised security and warmth inside. Smoke swirled from the chimney, creating ethereal patterns above the house. The farm sights mesmerized me, so Helmut and Greta unloaded their gifts from the cart while I sat and stared for a moment longer.

"Miss Lena," Greta called over her shoulder when she realized I hadn't moved. "Are you coming? This is the house, my dear."

I felt foolish dawdling, so I hastened off the cart and followed them to the door. They did not knock—I imagined Greta was a permanent fixture here—and opened the door and walked right into the front room.

"Herman. We have a gift for you," Helmut proclaimed as he entered the door.

I hesitated, peering around the door as Herman eyed the roast in Helmut's arms.

"Helmut. If you had a roast for me, why didn't you send it with Greta when she was here earlier? You make no sense, old man."

He clasped him on the shoulder in a neighborly way and turned to Greta. "Two trips out here in one day? You two are losing your minds."

"No, no. We brought you Lena!" Greta chimed in.

Herman's head rose toward the door as I entered, and a grin spread across this unfamiliar yet familiar face. In one step forward, he gathered me in his arms and squeezed my breath from me.

No longer a boy, Herman sported a full beard and muscles rippled under his cotton shirt. His tanned and weathered skin confirmed his outdoor profession. Farming life looked good on him. The same deep blue eyes crinkled as he smiled—as I remembered from childhood. His manly voice had deepened, but it carried the same timbre and cadence.

"God be praised. You are finally here!"

He held me at arm's length to get a better look at me. Aware my travels had worn on me, I tucked my hair behind my ear to become more presentable.

"My little sister. You have grown since I last saw you. You must tell me about everyone back home."

Herman was lost in the moment of our reunion, but I realized we were not in the room alone. Frau Greta quickly set up dinner provisions in the kitchen, while Helmut corralled a couple of tots in the corner, where he spoke gibberish to them.

"I think that can wait until you give me a proper introduction to your family," I said.

"I'm sorry. My excitement over seeing you got the best of me. You can tell me of your trip and family after these two go to bed."

He turned to the tots now on Helmut's lap and took the baby from Helmut. He held her close and introduced her to me. "This is little Hannah. She just turned one. She looks just like her momma, doesn't she?"

Herman choked a little at the mention of Katarina but remained composed.

"She sure does. What a beauty. Those golden locks. You will be beating boys off with a stick when she is older."

I reached for her, but she burrowed tighter into Herman's beard, refusing the gesture. Herman reassured her in a whisper that it was okay and turned to her brother.

"That's what I have Hans for." The three-year-old stood on the settee with Helmut. "Hans will help protect his little sister as they get older. He is strong for his age. Right, Hans?"

Timidly, Hans raised both arms akimbo to reveal imagined muscles in each arm. He also sported the golden locks of his mother, but his facial features reflected more of a miniature Herman and the uncles the child had never met.

"Oh, I can tell you are strong. Can I feel it?" I stepped closer to my nephew, bent down to his level, and gently squeezed each arm—marveling at the tiny muscles underneath his plaid shirt. He rewarded me with a smile and puffed out his chest.

I realized the children had not been told who this stranger was in their house. "I am your aunt Lena. I am going to stay with you. Is that okay?"

Hans nodded but didn't say a word. Hannah clung steadfastly to her father as though I planned to kidnap her if she let go of her protector.

Herman consoled me. "She will be fine when she gets to know you. It takes her a while to warm up to new people."

"I can tell she is a papa's girl."

I patted her on the back and stroked her pretty hair, but Herman flinched as he quietly said, "She never knew her momma."

"I'm so sorry, Herman. I didn't mean to . . ."

"It's okay, especially now that you are here. I don't know what I would have done without the help of Greta, Helmut, and a few neighbors. Everyone's help kept me going. You will like it here, Lena."

I hoped Herman was right. The country had held more surprises than I imagined or that his letters had invented in my feeble brain: slave auctions, *placées*, wild riverboat captains, monster stories, and, of course, Karl. So I wondered if this small Illinois community held other such surprises.

When I told Herman about my trip, it would be best to omit any mention of Karl. He would not understand how I had let a young man escort his unchaperoned sister around an unfamiliar town, and there was no need to invite scandal into my story when the encounter was certainly harmless.

In Alton, when Karl guided me about the town, we had purchased a couple of apples from a fruit stand, but the apple I ate was long gone. The aromas from the kitchen enticed my empty stomach until it responded with a loud rumble.

Helmut chuckled when he heard it. "I think we'd better feed this girl before she faints from hunger."

Frau Greta soon summoned everyone to the homecoming dinner she had prepared. Generous slices of cooked roast beef smothered in a plum sauce that Greta had retrieved from her summer preserves graced the table. She had saved the newly butchered meat Helmut brought for another time, since it would take too much time to prepare today. Luckily, she had left a roast for the family when she was there earlier. She'd added fried potatoes with onions and brought fresh bread. She also uncovered sugar cookies for dessert. The children spied the cookies immediately and wanted them as soon as they sat down.

Herman bowed his head to say grace. Even little Hannah bowed her head as he offered thanks for my safe travel and the fine friends who provided the meal. He ended with the common table prayer our parents had taught us as children: *Komm, Herr Jesu; sei du unser Gast; und segne, was du uns bescheret hast.* Amen.[4]

Happy that our traditions carried over to this new country, I felt a tear threaten my cheek. Momma and Papa would be so happy to see Herman and his young family gathered around this lovely meal in a Christian home. I would tell them how pleasing it was here in my next letter.

Like the omissions in my tale to Herman, I must do the same when I wrote home. A proper young lady would not allow a strange,

---

4   Come, Lord Jesus, be our Guest and let these gifts to us be blessed. Amen.

young man to escort her into unfamiliar surroundings. I needed to limit my story to the Krueger family and those like Frau Oldendorf, whom the Lord sent to accompany me in my travels. I wonder, though, if He also sent Karl. I can't imagine Karl in my future, but his parting words still echoed within me. *"I will definitely see you again, Miss Lena. You can count on it."*

"Lena!" Herman's voice broke through the din of my daydreaming. "Goodness. Where did you go? All that travel must have exhausted you. Let me show you to your room, and I will put the *kindern* to bed. We can talk more tomorrow."

"I can get the *kindern* ready for bed if you'd like, while you settle Fraulein Lena into her new room," Greta said while clearing the table and wiping the children's faces before I had blinked twice. "And then, we need to be on our way. It gets dark so early these days. Best get going."

Embarrassed that I had no idea what their conversation had entailed while I was living in my head, I simply followed orders. Herman led me upstairs to a small, front-facing bedroom. The window allowed full view of anyone approaching the farm. The twin bed was roomier than sharing sleeping quarters with my sisters at home. The same bright yellow curtains with tiny, embossed daisies I had noticed in the windows upon arrival cheered the room, and a homemade nightstand with a water basin and an oil lamp awaited me. It was not quite dark enough to turn it on yet, but dusk was descending.

A patchwork quilt with a log cabin design covered the bed. I supposed Katarina had fashioned it herself, since similar fabrics hung in the curtains, too. Everything was in order. Obviously, my arrival had been much anticipated. The room could not be more welcoming.

"This is lovely, Herman. You know how to make me feel special. But you are right. I think the trip overtired me. I will visit more with you in the morning."

He placed my bag near the bed. "You have no idea how much I've looked forward to you coming, Lena. I can now create some sense of normalcy for the *kindern.*"

With a quick hug, Herman disappeared from the doorway. As tired as I was, visions of Herman, the children, and Karl swirled in my head during my half-sleep. This was my life now. I would be happy and fulfilled here. So, why did I keep wondering if I would see Karl again?

Lord, thank You for safely delivering me to Herman and the kindern. Keep my mind clear and focused on Your will. Amen.

CHAPTER 7
Preparing for Christmas

"For to us a child is born, to us a son is given; and the government
shall be upon his shoulder, and his name shall be called Wonderful
Counselor, Mighty God, Everlasting Father, Prince of Peace."

Isaiah 9:6

Herman was right about Hannah warming up to me. Within a few days, she was toddling her first steps into my arms. Not being able to pronounce her l's yet, she called me "Ena." Hans spent fruitless time trying to correct her, but Hannah disregarded most anything Hans told her to do.

Hans was an attentive brother for a three-year old. He made sure his sister did not attempt the stairs by herself and kept a vigil to be sure she did not go near the fireplace or hot stove. I wasn't surprised Hannah began saying no to most everything. Her brother scolded her with no almost every waking minute. "No steps, Hannah. No, too hot, Hannah. No, you get hurt Hannah." The tot did not make a move without her brother telling her no.

That did not keep her from trying to be with him, though. As she became more stable on her chubby legs, she followed Hans from room to room, calling "Hans, Hans."

Both adorable children clung to their father when he was inside, but he busied himself outdoors in the barn with the animals or repaired implements with his shop tools, leaving the children to my care most hours of the day.

"How did you manage the *kindern* during harvest?" I asked Herman during dinner one evening. "I mean, chasing youngsters around at such a busy time. You are out of the house a good share of the day now."

Herman shifted in his chair as if I had scolded him for his poor fathering. "I have good neighbors. You have already met Greta and Helmut. Frau Greta practically adopted the *kindern* as her own grandchildren. It filled an ache in her for grandmothering, since none of her own family live nearby."

He nodded at the tots gobbling their dinner of mashed dumplings at the table. I waited for Herman to continue. Between bites, he realized I wanted more.

"I must take you over to meet Dagmar and Josef Bruns. God sent special people to help when Katarina died. Dagmar and Katarina had grown very close before her passing. The two of them helped each other navigate farm life together in a strange land. Dagmar was here for Hannah's birth and Katarina's death. If it had not been for the Bruns helping with the *kindern*, I don't know what . . ."

He placed his hands over his face to hide whatever emotion it might give away.

"I'm sorry, Herman. I didn't mean to bring up bad memories. I can tell there are good people here. I can't wait to meet more of them."

He raised his head to meet my eyes again. "This Sunday, we will go to church. You will meet more of the community then. We are in the season of Advent now, so the ladies will have decorated the church in holly and bows." He smiled as he remembered past Christmases. "Hans should be old enough to understand some of it this year. Christmas will be fun for him."

I knew, in his heart, he still thought about Katarina and how she would miss her babies growing up and celebrating Christmas with them.

"I can't wait. Two months on a ship. Time in New Orleans and on the Miss-is-sip-pi River. It seems like forever since I attended a proper church service."

I placed my small hand over Herman's massive farm hands, and we both smiled a familiar smile of family solidarity.

*O*continued to settle in at the farm with Herman and the children, which proved an almost effortless transition. Herman upheld the family traditions he loved in Germany, so everything felt familiar in this new country. The children's world revolved entirely around my own now. Although I had arrived only days before, the children treated me as if I had been there forever.

On the following Sunday, I dressed the children in their finest clothes, while making a mental note that I needed to be sewing soon. They would outgrow their snug shirts and dresses in their wardrobe within a month, and the time for layers against the cold December mornings would beckon additional protection. With no extra choices for insulated warmth on their little bodies, I wrapped both of them in warm blankets as I tucked them onto the wagon for the ride to church.

True to Greta's word, our destination was the little white church at the crossroads we had passed by as we crossed the Rattan Prairie on that first trip to Herman's. A small sign near the door read, "Zion

Lutheran Church," a German-speaking church. We parked very similar wagons and carts and tied horses in front of the church. I stepped toward the open double doors of the church, marked with a single cross each. I sheltered the bundled children from being swept away by a sudden gust of wintry wind before the doors swung shut again.

Herman led us to a vacant spot on a pew—not too close to the front, especially with small children, but not the last row either—that fit our little family perfectly. The last row of our church at home had been reserved for the chronically late or those with fussy little ones. Hannah and Hans had not shown signs of fussiness since my arrival, so I assumed they would be well-behaved through a worship service.

Traditional blue Advent paraments spread over the altar. A bouquet of pine greenery wrapped in a festive red bow peered above the table, where a Bible lay open, presumably set there for the service. The white candles, yet unlit, spired over the tall lampstands on either side of the altar.

Evergreens and holly sat in the windows of the narrow slits of stained glass on either side of the sanctuary. A red ribbon accented each window as well, and a white pillar candle towered in the middle of each arrangement. The Advent wreath near the altar held the candles for the four weeks leading up to Christmas. Only one Advent candle would be lit today, but an additional one would be added each week until the center Christmas candle joined them on Christmas Eve.

Hans nestled between Herman and me on the hardwood bench, and Hannah snuggled on my lap. I scanned the sanctuary and mainly saw young families like Herman's, sitting side by side. Greta and Helmut sat in the second row, and she turned to nod a knowing smile at us as we arrived.

A couple without children sat at the other end of our pew. The man, approximately Herman's age, shook Herman's hand as we slid into our designated spot. The young woman leaned over to whisper something to me, but I could not hear her clearly. I think she was offering to help with the children if I needed it. I smiled and nodded a thank you for her kindness.

The opening hymn began, and my attention redirected back to the minister. He was a serious young man with a booming voice that filled the church as he led the piano-accompanied songs. I recognized the hymn "Trostet, Troset Meine Lieben"[5] as a traditional Advent hymn from home. We sang:

Make ye straight what long was crooked,

Make the rougher places plain:

Let your hearts be true and humble,

As befits His holy reign,

For the glory of the Lord

Now o'er earth is shed abroad,

And all flesh shall see the token

That His Word is never broken.

I had traveled abroad to some rough places. Now I just wanted the Lord to help me be a faithful and humble helper to my brother. The Old Testament reading was Isaiah 61, and the Gospel text was

---

5   "Comfort, Comfort, Ye My People"

Luke 1:76–78 about preparing the way for the Lord. A fitting Scripture, since it was so close to Christmas. I let the Word soothe me.

With the worship service in my native language, it almost felt as if I had never left Germany, other than not having my other brothers and sisters here with Momma and Papa. In the years since Herman had left Germany, I could tell he had more than grown into his fatherhood title with distinction. Papa would be proud of him.

The minister ceremoniously dismissed the congregation at the end of Martin Luther's hymn, "Savior of the Nations Come." Since most remained reluctant to go out into the cold—and Herman wanted to introduce me to many of his neighbors—we milled around in the back of the church, and I tried to remember the names of all the hand-shakers. Herman introduced our pew companions as his dear neighbors, Josef and Dagmar Bruns.

"Herman told me about you. He said he was lucky to have you as neighbors."

Dagmar took my hand. "Oh, I think we are the lucky ones. Josef and Herman are nearly inseparable during the spring and summer. They work side by side as if they own the same ground. I don't think brothers could be closer." She glanced away. "I felt the same way about Katie."

No one had called Katarina "Katie" back in Frohn, but the loving term suited her well.

"I am sure it was hard on everyone," I offered.

"Yes. If you need anything, be sure to let us know. Herman was beside himself, waiting for you to arrive."

Not imagining my brother being over-anxious about much of anything, I smiled back. Then I remembered the sewing projects for the children.

"Dagmar, where do you shop? I need to buy fabric to make more winter clothes for the children. They are outgrowing most of the things at the house."

"Let me take you into town tomorrow if Herman can spare you. I will show you around our village. Both Widow's Mape and Tyron's General Store carry most anything you need. The town is growing."

Before I could finish planning my day with Dagmar, Herman cupped my elbow and guided me toward other parishioners he wanted me to meet. I tried to concentrate on the faces and commit their names to memory as if Herman might quiz me on the way home.

I was able to dutifully shake hands with everyone, since Dagmar had graciously taken the sleeping Hannah from my arms. I learned most everyone farmed or owned shops in the area.

"This is the Zimmer family," Herman introduced a family.

"I am Charles," the grown son of the Zimmer family said as he stepped forward. "Herman has been waiting a long time for you to come. Me, too."

I furrowed my brow and tilted my head at his strange proclamation. "Why would you be waiting for me to come?"

"Because there are no unmarried young ladies around here."

He grinned a slightly embarrassed grin, then jammed his hands firmly in his back pockets while swaying back and forth on his heavily booted feet. His hair, slicked back under a wide-brimmed hat, emitted a greasy sheen. Although he was easily my age, he seemed too young to be thinking of marriage. I doubted if he even shaved yet.

I had not come to America to be courted, but Karl's face would be the only one that came to mind if I had.

I paused to answer, and Herman supplied a fitting one of his own before I could. "Lena came here to help watch my children, Charles, not to get married. So, you'd better find yourself another girl to chase and leave Lena alone."

I was both thankful and annoyed. I could speak for myself, but thankfully, I did not have to hurt Charles' feelings by telling him to go away. I forgot how handy big brothers could be.

Charles was not that easily persuaded, though. "You can't keep her all to yourself, Herman. If she—"

"Wants to live with us," Herman said, finishing Charles' sentence.

The issue was closed in Herman's estimation, so he turned and marched everyone to the wagon, leaving Charles to stare after us. We loaded the children into the cart and headed back home, where, thankfully, the welcome sun cut the cold, and we sat more comfortably as we rode through the prairie.

The next day, to get Christmas preparations in full swing, Dagmar and I bought fabric, candles, and ribbons for sewing and decorating. I began making Hans a blue jacket and little Hannah a baby blue gingham prairie dress with a matching bonnet. I also spent the next weeks knitting her a cream-colored sweater to keep her warm, hoping the dress was oversized enough for her to wear into springtime. Dagmar tutored me through creating the floral patterns and the feminine finishing touches for Hannah's new clothes. Once completed, I wrapped their clothes in tissue, placed them in boxes bound in red ribbon, and hid them away until Christmas.

I divided the remainder of the red ribbons into a dozen bows for the Christmas tree. I tied each one with a pearl button in the middle to catch the light better. I found a woven star Katrina had fashioned for the top of the tree tucked away in a trunk upstairs. A box of red ornaments and white candle stems awaited the season in another box, and I readied them for the anticipated tree while the children napped so as not to spoil their surprise. We were ready for Christmas.

In our German tradition, Herman sent me to Christmas Eve service ahead of him, pretending he needed to tend to the animals. Josef and Dagmar welcomed the extra riders on their wagon. An evening service was not routine for the family, so Hans did not realize this was a ploy for his father to work without the children. While Hans and Hannah were safely away, Herman would set up the Christmas tree in the front room and decorate it to surprise us when we returned home. In high spirits on the way to church, we sang "O Tannenbaum" all the way, since Hans would not allow us to sing anything else.

We slipped into our pew and visited in hushed tones while waiting for the service to begin. Before the service began, the elder lit the window candles that were surrounded by greenery and holly. The candlelight beneath the stained-glass windows caused the church to bask in a spiritual glow perfect for a Christmas evening. Flickers of reds, blues, and greens danced around the room, illuminating the season's peace.

I thought Herman sat down beside me just before the opening hymn. I scooted over to ensure he had enough room, but I peered into a different set of blue eyes. The man was not Herman, but Karl!

Karl smiled at my surprise. "You have room for me?"

I did not know what to say. He occupied the seat before I could control my tongue. I would be rude to ask him to move. There was enough room for Herman when he arrived, but how would I explain a strange man to Herman?

"I guess," I stammered as the church filled for the Christmas service.

Dagmar tilted her head my way as if to ask, "Who's that?"

I repositioned Hannah on my lap and pretended not to notice the query. Moments later, Herman snuck in the church doors and slid in from the side aisle. He passed Dagmar and Josef and sat between Dagmar and Hans. I was happy he had not come up the middle and sat beside Karl. I counted my blessings.

I am sure the pastor spoke the familiar Christmas message about the Savior being born for us, but the whole message was a blur with Karl sitting next to me. His warmth radiated through both our coats, or maybe it was my body heat rising with the thought of having him so close to my family and me. His rich alto voice sang all the Christmas hymns with gusto. He could not be ignored. It did not help that little Hannah in my lap kept reaching for something sticking out of Karl's coat pocket.

"No, Hannah," I whispered. "Leave the nice man alone."

"Glad you think I'm a nice man," Karl whispered back. "She's adorable, by the way."

He held his hand out, and Hannah grabbed his finger. She almost flung herself into his lap, but I stopped her, tugging her back on my skirt and giving her the doll to hold. Why would Hannah take to a man she had never met? She was usually wary of strangers. This man was too much of a magnet.

We finished the service singing "Silent Night." But the idea of "heavenly peace" escaped me entirely. Before the congregation rose to depart, Karl took the small, wrapped box from his coat pocket that Hannah wanted and offered it to me.

"I brought you a gift. Merry Christmas," he said as we stood.

Great. I could dismiss Karl as someone who needed a seat for the Christmas service, but how could I explain to Herman why a stranger would buy me a present?

"You shouldn't have done that. I didn't expect anything from you."

I did not reach for the gift and shifted Hannah to my other hip as we stood staring at the extended wrapped box.

"I told you I would see you again. I knew you needed some time to settle in, and I wasn't sure which farm was your brother's, so this seemed the best thing to do." He pulled my hand away from Hannah and placed the small gift in it. "Go ahead. Open it."

By now, Herman and the Bruns eyed Karl and me. "Maybe I will put it under the tree." I did not know what was in the small gift box but opening it under this scrutiny invited too many questions.

"Open it, Lena."

Hans reached up to take the small gift, mimicking his sister's attention to the box, so I wiggled the top off the gift box. In it lay a silver chain with a water droplet stone pendant.

"It is to remind you of your voyage over all that water. Like you need reminding, I suppose, but I thought the teardrop stone was fitting."

Karl ignored the gathered adults and placed the necklace over my head.

Suddenly, Herman ordered, "And who are you?"

I still had no idea how to explain this situation, but introductions might be one way to start.

"Herman, this is Karl Muller. We met on the trip over here. Karl, this is my *bruder*, Herman."

Karl extended his hand to Herman, but Herman did not oblige.

"I've heard so much about you. Lena couldn't wait to get to you and your children. They are delightful, by the way."

Karl reached over and took Hannah's hand as she was trying to eat the ribbon from the box.

"I have heard nothing about you."

Herman kept us both in his line of sight, trying to gauge the interloper better.

"Well, I only helped Lena navigate her way from New Orleans to here. I live in Alton. I wanted to be sure she got properly to her brother. It is not always easy or advisable for a young lady to travel alone."

Herman shifted from the scolding admonition. "I suppose I should thank you for your help, but we can manage fine on our own now. Good night, Herr Muller."

Herman took Hannah from my arms before she ate the necklace Karl had draped around my neck, then turned and reached the door in two purposeful steps.

Karl grabbed my hand as I attempted to follow. "So, you didn't tell him about me at all?"

"No." What else could I say? What could I tell Herman? I liked a man I met on a steamship? Herman might likely lock me up.

"I've been busy with the *kindern*. There hasn't been much time for all those travel details." I looked at him a bit sheepishly and pursed my lips. "Besides, I didn't feel the need to tell Herman all about you when you are not the reason I came."

I hoped I sounded dismissive enough to this man who only treated me with kindness.

"But it can be."

He leaned closer, and I worried his romantic intentions might take over right there in the house of God. A kiss here would spell disaster, for sure. I had to get away. He filled my senses with forbidden ideas.

"We are leaving. Christmas is waiting at home," Herman interrupted.

I turned abruptly and followed Herman to the cart, leaving Karl in the church, watching after me. Some merry Christmas. I had not even said thank you for the lovely necklace I played with around my neck.

CHAPTER 8
Coming Clean

"Create in me a clean heart, O God, and renew a right spirit within me."

Psalm 51:10

I hummed "Silent Night" to myself all the way home, promptly lulling Hannah to sleep in my arms. Herman never looked my way, although we were seated on the same wagon bench with only Hans wedged between us under the winter blankets. He maintained his focus on the dark winter roads as if a creature might jump out at any moment.

Herman kept his steely blue eyes peering through the dark all the way home after the Christmas Eve service as if fearful of missing a turn on a road he had memorized from a multitude of trips. I could not read his thoughts, but certainly, he stewed over meeting Karl at church. When he was ready, he would unload a firestorm of German wrath.

We pulled up to the house, and I carried sleeping Hannah inside. Hans, still awake but rubbing his eyes, let his father guide him through the front door. The magnificent Christmas tree Herman had decorated in our absence stood by the front window. I was stunned. The reflective touches of red ribbon against the glass ornaments he had added to the pine brought the tree to life. Katarina had stored away more decorations than I had realized as an inheritance from her family.

Herman lit the small candles fastened around the tree with a small twig ignited from the kerosene lamp. The golden baubles flit dancing rays of magic into the room, illuminating a lovely white angel, who stood sentinel atop the majestic eight-foot evergreen.

I stood there with Hannah in my arms, almost wanting to wake her so she could see this Christmas Eve sight. But, alas, she would be delighted with the tree in the morning, and waking a sleeping baby did not seem wise.

Hans quit rubbing his sleepy eyes and stared wide-eyed at the miracle of Christmas before him. Then, he gathered his sleepy wits and squealed, "Chrithmuth is here!"

Herman scooped Hans up so he could see the spectacle better and giggled at his son through a deep throat rumble, all the while giving him a good-hearted squeeze. Katarina would be so proud of them. My heart constricted, too, as the Lord reminded me of my promise to this budding family. I could not abandon them for the attention of a man I had met on my journey. I could not allow Karl to distract me from my purpose here. Herman and the children needed me. This was home.

With the children tucked safely in bed, I debated whether to sit quietly by the cozy fire and the beautiful decorations downstairs and soak up the holy aura or head directly to bed. I hoped Herman might enjoy the time alone to reflect on Christmas and his growing family. I decided I was not ready to be confronted about Karl, and slumber beckoned for a more peaceful solution to an emotionally draining day. I also needed to be up early to fix a Christmas strudel for breakfast, which gave me another excuse to disappear for the evening.

Sweet dreams of a kind man in a green jacket delighted my slumber. He and the children danced under the same Christmas tree, singing carols and basking in the luminous candlelight. A combined joy and peace filled the air until a dark cloud covered the scene and the music soured. Then, in a puff, everything disappeared. I awoke bewildered.

I dressed for my breakfast duties. Herman was pulling on his boots to check the animals while I started the family strudel: apples, nuts, butter, and cinnamon wrapped in a cocoon of freshly rolled dough layers that had sat to rise overnight. I may not receive the top family baker accolades like my little sister Eva, but we all were trained in this yearly family tradition. Years of helping Momma in the kitchen made this delicious creation second nature, and it brought back so many loving memories of family. The delightful smells of the morning baking wafted upstairs, gently waking the children from their Christmas morning sleep.

Hans, helping his little sister down the stairs, tried to tell her about the big tree in the house. "It came for Chrithmuth," he told her. Hannah's eyes went straight to the angel atop the tree as she worked her way down each step, one bottom bump at a time. Her squeal of delight echoed through the house.

Herman entered the house to see his children enthralled with the joy of Christmas morning. Unlike the night before, enticing gifts now lay wrapped beneath the tree. Each package, surrounded by simple brown paper and tied with a red ribbon, had a child's name scrawled on it.

Herman put Hannah on his lap and instructed Hans to hand her a box with her name. Then, he pointed out one for Hans. Hans opened a well-carved wood locomotive with working wheels, two train cars, and a caboose. Each one was intricately painted in blues and reds with a black smokestack and trim.

Hans' eyes widened as he touched each piece and gently set them on the floor to check their rolling ability. He attached the cars and began "choo-chooing" them in circles. Little Hannah found a box of wooden blocks with brightly painted yellow, purple, and green letters and numbers carved on each side. All those extra hours Herman had spent in the barn entailed creating gifts of love for his children to give them a memorable Christmas morning. My smile crowded my eyes into slits that leaked tears of happiness at the sight.

My presents of a dress for Hannah and a jacket for Hans paled in comparison to the toys Herman had crafted. What child gets excited about receiving clothes for Christmas? Enthralled with their new toys, Hans helped Hannah build and rebuild structures for his train to navigate around the room. Hannah delighted in knocking down whatever Hans constructed, and the two laughed at the destruction. I could hardly pull them away to eat breakfast or get dressed. Herman sipped his coffee and watched them play, giving occasional instructions about making a bridge or tunnel for the new train.

By noon, Hans' and Hannah's steam ran lower than their train, so they lay down for short naps. The invitation for Dagmar and Josef to share Christmas dinner prompted me to busy myself with preparations in the kitchen while the children slept.

As I set the table before the guests arrived, Herman caught me unaware and held out a secret gift he had saved for me. I had been so busy with thoughts about the children, I had not bothered to create anything for my brother. Oh, how could I be so thoughtless? Herman had been nothing but kind and appreciative about my coming to his aid. He provided for his household, embraced all his adult responsibilities, and welcomed me with all the respect a brother owed a sister. I had difficulty remembering him as the same boy who grumbled about sharing a loft with his younger brothers back in Germany.

"Oh, Herman. I didn't think . . . I mean, I didn't get you anything."

He stood there silently with his hand outstretched, wordlessly willing me to take his offering. I took the gift from his calloused hand and untied the red ribbon. The brown paper fell away to reveal an exquisite jewelry box with silver trim around the tiny hinges. A small lock and key held the latch together in the front. I turned the key and opened it to see a dark blue velvet-lined interior. I stroked the kitten-soft fur before returning to Herman's gaze.

"It's beautiful," I said.

He fought back a tear as he hoarsely said, "It was Katarina's." He paused to gulp and then continued, "I thought about saving it for Hannah, but she won't need anything like that for a long time, and you are doing so much for us."

I reached up to hug him as I set the jewelry box aside, and I gave him a kiss him on the cheek. "I will treasure it always. And when the time is right, I will be sure it goes to Hannah. I'm sure her mother would want that. After all, what jewels do I have for such a wonderful box?"

No sooner had I spoken the words than I realized we both had the same thought. Karl! Just last night at church, he had given me a keepsake necklace. I had not dared to wear it today because it would only stir Herman's ire. Instead, I had walked right into a conversation successfully avoided last night.

Herman's disposition soured as he looked from me to the gift. "Tell me about that man who gave you the necklace last night."

"As he said, his name is Karl Muller. He was kind to me on the trip up the river, and we sort of became friends on the paddle wheeler."

"Men who are *sort of* friends don't give women jewelry. You have been here more than a month now, Lena. Why did you not tell me about him?"

"What was there to tell? He grew up here and knows the area, so he told me helpful things about navigating the Mississippi and Alton since he lives here and such. He was just friendly."

"He obviously wants to be more than friends. A young, unchaperoned girl should not become *friends* with a grown man." Herman nearly spit out the word "friends."

"There is no place to be alone on a steamship, *bruder.* I really would not say I was unchaperoned."

At least, that part was true. No need to tell him I spent nearly a whole day in Alton with Karl alone or that he almost kissed me.

"I was traveling with a German family I met on the *Olbers*, the Kruegers. Remember? I told you about them. I helped with their young *kindern* since they had a small son die on the trip. I tried to comfort them as much as I could. I guess you can say they chaperoned me well. I usually had three youngsters at my side, too." I smiled, remembering their attention. "They got off at St. Louis."

Why had I added that last part? I supposed I did not want Herman to expect me to produce them as proof somehow. With his icy stare holding fast, I rambled on. "We helped each other during our months traveling together. That way, it did not look to outsiders as if I was traveling alone, and Frau Krueger appreciated having someone else around to help corral the *kindern*. It worked quite well for all of us."

"And where was Herr Muller when you were supposedly chasing tots? I don't see a man like that being a nursemaid." Herman shifted his stance and folded his arms while waiting for me to explain.

"Herman, you would be surprised. The little boys got scared on the steamship because the engines were roaring. There was a race on the river or something and Karl—um, Herr Muller—took the family inside away from the noise and told them a story about a Native American chief, which kept their minds quite occupied. He is a good storyteller."

As I spoke, I neglected to reign in my enthusiastic appreciation for Karl, and I saw more clouds burrow into Herman's brow.

"He was being very nice to distract them like that. You can't fault him for being kind, can you?"

"Lena. You are young and naive. Men don't just do things to be nice. They conspire and beguile young maids for their own desires. And you think your Herr Muller is just being nice to you?" He took a step closer to emphasize his point. "You will not be seeing him again."

"What?" Why did my brother think he could order me around? "I cannot stop a man from attending church, can I? He did nothing to be shunned by us. He has been nothing but kind."

I realized this was not how I wanted this conversation to go. I tried to calm myself. "I know I did not come to America to find a man. You brought me here at your own expense to help you with your family, and that is what I plan to do. Do not worry that I will run off with the first man who looks my way, *bruder*. I am not a fickle female who is completely ignorant of the world. I know my obligations, and I will make sure Karl Muller knows the same thing."

Not wanting another retort from Herman, I turned my back on him to further attend to Christmas dinner preparations, leaving the jewelry box on the table. My hands busied themselves mashing potatoes, but my mind was on Herman and Karl. What a thankless thing to do. Here Herman had given me the sweetest gift, and I had yelled at him. He only wanted to protect me. On the other hand, Karl had done nothing but be a gentleman, keeping me from harm's way several times and then seeking me out to give me a Christmas gift. Why should I be angry with him?

I knew I had to break Karl's pull on me. He must shower his charms on some other damsel. I was committed to Herman's family for now. I could not ask him to wait until Herman's children are grown before he can come courting. He must move on.

I was lost in these thoughts as the children awoke and returned to playing by the tree. Dinner guests knocked at the door, and Dagmar and Josef entered with more gifts for Hannah and Hans. Opening the gifts, the *kindern* found that Dagmar had made Hannah an adorable rag doll with golden hair to match her young mistress. Hans opened a couple of picture books full of puppies and farm animals. The domestic scene restored the morning's joy, but Herman's demeanor forecast was partly sunny with a chance of more clouds moving in.

Herman said grace as we gathered around the dinner table. "Dear Lord, thank You for gracing us with Your presence this holy day of Your Son's birth. We thank You for our good friends, good health, and family. Especially, we thank You that You brought Lena here to be with us. She is an answer to many prayers and is here only because of Your bounteous grace and mercy. In Jesus' name, amen."

The prayer was sweet and heartfelt, and it reminded me why God had brought me safely to Herman's door, which was certainly the purpose of Herman's emphasis.

Lord, some of Your safe providence was manifested through the hands of Karl, even if Herman does not know that.

Dagmar asked for my Sauerbraten recipe while we dined on the marinated roast, specially chosen by Frau Greta for our Christmas dinner. She had prepared the *Mohnpielen*, poppy pudding, for the meal; and I needed her recipe for the sweet bread she had soaked generously in rum, milk, raisins, and nuts.

We women swapped recipes while the men spoke of plans for spring planting. Josef and Herman's farms ran adjacent for acres, and since neither could afford farm crews, they assisted each other in many duties. The two friends huddled together, speaking of seeds, roots, plows, and animals—as if no one else sat in the room.

With full tummies and a full day of excitement, the *kindern* slumbered early. Dagmar and Josef visited on into the evening. I learned Dagmar was five or six years older than I, but our womanly connection bonded us while the men spoke farm business to each other. Neither of us left our homes often, so to relax in the company of another female filled us with a sense of companionship and giggles the menfolk could not fill.

I had not noticed that the men's conversation switched to politics until Herman said, "I don't know why we need to get involved with what people do with their slaves. It's not our problem."

"Do you think the country will be all right when some states are free states and others are slaveholding?" Josef asked. "Some talk about a war, and then it will be everyone's problem."

"People always talk about war to scare people into taking a side. I don't plan to fall into that trap. I'm going to stick to myself, my farm, and my family," Herman said, looking across the room at Dagmar and me listening to their serious tone.

I should stay out of their conversation, but I felt prodded to ask, "Have you seen the way the slaves are treated? I saw some horrible things during my time in New Orleans. No one should be treated like that."

"What?" Surprised that I had entered their male-centric world, Herman scolded me. "Lena, you don't know about these things. They even had slaves in the Bible. We farmers need to leave things alone. It is not our affair."

"But, Karl . . . "

The moment his name escaped my lips, Pandora's box sprung open. I tried to close it again and bit my lip, but the damage was done.

"Muller? Did he fill your head with political garbage on your trip up the river?"

"We did not speak of politics at all. My eyes witnessed how those poor people were savagely treated. I was nearly struck by a horse's whip that a carriage driver meant for a black man crossing the street near the docks. Karl—Herr Muller—kept me from harm by moving me out of the way—even before we had officially met."

"What are you prattling on about? You had no business spending time at the docks of a city like New Orleans."

"I was *not* spending time there, *bruder*! I was being escorted by a woman from the German Society away from the *Olbers*. We hadn't even gotten too far before I was almost struck on a busy street," I said, stomping my foot. "Furthermore, just around the corner from there was an actual slave auction. It was the most pathetic thing I have ever seen."

"That is the last place that woman should have taken you. Don't these people understand how the sensibilities of young girls can be turned into melodrama?" Exasperated, Herman continued. "In any case, what is happening to the slaves in this country does not concern us. We need to mind our own business." He turned, intending to dismiss me and continue the conversation with Josef.

Dagmar and Josef glanced at each other uncomfortably and began to rise. "It is time we head home, I think. The time is late."

Dagmar handed Josef his coat and stepped into the kitchen for her empty dish.

"No need to leave, Josef." Herman had not intended to drive his guests away. "The evening is not that late."

"No. We should go. We had a great time." Josef looked back toward the Christmas tree. "Someday, maybe we will be the ones to invite you over to watch our children open gifts." Josef faced me. "And that was a terrific meal, Lena. You'll make a husband proud someday."

Lord, that's the last thing Herman needed to hear now, I silently prayed.

Dagmar returned from the kitchen and hugged me goodbye before Herman walked them to the door. By the time the door closed, I had climbed to the top of the stairs—escaping to my room before the conversation returned to Karl or slaves again. Exhausted from all the Christmas preparations, I found sleep still refused to find me as my mind recounted the day. But eventually, I slipped into a dreamless sleep.

CHAPTER 9

Slippery Slope

"So whether we are at home or away, we make it our aim to please him."

2 Corinthians 5:9

The winter days became blusterier. The wind and sleet made the outdoors miserable, but the *kindern* played happily with their Christmas gifts and did not seem to notice the dreary conditions as long as the home fires roared inside.

Herman, on the other hand, needed to venture outside to care for the animals and sometimes did not return to the warmth of the house during daylight hours. The stormy weather mirrored his miserable temperament when he re-entered the domestic tranquility of *kindern* playing. He never raised his voice about the disheveled state of play in the parlor. However, he did not joy in their merriment or offer to read Hans any of his new books. A permanent cloud followed him as he closed himself off from the rest of us.

I said little, not wanting his anger to erupt again about Karl. How could I convince him not to worry about this man who had interjected himself into our lives without invitation? I planned on staying with Herman and the *kindern* as long as they needed me.

Another Sunday rolled around, and I held my breath. Would Karl be in church? Should I pray for him to be there, so I could tell him to go away? Having Karl near would only upset Herman again. If Karl did not appear, telling him to go away still hung in the balance, yet I enjoyed his company so much. Herman could not keep Karl from attending church, even if he ordered me not to see him again. Whether Karl came or not, neither situation appealed to me.

The sun illuminated the previous week of snow on the reflective drifts of white-draped tree branches and blinded us during the sleigh ride into Bethel. The church glowed in the morning hues of gold as if God had taken up residency and awaited the worshippers to arrive and sing their glories to Him. Images of the people of Israel protected with God's fire as they entered the Promised Land descended on me. Surely, the Lord meant to lead me out of the winter doldrums today.

I scanned the pews for Karl after my eyes adjusted to the relative darkness of the sanctuary. He was not sitting in any of the pews. Charles Zimmer's eye caught me perusing the congregation as we entered, and he offered a brief wave. I averted my eyes to shuffling the children forward to our usual pew. I did not intend to encourage another suitor. Charles' intentions must stay unrequited.

I silently prayed that the sermon would enlighten me. I needed some spiritual guidance, for sure. The Old Testament reading came from Isaiah 62:1-5. I listened carefully for a sign and was shocked when I heard verses four and five mention marriage four times. This must mean God wanted Karl to court and then marry me. Why else would we be reading those verses today? My heart raced. Could this be the sign I had prayed for?

I told myself to calm down. The pastor continued reading Psalm 36:5-10. The last verse said, "Oh, continue your steadfast love to those who know you, and your righteousness to the upright of heart!" Continue? Love those who know you? That sounded like I should stay with Herman and the children. After all, I didn't know Karl that well, and I certainly couldn't continue a life with a man I had just met.

My imagination ran wild. The man had given me only a necklace—not asked me to marry him. What was I thinking?

"All rise for the Gospel reading in John 2:1-11, the wedding at Cana," Pastor Klein said.

A wedding? You must be kidding me. God, You have my heart and mind in knots. Please use the pastor's sermon to help me sort out this mess.

I hung on every word the pastor spoke. Pastor Klein exhorted, "The wedding at Cana did not reveal who was getting married or which important guests may have attended the event. Ultimately, the wedding itself is not the important part of the Scripture. It is not about the wedding; it is about Jesus. The wedding illustrates how God acts for ordinary people in ordinary situations."

If I took my eyes off myself and my problems long enough, where would I see Jesus at work? I looked down at Herman's precious children, nestled between us. I observed Hans flipping through the new books he was allowed to bring to the service and Hannah clutching her new ragdoll. They were the face of Jesus. I did not need fantasies of a wedding dancing in my head when God's work lay before me. I gave Hannah an extra squeeze and basked in this newfound happy state. I felt blessed that Karl had not attended services today to complicate the morning's revelations further.

Herman saw my gentle tug on Hannah before opening the hymnal for the post-sermon singing. I saw him smile as he watched me fall in love with his sweet urchins, and the tension in him seemed to relax. I am sure his prayers about our domestic arrangement unfolded as a blessing before him. The fear of losing me to a handsome stranger made him unnecessarily anxious and irritable just when life had begun to fall into an acceptable reality for his young family again.

Dismissed from worship, the congregation visited briefly inside before venturing out into the winter and made plans for social events to break the monotony of snowbound days before spring appeared again.

"It is turning out to be such a nice day. Why don't we go sledding?" Josef asked as he helped Dagmar wrap her scarf around her neck. "A hill near the creek would make a great sledding spot. Hans and Hannah will like it, I'm sure."

Herman looked at me, and I shrugged a "why not" back at him. "We can get a bite of lunch and meet you there afterward."

Excited about this new outdoor adventure, we did not notice Charles Zimmer approaching our group.

"I have some gliders from when I was a boy. I'll bring them over."

His comical ear-to-ear grin masked the adult demeanor he intended to portray. *Who invited you?* I found myself thinking.

I quickly chastised myself for my unchristian attitude. Instead, Herman nodded a thank you to Charles before boarding our horse-drawn sleigh, which confirmed his welcome.

After a warm dumpling lunch and a brief nap for the children, we bundled them up again and met Dagmar and Josef at the preordained site. The steep slope led down to the frozen streambed, but we found a gentler one for the tots.

Herman put Hans on a coaster by himself with instructions to hold on. "Uncle" Josef stood at the bottom of the run to catch him. Hans' eyes widened as he streaked downward, but the shrill sounds erupting from him displayed pure joy. The minute he slid to a stop near Josef's feet, Hans was pleading, "Again!" He grabbed the rope of his new adventure and scrambled back up like a snowy tumble bug, ready for another run.

Hannah caught her brother's delight and wanted to try her own ride. She was not big enough to slide by herself, so I climbed on the sled, and Herman placed her on my lap.

"Sit still, Hannah," I told the squirmy tot as I wrapped my arms around her.

I was centering Hannah on my legs when the voice behind me asked, "Are you ready?"

Charles' hand squeezed my shoulder. Unable to recoil from his heavy gloved touch because I was settling the wiggling Hannah onto my lap, I tried to stop his push.

"Almost," I said as I tugged Hannah closer to my chest.

Before I completely centered us both on the sled, the overzealous Charles abruptly hurled Hannah and me down the snowbank at breakneck speed. I tried to keep us upright and hang on to a squealing Hannah, but I leaned too far to miss a rock and flipped us over in a heap of fresh white powder. I still held her tightly, but the sled hit a nearby tree as it continued without passengers.

"Hannah! Are you all right?"

I held the sure-to-be-frightened girl at arm's length to look her over. With one gasp, she started laughing. Her cheerful giggles washed me in relief. Both Herman and Josef ran from opposite directions to assess any damage. Herman scooped Hannah in his arms, then turned on Charles.

"What do you think you are doing? You could have hurt them!" Herman yelled up to Charles, who still stood at the launch site watching the fury below.

"I thought they were ready. I'm sorry," he sheepishly said, jamming his gloved hands in his coat pockets. "I didn't mean to hurt anyone. I thought they were ready. Honest."

Herman strode up the snowy slope again with Hannah on his shoulders while Josef offered his hand to help me up. My ripped stockings clung to my bloody knee and dripped red rivulets in the snow.

"It looks like you're injured," Josef said as his eyes landed on the wound.

"I'm sure it's just a scrape. Nothing more."

The gash stung too much to tromp through the knee-high winter scape, however, and I did not feel like jaunting down the hill again.

Josef took the upended sled, and I plodded along behind him as he shouted up to Herman, "Lena got a nasty cut on her leg."

"What?" Herman looked from me to Charles. "You are too dangerous for this little outing Charles. I think you should leave."

Charles stood for a moment, unsure if Herman had the right to order him off the property. The unwelcome stare from Herman convinced him to reconsider his options, and he dragged his sleds behind him like a whipped dog making his way back to his family's homestead.

"Maybe we should call it a day, so Lena can tend to that cut."

Herman put Hannah down to check if anything else might need gathering up before leaving. Suddenly, Hans started to cry. "But, Papa, I want more."

"I have an idea," Dagmar interrupted from her uphill sentry position. "You two men can stay out with the *kindern* a while longer if you want. I'll see to Lena." She gave me a sisterly wink. "With Charles not here to be reckless, you two can keep the *kindern* safe. We can have hot chocolate ready for you when you come back."

Neither of them answered before Dagmar tugged my sleeve to escort me back to the farmhouse.

"I don't know why Charles thinks he can butt into our fun," I told Dagmar on the way back.

"That's easy. He is sweet on you."

"I am not here to find a beau. I am here to help Herman with Hans and Hannah."

"I know, but would you say that if the man with the necklace came sledding?"

My rosy cheeks held too much warmth for such a cold day. I could not profess ignorance to Dagmar's words. She had seen our exchange at church, though we had not spoken of it.

"His name is Karl Muller. We met on the Mississippi. I need to tell him I am not to be courting anytime soon. He must be sent away like young Charles. There is no place in my life right now for a beau." I breathed out my last sentence as if it hurt because it created such an ache in my soul.

"You can't live for others completely without considering your own needs, Lena. Herman cannot expect you to dedicate your whole life to his family. You may want one of your own someday."

"Well, someday is not now. So, let's not talk about it anymore."

I attempted to outpace Dagmar, but my leg hindered my gait, and we remained side by side all the way to the house.

Safely back at the farmhouse, Dagmar sat me on a kitchen chair and rolled down my stockings. "Let's look at that cut."

The cut was not too deep but ran six inches to my shin. A bandage stemmed the tide of blood and would keep it clean for a few days while it healed. Dagmar took the lead in concocting the steaming hot chocolate for the sledders while I rested my bandaged leg. A short while later, the men and *kindern* arrived home saying the children had tired of the cold. They stomped and shook off the accumulated snow from coats and boots.

All their winter items were tented near the stove to dry, and each sledder sipped from their steaming mugs. A little fresh snow cooled the children's cups. Hannah, overdue for another nap, slumped in her highchair. Both rosy-cheeked imps sipped their "coffee," as Hans called it, before Herman and Josef carried them to bed for a well-deserved nap.

That evening, after a late dinner, I opened my Bible to read. I read the Scripture that told me to "walk by faith, not by sight."[6]

"'Walk by faith, not by sight'?" I said out loud to myself.

Praying, I whispered, *I am trying, Lord. Please give me the faith and sight to do Your will. I am not sure Herman knows Your will for me, even if he thinks he knows Your will for him and the kindern.*

Then I read, "Whether we are at home or away, we make it our aim to please him."[7]

I silently continued my prayer. *I am so far from home, Lord. Even though Herman has made a wonderful home here, I do not have my momma or papa to help me make decisions. Whatever I do, I must do what is right by You. Teach me what is right for me, and I will follow. If I keep my faith in You, You will indeed show me the right way and put me in my right mind about all of this.*

---

6   2 Corinthians 5:7
7   2 Corinthians 5:9

CHAPTER 10
Winter Woes

"And perhaps I will stay with you or even spend the winter,
so that you may help me on my journey, wherever I go."
1 Corinthians 16:6

The pleasant sunny Sunday snow day dissolved into blustery storms again. The incessant storms varied from sleet to ice to hail to more snow. The *kindern* seemed to lose interest in their Christmas treasures and instead longed to run around outdoors. For two Sundays, the weather blew nasty storms across the plains, gathering gloomy temperaments along with the clouds. The risk of the *kindern's* health or the horses' well-being kept us from attending church services. We longed for an uplifting message from God and interaction with neighbors.

Housework seemed impossible. The distraction of two needful tots with diapering, feeding, and entertaining left items lying around willy-nilly. Laundry draped around the house in a never-ending attempt to dry diapers and clothing, since nothing dried in these drafty winter conditions.

I had to shoo the *kindern* from underfoot as I made meals or swept the floors, and they tried to entertain themselves by wrangling over each other's things. Constant handling left Hans' new books tattered and dog-eared and he recited every page by heart or told his own story based on the colored pictures to his captive audience, Hannah.

She repeated new words her brother taught her from the hours of attention. She toted her doll everywhere, introducing her to all her imaginary friends as her language skills improved daily. She named the doll Margie, but she called her imaginary friends John, Jick, and Jack. The way she jabbered about them, it was difficult to determine if they were all one person or several. With them, she had playmates at the ready whether Hans wanted to play with her or not.

Herman busied himself with the outdoor chores of feeding animals, chopping wood, or moving snow to make paths between work areas. He reread all the books and magazines available in the house when nothing beckoned him outdoors, and he grew restless for spring when he could work in the fields again.

Three Sundays had passed since the sledding day, and Herman insisted on attending church regardless of the weather. He needed to socialize away from the farm like the rest of us. We watched the skies and said our prayers so God would let us venture to town come Sunday.

Finally, God answered our prayers for clear skies on a crisp Sunday morning. Although the roads were iced over and the tree limbs struggled under the heavy ice coating, we bundled the *kindern* to escape the confines of the farm. Their excited little bodies wiggled into the warm outdoor-bound layers, since they wanted to run outside just as much as newborn lambs.

Herman prepared the sleigh, and we carefully inched into town at a crawling pace since the horse found it challenging to keep her footing. The bundled *kindern* chattered happily on the wagon seat, delighted to be outside again, even though they could see their breath circle in front of their faces. Their rosy cheeks hovered over their smiles, and they were terrific little snow babies on the way to church.

We arrived late, just as the congregation finished their first hymn. We quickly ushered everyone to our "reserved" pew, noticing many other places remained empty on this cold winter's day.

I listened closely to the pastor read Exodus 17:1-7. I had not been in the company of fellow believers outside my own home for nearly a month, so, certainly, God would speak to me today.

"Why do you test the Lord?" The pastor's words rang loud and clear.

Why did Pastor Klein or God Himself seem to speak directly to me in these sermons? I knew this passage pointed to the Israelites grumbling about their circumstances in the wilderness, but I felt convicted. True, I had not voiced dissatisfaction to Herman, but I often complained enough in my heart to distress my Creator. Was I testing God?

The pastor continued by reading Psalm 95:1-9. These verses reminded me to sing praises to the Lord and not complain. Maybe the dreary weather dampened my usually sunny disposition. Happy to be reminded in God's Word that He is deserving of praise no matter our circumstances, I straightened my posture and smiled, bracing myself for more timely instruction.

Satisfied, I looked over the congregation. The sanctuary gaped with large, empty pews. Those who lived in town and on nearby farms sat in their respective seats, and I made mental notes of those absent: the Bartels, the Schmidts, the Neumans, the Koenigs. Then I noted one person *was* present.

Karl sat alone on the far side of the church, not too far below the pulpit. Why had I not noticed him there before? We had not spoken since Christmas Eve, and it was now February. Of course I had not forgotten him. That was impossible. He might not fit into my life here, but I would never forget him. I did need to pay attention to the sermon and stop my wandering thoughts, though.

The pastor continued the Scripture readings, and I heard him say, "'Exercises self-control in all things.'"[8] Like I needed reminding.

The Lord tested my resolve as Karl peeked over his left shoulder at me. He winked before he turned forward again like a dutiful congregant. My heart raced and refused to be controlled, even though I willed it to behave. I breathed a few shallow breaths and returned my focus to the congregation's instruction to rise for the Gospel reading about laborers in the vineyard.

Lord, I silently prayed, *keep reminding me that You sent me to work in Herman's vineyard and not to be spirited away by another.*

Church ended with a triumphant hymn, but a less triumphant duty lay before me—I needed to speak with Karl. I had practiced my dismissal speech many times in my mind over all those dreary indoor days on the farm. Not a single practiced scenario came to mind now as he strode toward me in the flesh. His tall frame, wavy, blond locks, and determined stance created a vacuum in my head.

Herman may not have seen Karl sitting in church during the service, but Karl made himself more than evident now. He arrived in front of our family and offered his hand to Herman. Herman hesitated to reciprocate the manly gesture.

"Hello again," Karl began.

---

8   1 Corinthians 9:25

"Long way to come to church for an Alton man, don't you think?" Herman grumbled as he gave me a sideways glare.

"It's a free country. I believe I can worship wherever I please." Karl turned to me. "And today, I am pleased to worship here."

The mischievous twinkle in his eye was unmistakable, and Herman shifted in his Sunday shirt as if ready to pounce.

"Herman, may I speak with Karl—um, Herr Muller—alone for a moment, please?"

Herman's eyes narrowed. "I can tell him what we discussed," I added in an undertone to gain his permission.

Herman scanned Karl up and down, took Hannah from my arms, and said, "Make it quick. The weather doesn't look any better for the ride home."

I exhaled the breath I did not know I held and mouthed a thank you to Herman as he turned away.

I turned to Karl as he asked, "What you discussed? About me?"

I took another deep breath and nodded. "Yes. It was so nice to see you at Christmas and all, but . . . "

"But what? Didn't you like the gift?"

"No. I mean, yes. The gift was lovely. I mean, it doesn't have anything to do with the gift."

"What *does* it have to do with?" He stepped closer, so I tried to step back to keep my composure but bumped into the pew behind me. "Do you need to get away from me?" Karl raised an eyebrow at my distressed position against the wood furniture.

"Actually, yes," I stammered.

"I don't understand. I thought we had a fine time on the Mississippi and that day in Alton. I want to get to know you better, if I can." He took my hand in his and stroked the back of it. "I think you and I could have a future together if we tried it."

"You must remember why I came to America." I shook his hand from mine and tucked the tingling appendage behind my skirt. "I am here to help Herman raise his children. They need me. I can't leave them now that they are depending on me as they do."

Frustration cracked my voice. I knew sounded more like a whiny, little girl than myself, and I did not sound like a confident woman telling a suitor his advances were no longer welcome. That was likely because I wanted to welcome them but knew I could not allow those thoughts in my head.

"So, Herman is telling you to get rid of me? No wonder he treats me like a pariah every time I meet him. I think the guy might slug me if we weren't in church."

"It's not just Herman. It is my choice, too." Karl furrowed his brow. "I gave him my word. He paid for me to come here. I am here for Herman. You never would have met me had he not sent for me in the first place. I am not at liberty to accept your attention, Karl. You have been nice to me, but you must leave me alone now. Understand?"

I realized my voice had grown louder, and other churchgoers turned their heads, listening to our every word.

"He can't hold you prisoner just because he paid your way to cross the ocean, Lena. That makes him no better than the slave traders. He can't keep me from seeing you." He straightened his tall frame and gritted his teeth as he looked toward where Herman departed through the church doors.

"No, Karl. That is not fair. Herman is family. You can't see me anymore. You must stay away. I committed to work in Herman's vineyard, just like the vineyard workers in today's Gospel lesson. I will stay as long as he needs me. It would not be right for me to ask you to wait until he no longer needs me on the farm. It is best you just go."

"That's not right, Lena." His face remained clouded. "You know I like you. I more than like you." He wiped his face with his hands. "But if you tell me to go, I will." Karl jammed his hands in his pockets to keep a civil composure.

"It has to be this way, Karl. I'm sorry."

Karl turned and strode out the door. The few congregants left in the church started impromptu conversations between themselves, as if they had not overheard the whole exchange. I guess I gave everyone something to talk about. The grapevine gossip of this relationship status would spread through town in no time.

I shrugged off the public humiliation and found Herman and the children with the Stolzes, passing the time in their home next to the butcher shop while they waited for me. The wind whisked me through the door, which closed in a loud slam as I stood shamefaced in front of my waiting family.

Herman scowled at the unceremonious approach. "Well?"

"It is done. You needn't worry about him anymore."

I forced a lighthearted lilt into my voice as if the previous conversation required no more effort than telling Karl to have a delightful lunch.

Frau Greta gave me a sympathetic squeeze on my shoulder. "Don't worry, child. You are young. There are many more nuts in the strudel."

Herman had not told her why I had spoken with Karl after church, so I nodded and accepted her misaimed advice. Let her remain in her false assumption that we parted due to a lover's spat or something. I did not tell her I had chosen not to search for any *nuts* here at all. The town gossips would tell her every word of the discussion soon enough.

Herman wanted to hurry home, but the town butcher—who had the choicest meat and largest heart—invited us to eat with his family. After so many days indoors, we starved more for human interaction than delicious food, so we happily accepted their kindness for both.

After the warm meal, the *kindern* drifted off to sleep, and we thought it best to hurry them home. The roads had not improved any throughout the day, and more clouds rolled in on the horizon. We loaded the sleepy *kindern* on the sleigh, and Herman urged the anxious steed home.

The clouds darkened, and the wind howled louder, so Herman insisted the mare pick up the pace on the slick road to arrive home before being caught in the impending storm. The faster the horse hurried, the more unsteady her gait became as her footing slid on icy patches. Without warning, a gust of wind spooked the horse, and she slipped from the road. The sleigh lurched into a ditch of drifted snow where it promptly overturned, dumping us all out into a waiting snowbank. Herman's side went down first. He hoped to steady the sleigh by holding the reigns and guiding the mare back to the road. Instead, since he was not protecting his own fall, he fell under the sled runners before the sleigh slid to a stop. He stifled a scream as they sliced across his boot and ankle.

Instantly, the *kindern* were jolted awake as the impact threw them out of the way of the wreckage and into the soft roadside snow. I landed unceremoniously alongside them. Snow covered all of us, and the *kindern* started wailing and shivering.

"Are you all right?" I asked the *kindern*.

I ran my hands over each of their limbs to check for injuries. Thankfully, their tears stemmed only from being scared and not from any wounds.

"There, there," I consoled.

Hugging them closely and reassuring them they were fine, I then ran to the other side of the upturned sleigh to see about Herman.

Herman had not fared as well as the *kindern*. The snow under his foot had turned crimson, and he covered his ankle with his hands and snow to pack the injury and halt the bleeding. I took my hand-knitted scarf from my neck and wrapped the mangled mess at the end of his pant leg to hide the bloody wound from the *kindern*. I feared taking off the mangled boot would expose him to too much cold and increase the bleeding. I also had no desire to see the wound myself. I swallowed to keep from fainting at the sight of all the blood pooling in the snow, which soon became the size of a wash basin.

Herman struggled to his side, trying to sit up so he could see his horse flailing in the snow.

"Did she break anything?"

The more Herman strained, I could tell the more pain he inflicted on himself, and the more his wound bled.

"Stay still. You cannot see your horse when I am seeing to you. You look seriously hurt." I tried steadying Herman against the snowbank.

The animal struggled on the ground, trying to stand again on the icy slope but only emitted anguished squeals. I knew it did not look good. Herman likely thought the same.

My nursing skills would not hold for long, and I surprised myself by not passing out from the nasty sight. Tending to an injured horse would take more stamina than the good Lord had given me. At home, the boys took care of the livestock, and the girls kept to domestic chores. I had learned to ride but never bonded with the beasts like some girls. As I saw it, horses provided transportation and were not intended to be friends. My heart ached for the poor beast, but I didn't know how to help.

At that moment, the sky angrily erupted, and a hail and snow mix pelted us. The *kindern* continued wailing loudly as they huddled together in the snowbank.

Lord, can this be any worse? I prayed. *Please help. I don't know what to do. How can I take Herman and the kindern home if the horse is injured? He won't be able to walk on that foot. We need help.*

At that very moment, the shadow of my personal angel blocked the strained sun peeking from a wayward dark cloud and hovered over me. Karl.

"How?" I said out loud, though to no one in particular.

It did not matter how. God had sent Karl to help us—to help me—again. I dare not send him away now. Karl assessed the situation as he dismounted his horse.

"Herman, it looks as if your horse has broken his leg and is in pain. I'm going to put him down for you, okay?"

Herman nodded through his pain and let Karl take charge.

"Lena, gather the children. I'll right the sleigh and put Herman on it. My horse can take you all home when I hook her to it."

As I turned to collect the *kindern*, I heard the fatal shot of the injured horse. Within minutes, Karl had harnessed his roan mare to the sleigh and loaded everyone. Herman lay propped up in the back of the wagon where Karl rewrapped my poor bandaging job.

He then took Herman's usual place at the reins, and his sure-footed mare trotted us home through the ever-increasing storm. The *kindern* huddled on my lap under a blanket as I shielded them from the whipping winds and hail.

"There it is."

I pointed out the Neubauer homestead as darkness fell on the farm silhouette. Karl's horse pulled the sleigh close to the front door, and I shuffled the cold and miserable *kindern* inside while Karl assisted Herman through the front door. Although initially reluctant, the weakened Herman leaned on Karl and hobbled into the house. I pointed the way to Herman's room, and Karl helped Herman to his bed, where he propped up his damaged foot on some pillows I gathered from the cupboard.

"I can try to make him comfortable now that you have him here," I offered as I peeled back Herman's tattered boot, trying to not wince at the bloody mess inside.

My gag reflex nearly overwhelmed me at the sight of so much blood in his shoe, but I kept swallowing and managed to dislodge it without unwrapping too much of Karl's pristine bandaging.

"I think I should fetch the doctor for you," Karl said. "I'm sure he needs some sewing up if he is to use that foot again."

Herman started to object, "I don't think you need to fetch a doctor in the storm." But the mere effort of the protest turned his face white, and he fell back on the bed and nearly blacked out.

Karl turned to me. "Do you have something to take the edge off Herman's pain? I'll head to town for the doctor, and if the weather doesn't get worse, I'll be back tonight."

Karl grabbed his hat and set off before anyone agreed or disagreed with his plans. I grabbed the whiskey that we kept just for emergencies and gave Herman a small shot to help with the pain and swelling. I nudged him awake again and helped him sip before he slipped into a fitful rest.

Herman sank further into his bed, spent from the injury and loss of blood. I filled the *kindern* with warm milk and donned them in fresh pajamas and readied them for bed, where the exhausted imps dozed off immediately.

I peered in on Herman. He slept fitfully, uttering soft scourges under his breath at his foot, the weather, the horse, and, unfortunately, Karl. I hoped Karl would return with medical help soon, so the doctor could ensure Herman would use that foot again. Admittedly, I was glad I did not have to redress Herman's wound again either, since God had not given me the constitution of a nurse. I kept a vigil in the front room while I waited for my God-sent knight to return. God always seemed to send him to rescue me.

Lord, why do You keep him so close when I am supposed to send him away?

CHAPTER 11

Helping Hands

"May he send you help from the sanctuary and give you support from Zion."
Psalm 20:2

Karl was true to his word. He and Doc Howard arrived on horseback, bag in hand, while the *kindern* slept upstairs. I had watched after Herman, who settled into a fitful slumber in the interim. Every time he had moved in his sleep, he jerked against the pain of his foot, grumbled incomprehensible abuses, and tried to reposition himself into a restful posture.

Herman roused when the doctor arrived and unwrapped his nasty wound. I swallowed hard and backed away. The blood drained from my face, and I slipped out the bedroom door and eased myself into the nearest chair, where I could not see the doctor stitching up Herman's foot. Karl stayed in the bedroom to assist the doctor as Herman bit down on a clean cloth I gathered for them from the bureau. Herman screamed through the muffled cloth, and I covered my ears, hoping he would not wake the *kindern*.

I heard Karl trying to restrain my hurting brother, but no sounds echoed from the *kindern* upstairs. I scolded myself for not being a better nurse. The doctor would have another patient on his hands if I returned to Herman's room before he completed his work. What a sorry sister I was! Herman's stifled moans finally eased, and I wondered if it was safe for me to return.

Karl found me cowering outside the bedroom. "You okay?"

He towered over me as I sank further back into my overstuffed chair, but I felt it best to stay there a moment or two longer to ward off impending dizziness.

"Ja." I sighed. "I'm not very good with blood and doctoring. I'll be okay in a minute."

Karl smiled a lopsided grin as if this weakness endeared me to him even more than before. "Okay. Stay put for a while, and I'll take care of things outside for you."

Karl sauntered outside in the dark before I realized what remained to be done. Since arriving home, I had fussed inside over the *kindern* and Herman, but I hadn't thought about the sleigh left out in the storm or animals in the barn who must be fed. To have a clear-thinking person around in a crisis steadied my nerves.

The doctor emerged from Herman's room and stood in the doorway, watching me much like Karl had moments before. "You okay, Miss?"

"I'll be fine, thank you. How is Herman?" I straightened my dress to appear more composed and forced myself to stand before him.

"He cannot stand on that foot for several weeks, and he should prop it up to help it heal. If he tries to use it too soon, I may have to take it off completely. The foot was almost cut clean through, and I'm not sure he will be able to feel his toes when and if it heals. Your job is to keep him off his feet and keep the wound clean. I will stop by next week to check on him. If he gets a fever or an infection sets in, send for me." Doc Howard gave me another discerning look. My pale complexion did not escape his gaze. "Will you be able to change the bandages every day?"

I blanched at the implication that I had failed as a nurse in caring for my brother. "I'll do my best," I offered. "We will make sure he has what he needs. I promise."

We? What was I saying? Did I expect Karl to stay around and help, or maybe Dagmar could make a daily stop? I am sure Dagmar would make an excellent caretaker, but could I impose on her to come regularly?

I reclaimed my composure and walked the doctor to the door. The storm had left a calling card of fresh snow, blanketing the surrounding slopes. Ice hung from the eaves of the house. I threw on my wrap after thanking the doctor, then walked outside to check on the state of the barn and any neglected animals. It appeared as if Karl had left the lantern lit, and I needed to extinguish it before heading to bed. Stars dotted the night sky, and a nearly full moon lit the way to the barn.

Through the open barn door, I saw Karl tinkering with some of Herman's tools that hung over the workbench. "What are you doing?"

These were Herman's prized possessions brought over from Germany, and Herman would not be pleased that another man disturbed them in his absence.

Karl spun around. "Oh, I didn't hear you come in. That fresh snow must have cushioned your steps." He looked closer at my disheveled appearance. The night drew unexpectedly long, and it had begun to show. "Or maybe I was just deep in thought sorting through these tools. Your brother has a nice assortment here. I can put these to good use while I am here."

Did I detect a smolder in those blue-gray eyes? While he was here? Was he planning on staying? I shook the fog from my brain and repeated, "What are you doing? I thought you'd be leaving when the doctor left."

"I figured you needed some help while Herman recuperated, and I came out to see what you might need." He gestured toward the animals. "I fed your stock, and I am looking at the tools your brother has so I can fashion him some crutches when he feels up to it."

"You don't need to do all that." I softened. A guilty nudge warned me to be suspicious of his motives, although Karl had been nothing but helpful since the day I met him. "You've done so much already."

I started to urge him away but instead blurted, "I don't know what I would have done out there if you hadn't come along." The tears began to fall.

Karl took a couple of long strides to span the distance between us when he saw my tears, but I put my hand up to stop him from touching me. He abruptly stopped and remained still while I tried desperately to regain my composure.

I closed my eyes and silently prayed, *Lord, give me strength to resist the charms of this wonderful angel You have provided to help us in this time of need.*

When I opened my eyes again, Karl stood close enough to touch. I resisted the urge to hug him and said softly, "I'm not sure having you here is such a good idea, Herr Muller."

He cocked his head as if waiting for me to change my mind. "So formal, are we?"

"I do appreciate the help, though." My eyes darted around the stalls. "This was always Herman's area, but I could learn to do everything out here if I could impose on you to show me."

I did not sound confident, but the Lord did not create an inept female in me. If others managed these tasks, so could I.

"I can't leave you alone to mind the kids, the livestock, and Herman. I promise to keep my distance, and we can say our goodbyes when Herman is well enough. Okay?" He held out his hand, but I could not risk shaking hands, however innocent, because of my weakened resolve.

"Don't you have a job? Isn't there other work you need to be doing? You can't just hang around here for weeks on end. Surely, someone will miss you."

I grasped at straws. I did not want him to go, but I could not ask him to stay either. He did not belong here. Herman would have my hide if I allowed that to happen.

"I asked Doc Howard to let my office know I am needed elsewhere for a while. Let's call it a family emergency." He winked. "They can get along without me for the present. Things usually slow down in the winter, anyway."

"What things?"

"When it snows, tracking runaways is too easy, and the weather makes it more dangerous for escapees to be out and about. So, we aren't helping as many folks through our office as in fair-weather months. I can be spared until your brother is better."

I tugged my wrap closer. What Karl said made sense, but I knew little about what he did for the slaves. I hesitated to ask more. Everything about him remained so mysterious.

"If that is true and you can spare the time to stay and help us for a while, I accept. It is late. You can look through Herman's tools in the morning. I'll find you some bedding, and you can bunk on the couch tonight. We can explain this to Herman in the morning." I refocused the conversation on Herman, and it sobered my senses as I retreated toward the house.

I did not expect Herman to be pleased with Karl staying under his roof, even if we sorely needed his help. I peeked in on my sleeping brother again while gathering some bedding for Karl's couch accommodations. The doctor must have administered something to help him sleep because he did not toss and turn as he had before. Soft snoring pulsed from him as the covers fluttered with each breath. Karl took his coat and boots off when I brought his bedding into the front room, so I placed his blankets on the settee cushions and turned without saying a word. Too tired to speak, I resigned myself to this arrangement, at least until morning.

My head spun from the day's events, but I drifted off to sleep as soon as I sank under the covers. The upended sleigh had jarred my bones more than I had let myself realize—until now. The inviting bed proved the perfect solace for the aches that spoke to me.

The gingham comforter melted into a fur-lined muff, and I drifted into dreamland. The blowing winds sprayed fresh snowflakes into my face as the carriage sled raced along a glorious white landscape of sparkling trees, guarded by hugging drifts. Seas of white glistened in the morning sun, and the frozen stream etched tiny ice sculptures the locals merited to Jack Frost. Back in Germany, the cause of the wintry beauty fell to Frau Holle. She made her bed and shook the feather pillows over the German countryside on winter nights.

What a glorious ride. The sun beamed; the snowflakes danced; and the crisp air refreshed my every sense. My hands stroked the soft interior of the fur muff, and another warm hand soon reached inside and touched mine. The softness moved as another warm hand touched mine in the furry tunnel. The hand led to a strong arm, and my gaze traveled up the masculine arm to a gentle smile. Familiar blue-gray eyes watched me. The twist of blond curls escaped his jaunty hat, and I sunk into his welcoming arms—my protector and deliverer. God provided him for me at every turn.

As I leaned into my pleasant dream, Hannah and Hans burst into my room. "Aunt Lena. Get up! Get up! There's that man downstairs!"

Hannah stuck her little thumb in her mouth, nodding her blonde curls at her brother's proclamation.

I gathered my morning alarmists onto the bed. "It's okay." I hugged them for reassurance. "Remember Herr Muller? He helped your papa when we crashed yesterday. He is going to help us until your papa is better." Their leery eyes nodded back at me. "Do you think we should go downstairs and fix some breakfast?"

That perked them up. Everyone hopped off the bed.

"Slow down, you two. Let me get dressed, and we will make oatmeal." As I straightened my nightdress, I noticed a bruise forming on my thigh. I did not come away from the wreck altogether unscathed, I see. I turned back to the *kindern.* "Hans, do you want to help your sister find some clothes for today? I will be right there to help in a minute."

He dutifully took his sister's hand and led her out the bedroom door. When the three of us were finally dressed, we traveled downstairs to find blazing fires stoked in the stove and fireplace.

Karl stood nearby. "I hope you don't mind. I found the coffee and made myself a cup."

"No, of course not. It is nice to have the fire going this early. The *kindern* are hungry."

Hannah and Hans were in their seats, awaiting the promised meal, before I grabbed the saucepan from the cupboard. "I'll cook some oatmeal for you and check on Herman."

"I looked in on him a minute ago. He is still asleep. The doctor must have given him something to knock him out. I'm surprised you didn't sleep longer. You had a big day and a short night yesterday."

I looked over at Hannah and Hans and chuckled. "Ever try to stay in bed with these two around?"

His smile grew. "No, I guess not. They were startled to find me here this morning. I never saw two tykes fly up a stairway so fast." He eased himself into a chair at the table and made a funny face at Hans to show the little ones his not-a-monster side. Hans and Hannah giggled. Hans tried to make the same face back at him and then tried a few of his own. Everyone laughed at the antics.

"They were definitely startled." I smiled. That dream, still fresh in my thoughts, rose dangerously near the surface.

After finishing a bowl of oatmeal, Karl excused himself to complete Herman's morning chores and find the right tools to fashion some crutches for Herman when he sufficiently recovered.

I waited for Herman to awaken for breakfast before I told him about my arrangement with Karl. Serving him a meal, I could handle. However, telling Herman that Karl slept at the farm last night and would be here for a while might not be so palatable.

Lord, give me the right words, I prayed, *so Herman will not be upset with Karl or me. If You sent Karl to help us, Herman must be made to understand, right? Please give me the wisdom and strength to do Your will. Amen.*

The *kindern* scampered off to fill their childhood desires in the front room. I absentmindedly put the dishes away as I tidied the kitchen and decided to gather some sausages from the cellar for dinner. It was time to check on Herman again. I half-hoped he slept, but he was bound to need more pain medicine for his discomfort by now.

I hesitated outside his bedroom door. If he were awake, I must tell him about Karl, though that was a bucket of worms I would just as soon leave alone. I steadied my breathing to turn the doorknob quietly—no need to rush the moment.

Startled back to my senses by rustling and grunting sounds, I pushed the door fully open. "Herman?" I timidly stepped inside. He struggled to twist himself from under the covers. "What are you doing?" I rushed over and repositioned the blankets around his torso.

Herman pushed my hands away. "Lena! Stop that. I need to get up."

"I am keeping you in bed, as the doctor said. You can't put any weight on that foot. Do you want him to come back and cut your whole leg off? You need to listen to reason."

"The doctor can take a flying leap." Herman pushed my hands away again and tried to get his aching foot to the floor.

I stepped back. Herman usually kept his temper under control and seldom spoke so coarsely. It alarmed me. He continued his tirade as he tugged the untucked blankets from beneath him, but his overzealous jerking caused them to catch on his elevated leg, and his face paled. He stopped to recompose himself.

"It is daylight outside," Herman said. "The animals don't care what the doctor says. I must go out there and get morning feed." The full force of his anger unleashed on me. "Why'd you let me sleep the morning away?"

Herman tried again to swing his legs out of bed, and sweat formed on his forehead from the exertion.

"Now, you get right back in that bed, Herman Charles Neubauer! Your animals are taken care of. Your job is to heal that wound of yours."

I bravely stood tall beside the bed to prevent his legs from sliding on the floor as he intended. He paused from his struggle with the bedding and cocked his head as what I said took root. Puzzled, he sighed and frowned at my determination to keep him horizontal.

"Really? You fed the animals?"

I tried to hold his gaze as I stammered, "W-w-well, no. Karl is taking care of them for you."

"What!" He almost stood upright by pushing his good leg against me but lost his balance without support from his injured foot. He tumbled unceremoniously on the bed again, hurting his pride more than anything else, and wincing when he jarred his foot.

"You tell that *dummkopf* to keep his hands off my animals and my farm!"

"Now, you listen to me, Herman. You are in no position to turn down his help. You can't take care of things right now, and I tend to the *kindern* and the house all day. Isn't that why you sent for me? This farm is more than a one-person job. Karl is kind enough to help us out, and you will let him!"

I seethed the last phrase through clenched teeth. Herman started to protest, but I continued my defense.

"And another thing. I would never have gotten you and the children home from the accident if Karl hadn't come along when he did. You owe him a tremendous thanks for taking care of us, rather than treating him with the contempt you are."

I stepped aside, ready to retreat after gaining a momentary upper hand. Herman considered my words, but his stubborn German streak was not finished with this debate.

"Where is he staying?" His even tone did not disguise his foreknowledge before I revealed my answer.

I looked away, presumably to check the weather through the window. Herman might explode again if I did not carefully choose my words. I softly answered, "I made a bed for him on the couch in the front room last night."

The mercury on Herman's face rose to replace the relative resolve of a moment ago. Then, through clenched teeth, he muttered, "He's under my roof?" He almost elevated from the bed.

I rolled my eyes. "Where else was he to go? You don't think I should make him sleep in a freezing barn, do you?"

Herman released the breath with an imperceptible "Why him?"

"Who else?" I volunteered. "No one else came rushing to help." Herman struggled to control his temper with a grimace that exposed his underlying physical pain. "I came to give you your medicine and feed you some breakfast." I offered my olive branch of oatmeal and coffee.

"*Ja.* I could eat something. *Danke.*" He sunk back into the pillows, the fight in him waning. "If I were a hundred percent, you'd not get off so easy."

I smiled. "*Ja*, I know. Just relax and heal. Let us handle things for a while." I propped his pillow higher for him to feed himself from the tray I had brought to the room.

He called after me as I left him to eat, "He's not staying a moment longer than necessary."

"Yessir," I said more to myself than my brother, since he preferred the last word in any argument.

Lord, I cannot let Karl become a permanent fixture in my heart.

CHAPTER 12

The Truce

"For he himself is our peace, who has made us both one and has broken down in his flesh the dividing wall of hostility."

Ephesians 2:14

With Herman's breakfast delivered, I gave him time to eat before attempting to check his bandages. I returned to an empty tray and girded my loins for a peek at his wounded foot. So far, the wound looked as if it was healing, but I could not bear exposing myself to the raw injury for long. My stomach gymnastics lost control, so I quickly rewrapped his foot and hoped the bandage would hold until a more able-bodied soul could look at it.

Herman's strength slipped away again—either from the vigorous morning exchange or the administered medication. Either way, he drifted back to a restful sleep after his meal.

While I helped Herman, the *kindern* stacked couch cushions on the floor and leaped on them from the furniture. Their giggling wafted throughout the house and lifted the mood with their innocent activity, superseding the tension of the Karl-versus-Herman juxtaposition.

Suddenly, Hannah yelped an urgent wail, and I jumped into action. "What happened?" I scooped her from the floor, where she had missed the cushion and bumped her head. "Oh, poor Hannah. You're okay." She snuggled into my shoulder and popped her thumb into her mouth, stopping the wail. Hans pointed at the offending floor. "It's okay, Hans. No one is blaming you."

Karl opened the door cautiously. "I heard a scream." He surveyed the crying child in my arms. "Thought I should check and make sure everything was all right."

"Everything is okay. Hannah bumped her head when playing."

Karl awkwardly stood there, wondering if he should go back outside again.

"You look cold. It is almost lunchtime. Why don't you come in and warm up while I fix us a bite? I have soup simmering on the stove."

Karl took another step inside and accepted the invitation. "How's Herman doing?"

"He's sleeping again. I gave him more medicine and rebandaged his foot. Someone with better nursing skills may want to take a look at it, though."

After lunch was prepared and everyone had eaten a bowl of lentil soup, I sent the *kindern* upstairs for an afternoon nap while Karl put his coat back on.

"Wait," I said. He stopped and awaited further instructions. "I want to ask you something before you head back out."

Karl shed his coat and continued to wait.

"How did you happen along just when we needed you yesterday? I prayed, and you appeared like a miracle, but I can't figure out why you were out that way in the first place. Can you explain this to me?"

"I have never been called a miracle before." He pondered this thought for a moment. "I was out looking for some other safe homes for the runaway slaves we help. The safe houses we use around Alton are becoming compromised. I had a lead about some people in this area who might be willing to help. I was riding back from a farm to the north and noticed your sleigh. I was curious about where you lived and watched for a while. Then, I saw your horse stumble and the sleigh flip. So, does that make me a miracle?"

"I think it does. God put you there to be our help in time of need. He seems to use you often as my protector."

"I don't mind protecting you at all. It is my pleasure." He tipped his hat.

"Did you find some safe houses out this way? Tell me more about what you do."

Karl sighed. "This may take a few minutes." He glanced around the room and shifted. "My work is rather secretive."

"Are you afraid to tell me? Do you think I will tell somebody?"

"No. But sometimes, knowledge can be burdensome. It is easier for some folks not to notice what is happening before them, rather than worry about things going on under their noses."

Ripples traveled down my spine. If there were things going on around here that might affect the family, I wanted to hear more. "Leave your coat off and sit a spell. All is quiet now, and there may not be another chance to talk for a while."

Karl draped his jacket over the back of the chair and eased himself onto the divan. "Remember when I told you about the Underground Railroad?"

"You said it was a way of helping runaway slaves get to Canada."

"That's right. It's not an actual train but a network of people who help fugitive slaves obtain freedom. We use code to help them. Conductors guide runaways to safe houses. Safe houses are called stations, and those at the stations are called station masters. There is no steaming iron horse on the rails for this."

"So, you were looking for new stations or station masters when you rode out here on Sunday in the storm?"

"Yes. I was less likely to meet anyone on the road in a storm. Slave hunters discovered some of the stations in the Alton area and recaptured some of the fugitives and took them back to their masters. In Underground Railroad terms, they are called cargo."

"I thought you said Illinois was a free state."

"It is, but there is a law called the Fugitive Slave Act. I doubt you know it."

I shook my head. In the few months since arriving in America, I'd had no exposure to the politics or laws here. Herman occasionally grabbed a German-language newspaper in town, but I admit I was more drawn to the latest fashion and local gossip rather than any political articles. No need to admit that to Karl, however, and sound like a foolish schoolgirl.

"That Fugitive Slave Act law allows slaves to be recaptured in free states. Anyone who helps them may be punished for their involvement. So, even though we are in a free state, fugitives can be kidnapped. This does not prevent them from taking free men on occasion as well. That is why some free states have passed personal liberty laws or anti-kidnapping statues to try to stop this atrocity."

"So, just getting to a free state is not enough for those who escape slavery?"

"I'm afraid not. So, many travel to Canada, where U.S. laws cannot touch them. The Underground Railroad helps them travel that far north if they want to go there. Others find family to live with or other places to settle."

"How do you find people willing to risk punishment to help people they don't even know? You don't just ride around hoping to find a brave soul, do you?"

Karl grinned again at my oversimplification of his abolitionist role. "I receive referrals from other sympathizers. Ministers are often on the frontlines because they understand the hearts of their congregations. I was following up on some of those referrals from church when I spotted you."

"Who did you visit out here?"

My mind searched the area for possible station masters in my midst. They must be brave to help move this precious cargo to safer places, but I did not yet know too many people here very well.

"I do think there are some willing farmers around here, but I won't burden you with names. It is best to keep them a secret as much as possible."

"I didn't think of your work as so secretive before. In New Orleans, your boldness fascinated me, but I worried about you, too."

"That may not have been as bold as foolish." Karl shook his head at the recollection of the beating he had received at the slave auction. "It is more dangerous for those escaping cruel masters than for me. I'm not the one being chased ordinarily, but it is still wise not to be too obvious about what I am doing. Not everyone approves of what we do."

"I don't think Herman would agree to his house being used as a station."

"I hadn't even thought of asking him, since he glares at me hanging around you like a fox guarding the henhouse. Did you tell him I was here?"

"Yes."

"And?"

"And what?" I averted my gaze, pretending I did not know what Karl wanted me to explain.

"How did he take the news? I don't think he will welcome me with open arms."

"Well, no. He wasn't thrilled, but I told him he was in no position to turn down your help and that you would stay as long as we needed. Is that okay with you?"

Karl could hardly contain his laughter. "You really said that to your brother? You are a formidable opponent, Fraulein Lena. I wish I had seen your brother's face when you laid down the law."

"I had the advantage, since he can't move out of bed now. I'm sure it wasn't as glorious as you think. But I guess I didn't do too badly for myself, now that I think about it."

"I am working on carving him a set of crutches while I am outside. I hope I am not arming the enemy against you. Just remember, I'll always be your protector when you need me. He can at least hobble around again when I am finished, but it may be difficult for him to catch you for a while." Karl stood at the door, hesitated, and looked back. "In the meantime, I'll try to stay out of his way as much as possible."

I hoped Karl would stay longer than the time it took to carve crutches. Herman may be able to hobble around, but I doubted he would be able to do his chores for some time.

Lord, I prayed, *is it wrong to ask that Herman not heal too quickly? This may be the only time I will have with Karl. Thank You for understanding. Amen.*

❧

*K*arl kept his word about making himself scarce during the day. He puttered around in the barn, took his horse out for some exercise, and otherwise occupied his time away from the house. He ate his meals with little conversation and directed most of his attention to the *kindern*. They warmed up to his teasing and looked forward to his brief time inside.

Being confined to his room, Herman kept occupied by reading a worn copy of John Bunyan's *Pilgrim's Progress* and planning the spring planting. He was anxious to be up and about, though. I brought the *kindern* in to visit him for a few minutes each day, where he could read Hans' new books to them. But I stood guard to be sure a rambunctious child did not jump on his bandaged foot, since they were never aware of their appendages. I spent a sizable portion of every day mopping up after their spills and tumbles. Herman's foot did not need to be reinjured because his children wanted to use his bed to bounce around.

In a week, Karl carried in a well-crafted set of crutches.

"Wow. This is what you have been doing all those hours? These aren't just crutches. They are a work of art. You whittled some designs on the side, too. What are they?"

"I doodled some ideas I thought Herman might like. On this side is a cross with a snake encircling it, like the one Moses used to heal the people from snake bites in the Old Testament. I thought he might appreciate the symbolism. The other side has shafts of wheat to symbolize the farm and remind him about the Bible verses about the sower." I stared at the intricate carvings, speechless. "I had extra time on my hands, I guess, trying to keep a low profile around here," Karl added sheepishly.

"This is more than doodling. You're quite an artist."

"My father taught me a little chip carving when I was younger. It comes in handy when I have time to create something. Anyway, these should help Herman move out of his room before long. I'm sure he is itching to be up and around, having been cooped up and looking at the same four walls."

"*Ja*. It's been tough keeping him still. I'm trying to scrounge up enough distractions for him. I don't dare leave the *kindern* with him, though, or we'd need to stitch him up again in no time."

Karl chuckled. "*Ja*. They are a lively bunch—like they should be," he said as he handed me the crutches. "I have another gift for him, too. If you are looking for things to occupy him, he might want to read this." He handed me a copy of *Uncle Tom's Cabin*. "This is one of the bestselling books in America now."

"What is it about? Herman loves American adventure stories. I think he's read everything from James Fenimore Cooper."

"Cooper wrote about America a hundred years ago. *Uncle Tom's Cabin* is about what is happening in this country now. This story will teach him all about the horrors of slavery."

"Goodness. I don't know if he will accept that. He doesn't think slavery has anything to do with us."

"You saw how the slaves were treated at that auction in New Orleans. That is only one hair on the dog of their inhumane treatment. No Christian should stand by and let others treat people that way." Although Karl's words were measured, they clipped off his tongue.

"I felt terrible about those poor people in New Orleans. I just don't think Herman feels the same way." I realized we were standing close enough to touch, so I stepped back and asked, "You want to give the book to Herman?"

Pausing, he said, "That probably is not the best idea. I am trying to give him a wide berth. He is sure I will steal you away from the farm, and he needs you now more than ever with his injury."

"You made this beautiful gift"—I pointed at the crutches—"and he does need another book or something to take his mind off his foot. Give him a chance to thank you in person," I said as I warmed to the nearness between us.

"He can thank me later if he wants. Now, I should find another outdoor project."

Then, without waiting for me to answer, he was gone.

Lord, I prayed, *I realize I can't keep Karl close and yet not pursue a future with him. I want to help Herman and also have Karl in my life. I suppose I should be thankful for this short time when I have both, although our time together is only temporary. Thank You for that.*

I took the newly hewn crutches and the book and lightly tapped on Herman's door. *"Ja?"*

I stepped in, carrying the precious gift of mobility in my arms and the book tucked neatly into my apron. "I have something you are going to love."

Herman looked up from the papers he had strewn on the bed in a makeshift desk. "Oh?" His eyes halted on the carved crutches. "Wow. Where did you find those? Pretty fancy."

"Aren't they? Karl made them special for you." Herman's delight drained from his face, so I hurried on. "He is an artist, isn't he? The best part is that you will be able to leave that bed soon." Herman's eyes lit up again, and he threw back the covers. "I didn't mean now," I added.

Herman retrieved his disheveled papers, placing them to the side before fumbling with the covers again and swinging his legs around to the floor.

"Hand me those things and let me try these works of art."

I knew the futility of arguing the point with him as I held his freedom before him. I helped him untangle the bedding from around his feet and let him grab the crutches. He would have hopped across the room to reach them if I had kept him from them any longer.

"Slow down. Even if you have these, you aren't running around the farm yet."

"You are not telling me what to do, little sis. I have a farm to run, and before long, I will need to be in the fields, hurt foot or not."

"If you don't let your foot heal properly, you will be limping around the farm for the rest of your life. The doctor hinted that he may have to take off your foot altogether if you do not give it time to heal properly. Is that what you want?" He did not answer. "For now, you should practice in the house. The warm winds are causing an early thaw outside, and that means more mud."

I read Herman's scowl. *I will not say you are right, but you make sense, even if I don't want to admit it,* I thought. He took a couple of tentative steps.

"These will work fine, I think. Just the right height for me." He nodded an appreciative grin and added, "Tell him I appreciate the gift."

"You can tell him at supper, since you can come to the table now."

Herman cocked his head as if he did not realize Karl ate his meals with us while he convalesced. He lumbered a few more steps into the living room, but his strength drained quickly from his effort. I helped him into his favorite chair and propped his injured leg on a stool.

"While you are still immobile, I also have a new book you can read."

I gingerly took *Uncle Tom's Cabin* out of my apron pocket and placed it on his lap.

"What is this?" Herman eyed the book suspiciously, then turned it over to examine the cover more carefully.

"The book is about the goings-on in America. Karl thought you might like it."

I left him to explore the pages more on his own. I could see that trying the crutches had exhausted him more than he admitted, and within a few minutes, he nodded off into soft snores before he could even open the book.

The *kindern* played upstairs, unaware of their father's progress below. I peeked in on them to ensure everything was in order and then opened my Bible for some alone time before making dinner preparations. The Bible fell open to Ephesians 2:13-14.

After reading it, I prayed, *Lord, are You telling me I should share this idea of peace with Karl and Herman? I can try. We haven't had family devotions in a while, as we did when we were growing up. Maybe Herman will let me read some tonight. Please soften Herman's heart. Amen.*

CHAPTER 13

A New Season

"Truly, truly, I say to you, unless a grain of wheat falls into the earth and dies, it remains alone; but if it dies, it bears much fruit."

John 12:24

By the time dinner was ready, Herman had situated himself and his injured foot at the head of the table. Karl came in, and the two men nodded a stiff greeting to one another. The *kindern* could not believe their good fortune of having Papa and Karl at the table to entertain them.

"Dinner is ready, but first, I'd like to start this meal with an evening devotion if I could." Before any protests, I continued, "We used to always have them when we were growing up, and I thought this would be good for the children."

Herman gave me a wary look and proclaimed, "But the head of the household always read the Scripture for the family."

"True, but you are recovering, and I thought I'd get things started if that's okay. You can continue the tradition when you are yourself again."

"I'm not an invalid, Lena."

"Okay, but can I at least share some things I read today?"

Herman nodded a reluctant okay. Karl sat amused at the brother-sister exchange and said nothing,

"Ephesians 2, verses thirteen and fourteen say, 'But now in Christ Jesus you who once were far off have been brought nearby the blood of Christ. For He Himself is our peace, who has made us both one and has broken down in his flesh the dividing wall of hostility.'"

"Lena, do you plan to make this a sermon?" Herman asked, shifting loudly in his chair.

"No, but I am not finished. In chapter 4:2-3, it says, 'With all humility and gentleness, with patience, bearing with one another in love, eager to maintain the unity of the Spirit in the bond of peace.' And in chapter 5:1-2, it says, 'Therefore be imitators of God, as beloved children. And walk in love, as Christ loved us and gave himself up for us, a fragrant offering and sacrifice to God.' Aren't these wonderful attributes to teach your *kindern*, Herman?"

"If you are doing this for the *kindern*, then why aren't you reading chapter six, where it tells *kindern* to obey their parents?"

"You didn't want me to read the entire book before dinner, did you?"

I rose to retrieve the hot dishes of sausage and red cabbage from the stove and set them on the table.

Karl added, "You could read more from chapter five about the duties of husbands and wives." His crooked grin punctuated his comment.

"I must say, Herr Muller, I didn't realize you knew your Bible so well," I retorted. I could see he was pleased that he caught me off guard. "Besides, no one here is in either of those roles, correct?"

I returned to serving the evening meal to hide the heat rising in my cheeks. This way, I could blame the steaming food for my flushed face, rather than Karl's implications of the bond between husband and wives.

The rest of the meal fell into pleasantries as Karl updated Herman on the chores he had attended to in Herman's absence. Herman thanked Karl for the beautiful gift of the decorative crutches but neglected to say anything about the book.

When Herman questioned Karl's need to keep hanging around, Karl said, "What I was doing at the office can wait a bit. Not too many fugitive slaves making a break for freedom in these winter conditions. I told my coworkers that a friend needed my help for a while and that I'd be here until he was back on his feet."

"Friend? I don't know you. In fact, I am not even sure what you do, Herr Muller."

"Please, call me Karl. Isn't that what friends do? As for my work, I am part of an organization that helps emancipate slaves. Alton is strategically located across the Mississippi River from the slave state of Missouri. Some slaves travel across the river to the free state of Illinois. When they do, we help harbor them until we can send them farther north to freedom. Sometimes, we write freedom suits for them. The day you had your accident, I talked to some folks in the area about helping us with our cause. Some of our homes in the Alton area have been . . . compromised."

"Sounds like a lot of trouble for people you have never met."

"Sort of like helping people whom I do not know well? Like here?" Karl smiled back.

"I guess so. I think you may have other ideas about being here, however."

Herman glanced my way as I pretended I had no idea what they were talking about.

"I received your message that Lena is not eligible for marriage, Herman, and I honor that." Karl shifted in his seat. "But for now, I'm enjoying a nice meal and helping out some folks in need."

Herman reluctantly agreed to Karl's offer to stay. My heart burst from all the goodwill exerted at the dinner table. I knew the Lord had answered my prayers. Even the *kindern* didn't spill or make mischief during the entire meal, which alone was an answer to prayer. I only hoped the truce would last.

⚜

The strain of a tense chain rattling between Karl and Herman loosened more each day. Herman found no fault in any of Karl's ministrations around the farm.

My fickle heart wavered between hope and fear. I prayed long and hard for the two to become friends, like Herman and Josef. The rhythm of work and rest melded Karl into a welcome addition to our farm life.

Every time I watched Karl play with the children or talk with Herman about plans for the farm, I knew the days of Karl's presence were getting shorter. Karl brought Herman a copy of a booklet, *The Old Farmer's Almanac,* and helped translate any terms Herman fumbled over. Karl also became Herman's sounding board for any farming advice in Illinois that may have differed from Germany.

Herman mulled over all the new concepts and was anxious to return to his duties. I dreaded the time of Karl's departure, but I knew I should not worry.

Lord, create in me a still heart, I prayed constantly.

Spring finally called with full force. The young trees Herman and Katarina had planted sprouted tiny promising buds. A few purple crocuses rose through the once-dormant, snow-covered soil, giving colorful life to the barren ground. The robins reappeared and sang their praises to the new season as they gathered sprigs for their nests.

One glorious morning, I discovered a waffle iron among Katarina's wedding gifts and decided to serve an ambitious breakfast of waffles to my family. Yes, I thought of Karl as family, too. Watching him work the farm and play with the *kindern* spread a contented warmth through me when he flashed his lopsided grin my way.

"Waffles? What's the occasion?" Herman's crutches clipped into the room with more speed each day and snapped me out of my daydreaming.

Karl had slipped outside for the morning chores but would return to eat breakfast at any moment. He had established a routine so natural that I could set a clock by him. Forbidden daydreams of a permanent life with him plagued my waking hours.

"It was such a glorious morning, I couldn't help it. With the robins singing outside, issuing in the spring breezes, it seemed like a celebration day to me."

I turned back to stirring the waffle batter. I did not realize I hummed "All Hail the Power of Jesus' Name" until young Hans joined the chorus with a near shouting, "'Crown him Lord of all!'"

Karl, now standing in the doorway, and Herman in his seat at the table burst out laughing at our impromptu morning choir. Little Hans beamed at all the sudden attention, and Hannah banged on her highchair tray, enjoying the lively spirits.

Karl's smile crinkled his eyes to near slits. "It smelled too delicious to stay away any longer. To be greeted with a song is almost too much."

"I wasn't planning on a show, but you are welcome."

I graced my audience with a brief curtsy before placing Karl's waffle in front of him. I brushed his shoulder as I leaned across the table to deliver the syrup bottle, and an involuntary shiver radiated through me, causing me to stumble.

Karl gently grabbed my extended wrist. "Whoa there. Don't fall."

His voice was barely audible. The family was engrossed in their morning good fortune of waffles and likely did not overhear his words of caution. My eyes darted back to Karl, where his gaze never left me.

"Meet me outside after breakfast," he whispered.

His breath intoxicated me, and my cheeks turned crimson. I had no power to answer. He released my arm, and I nodded as I returned to prepare my waffle.

Karl's words haunted me. Why he wanted a secret meeting with me after all these weeks together tempted me to run outside immediately, but instead, I ate my waffle absentmindedly.

By the time I cleared the breakfast table, Karl had gone outside. Herman struggled with his boots to follow him.

"Herman?" He glanced up but continued tugging a stubborn boot over his injured foot. "Dagmar says she has some vegetable starts I can plant in the garden when it is warm enough. It looks like such a lovely day. Will you watch Hannah and Hans a while, and I'll run over to get them?"

"Why don't you take them with you? She loves the children, and they need some outside time, too."

"That is true, but it would be nice to have a little woman time with her. You've had Karl to talk to all these weeks. I'd like some quiet time without the little ones for just one morning," I pleaded in my most obedient, sisterly voice.

Sighing, Herman relented. "I suppose you are right. I am sure it can be a bit lonely for you out here. I sometimes forgot that with Katarina." He stared at the floor. "I should have let her socialize more. I think she would have been happier here." Sadness crept across Herman's face.

I hugged Herman and said, "I'm sure she was always happy with you. You were all she ever wanted." Then, with another squeeze, I added, "You can have some time with the children, and I'll be back in a bit."

I draped my shawl over my shoulders and slipped through the door before he thought of another reason for me not to slip out alone.

Karl was in the barn, where he spent countless hours staying out of sight. "You got away fast. How did you keep Herman from following you?"

"I told him I was going over to Dagmar's. So, whatever it is you wanted . . . "

"Lena, it is time for me to go."

"Why? You can't go. Things are going so well. I don't want you to go. The children love you. Herman has accepted you. I . . . " My mouth ran faster than my brain.

"You knew I couldn't stay forever. Herman can hobble around well enough on his own, and I'm surprised he hasn't kicked me off his place before now."

"I think he enjoys having male company. I wouldn't be surprised if he isn't just getting lazy watching you work."

Karl smiled. "That will never happen. You should hear all his plans for this place, and he is itching to work the land again." He focused his attention back to me. "Your job will be to keep him from overdoing it. Maybe your neighbor will give him a hand occasionally if he needs it."

"Karl, why can't it be you?" Tears pooled behind my words.

"Lena, I'd love to have you in my life, but I have a job I must return to. I can't just move in here. You and Herman have made it very clear that you can't be mine."

He embraced me. "You are all I ever think about. Your soft, brown hair; blue eyes; and soft, pouty lips . . . "

Then, our lips met, and I evaporated into his arms. I wanted the kiss to never end, but at last, he pulled away with a sigh.

A spring breeze threatened to topple me through the open barn doors. I never imagined such a moment in his arms being so gentle yet strong.

"Why must you go now? I need more time." I tightened my hold on him, but he pushed me away.

"Lena, you must have known. The waffles and the singing this morning were a wonderful send-off."

"I guess God knew. He just didn't tell *me* the little secret of why we were having waffles today," I said, shaking my head.

"I love it when you credit God for every little thing. Now, you'd better go to Dagmar's like you told your brother. I don't want him angry with you," he said, turning me toward the door.

"Will I see you again? I don't want to say goodbye." The tears rolled down my cheeks in earnest.

"Don't worry, Lena. I will always be around if you need me. Don't say goodbye. It is such a harsh American expression. Say *auf Wiedersehen,* until we meet again."

After a quick peck on my lips, he nudged me toward the door. "Off to the neighbors with you."

When I arrived at Dagmar's house, my eyes were puffy, and I was an emotional wreck.

"Lena. What's wrong?" Dagmar whisked me inside, and I divulged my entire morning to her.

"Josef will help Herman whenever he can. The two have been the best of friends ever since we arrived here. I think Josef has missed him since Karl has been there to help. He hasn't had enough to keep him occupied during the winter months. And we don't even have *kindern* to distract him."

Dagmar's yearnings and unrest were palpable. I realized visiting her was not my idea but the Lord's. She needed a listening ear as much as I did. We'd had little social time during the blustery winter, since the weather kept most everyone cloistered inside. Without the confidence of other women, the winter months grew icy beards.

"Does Josef want children?"

"He doesn't say too much about it because he knows my heart aches for them. Sometimes, he talks about who will take over the farm and such." Dagmar looked up. "I'm happy to have Hans and Hannah to dote on. After Katarina died and before you came, I tried to be a substitute mother to them in a way, but ... "

"I'm sure Herman appreciated your help. Hans and Hannah adore you. You make such beautiful clothes for them, too. I am not the seamstress Katarina was. In fact, my younger sister, Heidi, can sew circles around me. Fortunately, Hannah will have someone handier with a needle to show her how to sew when she is older." I took

Dagmar's hand. "Children come in God's timing. Maybe it is just hasn't been your time yet. I will pray for you."

"Thank you, but I don't think I have the faith of Old Testament Sarah, who waited a near lifetime for a baby."

We stood, and I gave her a hug. "Well, I told Herman you had some vegetable starts for me to plant. I sure hope you do, or I will have some explaining to do when I get back."

Dagmar laughed. "You came to the right place, my friend. I can spare some I've started out back. I have some strawberry shoots you can put in your garden, too. I'll give you all you will be able to carry home by yourself. In the summer, we can make preserves together."

Loaded with all the plant starts that would fit into my basket, I drifted home. Karl would be gone by the time I returned. I would miss watching him work around the farm and playing with the *kindern*. What would my heart do now?

Lord, I prayed, *help me face my days without Karl being nearby. The farm will not be the same with him gone. I am not the only one suffering from loneliness. If it is Your will, grant Dagmar the family she so yearns for. She would make the best mother.*

CHAPTER 14

The Ring of Freedom

*"Yet because of false brothers secretly brought in—who slipped in to
spy out our freedom that we have in Christ Jesus, so that they might
bring us into slavery—to them we did not yield in submission even for
a moment, so that the truth of the Gospel might be preserved for you."*

Galatians 2:4-5

Farms are flurries of activity during springtime. My father worked in a sawmill back in Germany, so sustaining a living from a farm was new to me. Sure, Momma and Papa had a garden and a few goats to help feed their growing family, but Papa supported his family by running the lumber mill.

Papa always had a few coins for Heidi to buy ribbons for her sewing projects or extra ingredients for Eva's baking, and Martin was never short of books—mainly because he traded for many of them and nearly lived in the library. His shelves bowed from the heavy, bound volumes laced with Roman or Greek heroes. Money could always be found for such things in the most challenging times because Papa provided for his family.

Herman's farming required planning in the winter to plant and care for crops in the spring. The gift of *The Old Farmer's Almanac* explained weather and soil conditions to produce the best crops in the region. While being laid up for over a month, Herman used the time with Karl to map out detailed plans for the farm and a spring planting regiment.

With Karl gone, Herman joined forces with Josef. They worked side by side on their adjoining farms, sharing equipment and camaraderie. Josef spared Herman's injured foot by walking the fields alone as much as Herman allowed. Herman relented to riding in the wagon or mounting his new mare, since complete healing was still months away. Thankfully, his injury healed without infection, and his halted stride lengthened with more purpose each passing day.

Dagmar and I daily prepared large meals of meat and potatoes for the men's exhaustive appetites, and the sisterhood between us grew as close as the brotherhood of the men. Chasing Hannah and Hans around helped fill the haunting void of Dagmar's childlessness, but I could see it also strengthened her yearning for her own quiver of little ones. The children answered to us equally and had little chance to engage in too much unobserved mischief.

Besides chasing children and cooking meals, Dagmar and I each tended home gardens as the weather warmed. The root crops stored well through the winter; so we each planted rows of potatoes, turnips, carrots, beets, and parsnips. The above-ground crops needed more vigilance to keep the critters away. Deer liked squash and tomatoes the best. Rabbits attacked the lettuce and cauliflower. The growing season did not end before plenty of peppers and cucumbers found their way into pickle jars, and beans sat in stored sacks for year-round eating. The wheat and corn in the fields were cash crops. God blessed us with His bounty.

A weekly trip into town for church and occasional weekday stops at the market for supplies were all of the outside world we needed. In those brief stints, I kept an eye out for Karl, but he never appeared at church or town. Herman fell into his pre-accident routine again, and he seldom was in the house during daylight hours. For him, idleness was a sign of a man's weakness.

The children did not ask about Karl's absence. It was as though he had never been a part of our little family during those dreary winter months. They horsed around outside and grew faster than the garden weeds. I was the only one who suffered from the hole Karl had left in my heart, and long summer days of farming and the southern Illinois sun and humidity certainly couldn't fill it.

On the Sunday before July 4, the church buzzed with excitement about the upcoming holiday activities.

I leaned over to Dagmar sitting on the other side of Hans in our pew and asked, "What is special about the Fourth of July? Isn't it the same as other summer days?"

"No, silly. The Fourth of July is Independence Day. The town plans a big celebration. The children and you cannot miss it. Everyone in the county will attend."

"Oh? No one told me about this."

"Ja. We pack picnics to share, and the children play games. By evening, everyone dances to a fiddle band. Alton shoots off their cannons over the river. You can hear them in Bethel. It is a big celebration."

"I had no idea. I'll need to look through Katarina's recipes and make something delicious."

I hoped Karl would attend such a momentous event. It had been too long since I'd seen him. I'd given up watching for him in church since he had left the farm—adding to my weekly disappointment. A glimpse of him would have lifted my spirits.

Lord, I prayed, *You have given me a good life here with Herman and the children, but I so long for a husband of my own. Is that too much? Only You can help me satisfy the two loves in my heart.*

For the Fourth of July celebration, I found Katarina's favorite German cheesecake recipe, and I think my little sister Eva would have been proud of my rendering. I pulled out some pickled beets that lingered in the root cellar and created a baked meat dish of my own from fresh ingredients in the garden. True to Dagmar's description, everyone from the surrounding village came in their finest dress. Lavish dishes of potato salads, greens, pies of all varieties, strudels, and cakes graced the long table set up outside the church.

Herman and the *kindern* had smiled their way into town, anticipating a day to relax and interact with friends. The fields of corn were taller than the adult men and waited for harvest within the next few weeks. The wheat emerged into tall, wavy, bronze seas under the farmers' tutelage. A holiday to celebrate our adopted country fit the joy of the summer bounty. Herman bragged on his accomplishments with the menfolk and listened to ideas to produce better years to come.

Of course, the *kindern* were underfoot around the food tables during the picnic preparations. It was difficult to keep their fingers out of the food with all the delicious aromas wafting into the summer heat. Someone had baked a pie with ample cinnamon. A hint of garlic roamed from another dish. It was understandable that the *kindern* wanted to go Hansel and Gretel on the food table as if it were a house made of sweets, but the diligent mothers kept the children at bay until it was time to eat.

Amidst the hustle and bustle, a black couple caught my eye as they hurried to the backside of the church. Odd. I had not seen any black people since arriving in Bethel. The last ones I encountered were on the steamship, *Diana*. I had also seen others on the banks of St. Louis, working the docks or assisting their masters with cargo. I considered how the free state of Illinois revealed very few black people. Carrying on conversations in German or Irish in this area was almost as popular as English. I knew no one who spoke an African dialect or that Creole I had heard in New Orleans.

As my gaze lingered away from our family, Herman asked, "What is it?"

"I thought I saw something by the church."

"Of course, you did. People are everywhere today."

He scoffed at me. His mind was set on other things, and he must have thought me a silly female. He turned back to another distraction of children organizing a game of tag.

No need to explain myself to Herman, especially when I wasn't sure what had caught my eye. I followed the *kindern* to their organized games. At four-and-a-half, Hans was old enough to play tag with some school-age boys, who let him join them. He loved to chase Hannah and the few farm animals we let him pursue, but two-year-old Hannah could never catch her brother. She shuffled around, trying to follow the other girls at the picnic, until the clover became more interesting and she plopped down to pick them.

The Bruns rode up in their wagon. Dagmar wore a smart cotton frock with small daisies on a cornflower blue background. She had made Hannah a pinafore with leftovers from the same fabric. I had dressed her in it for the celebration because it was the newest and cutest outfit she owned.

Dagmar scooped Hannah up from her clover expedition and lovingly squeezed her. "How's my girl?"

To an unknowing observer, anyone would think Dagmar scooped up her own child, since they wore matching mother-daughter dresses. Hannah squealed with delight from Dagmar's luscious hug and the raspberry kiss on her cheek.

I wore my simple travel dress I had arrived in last fall—the same one I wore on Sundays and for holidays. Each time I put it on, it became shabbier. The embroidery around the collar was frayed. The fabric thinned at the elbow and where I wiped my hands on the skirt when I was without an apron. I needed time to create something new. Maybe Herman would allow me to look through some of Katarina's things. Although she was not as tall and of slighter build, I imagine some of her dresses might fit with little altering.

When Herman harvested his crop this year, I planned to ask for funds to make new clothes for his family. I did not want the family to look poor and threadbare, which would reflect poorly on Herman.

By midafternoon, several people used a small, raised porch to speak about American freedoms or present their political platform. The mayor greeted everyone first. Most attendees only half-heartedly listened while children continued to play tag and other unstructured games.

The mayor droned on, but the crowd was relatively disinterested in speech-making on such a fine day. Then Congressman Lovejoy regaled us about his times in the Alton area but reminded folks of the sinister times when pro-slavers destroyed his brother's newspaper business, causing his brother's untimely death. These events happened years before Herman and I had arrived in Illinois and seemed like ancient history. Eating and socializing took precedence for neighbors who rarely visited with each other while tending to the immediate needs of their remote farms and families.

The mayor returned to the podium after the congressman finished. "And now, ladies and gentlemen, I have the pleasure to call Mr. Karl Muller to the stage to introduce another special speaker."

Karl bounded onto the platform without using half the steps. My heart swelled at his athleticism, grace, and prowess. I wanted to say, "This man is mine." Although I had sent him away without any commitment, he still held my heart. I wanted to tell everyone to be quiet. If they did not want to listen to my Karl, I sure did.

"Ladies and gentlemen, this is a day to celebrate independence. We are fortunate to live in the great state of Illinois, where we can live free—black and white."

Heads turned as he approached the controversial topic. Was he going to use this platform to speak of the slave issue? Herman focused on Karl's speech. I had never overheard the two men entertain the slave topic during Karl's stay, but I knew their views chafed the other's sensibilities.

"I have the great honor to introduce a businessman from Chicago who has the distinction of being a voice for the black men and women in Illinois. Mr. Jones advocated for equality before the law, whether a person's face was black or white. He necessitated repealing the Illinois black code laws, which now allows freedom to our black neighbors. They are no longer subjected to fines, imprisonment, or removal from the state simply because they lack proper documentation. Nor are they subject to being sold at auction for inability to pay these unjust fines. The governor himself honored Mr. Jones with a cannon salute for his faithful service to the cause of his race. We are pleased to have this chance to hear Mr. Jones speak to you fine folks today. Please, put your hands together for Mr. John L. Jones."

CHAPTER 15

Strangers Among Us

"For we are strangers before you and sojourners, as all our fathers were.
Our days on the earth are like a shadow, and there is no abiding."

1 Chronicles 29:15

A black man speak to us? I had seen them working on the docks and being mistreated but never imagined that one would speak to a white crowd. This surprised me as much as meeting Miss Eula sashaying around New Orleans in her fine clothes and parasol had. How could the same race of people be slaves and yet hold positions of honor in the same society?

A stout black man, wearing a well-tailored dark blue suit, mounted the platform. As he did, a few black families appeared in the audience, hanging back from the others but close enough to listen. Tots clung to their mothers' skirts with wide eyes as if the strangers might snatch them up.

Mr. Jones jumped right into his speech by thanking the patrons for the opportunity to address them. "The only way we can all be free in this country is if we work together as neighbors. The free black men and women here stay to themselves out of fear." He pointed to the growing number of black families now in plain view. "Fear that someone will snatch them away from their loved ones and throw them back into the bonds of slavery. With the Fugitive Act of 1850, no one is safe."

Mothers held their small ones closer, and fathers surveyed the gathering to defend their loved ones if the need arose. "Even if a man was born free, a slave hunter could legally steal them away because of this law. These freedom-loving, God-fearing people are at your mercy." He gestured again to some of the emerging black families standing nearby.

"Where did they all come from?" I whispered to myself. "I've never seen any of these people before."

"Do you realize that almost five hundred blacks live in Madison County?"

I jumped, realizing Karl had come to stand behind me. I watched the events so intensely that I had lost track of him.

"You need to stop sneaking up on a person like that."

"I wasn't sneaking."

His impish grin filled my senses. A rumble rippled through the crowd, but I had missed Mr. Jones' comment. "What did he say?"

"He just told them the national black convention would be held in Alton in a couple of months."

"Really?"

I surveyed the other listeners. Some men were noticeably upset and shouted concerns.

"We don't need more freeloaders here!"

"How will we keep our families safe?"

"I'd better help." Karl gave my arm a quick squeeze and disappeared.

Leaving my side, Karl returned to the podium in a few quick paces. "Ladies and gents, there is no reason for alarm. The men arriving for the convention will be here to conduct business and return to their home states. We should be honored to host such a prestigious event. Alton is a growing city that we can be proud of.

"In fact, we just received word Alton will also host one of the debates between Mr. Lincoln and Mr. Douglas. Many of you are mindful of the issues facing us in this state and in the nation. I invite you to attend this debate and see these candidates in action when the time comes."

Karl turned his attention back to the speaker. "Please thank Mr. Jones for coming from Chicago to address us today." The white crowd returned a half-hearted applause, whereas the black families gave congratulatory nods. "And I return the podium to our fine mayor."

Karl escorted Mr. Jones from the platform and returned him to his entourage, who hurried him back to the train station before any harm befell him. Anything the mayor said would be anticlimactic now. The murmurs focused on so many black families appearing in their midst, alarming some of the women. How did we not know so many lived nearby? With more coming to free states from all over the nation, I was certain the German newcomers feared for their safety after hearing about plantation riots and other Southern uprisings.

Lord, please let everyone live in peace and harmony here. We are all Your children and need Your grace, I silently prayed.

Unrest followed the speechmaking. Men assembled in small groups, grumbling to one another about so many black folks at their celebration. I overheard some of their conversations.

"Where did they come from anyway?"

"They don't belong here, mixing with our families."

"Maybe we'd better run them off."

"*Ja*, no need having them spoil our holiday."

"Look at them just standing there like they ain't got something better to do."

The voices grew louder among the congregants, and I worried about their negative comments affecting the otherwise fun time at the picnic.

The black families stood away from the others and did not try to mix with anyone outside their group as they processed Mr. Jones' news about the black convention. They visited with their own families and ignored the growing resentment toward them near the church food table. Children no bigger than Hans and Hannah held their parents' hands and watched the other children play games they dared not join.

Unaware of the growing tension between the newcomers and the European immigrants, Hans ran over to a black boy about his age and grabbed his open hand before anyone thought to stop him.

"Wanna play?" He tugged the astonished lad to free him from his mother's grip, and they trotted together toward the grassy field where several boys continued to play tag.

"Jasper! C'mere!" the boy's father yelled after them.

The older children looked up when they heard the shouting black man, appalled that Hans held the hand of a black boy. The two skipped into the play area as if they were buddies. Jasper ignored his father's command, basking in his newfound freedom with this friendly boy. But the older white boys ran toward the happy pair and attacked Hans' new friend by pushing him to the ground and kicking him.

Jasper's father was on the scene in two strides and whisked his son out of the fray before the third kick. "Get off him!" He pushed a tall, blond boy aside and lifted his battered son into his arms. He turned to the play yard mob. "What's wrong with you? You're ten times bigger 'n him."

Jasper's father motioned his wife and daughter to follow him while he carried his sobbing son away from the disturbance. "Lu, gotta go."

His small family sped around the church's other side, leaving behind their picnic lunch under a nearby tree to escape the playground bullies and their parents.

Another tall, blond boy yelled toward the adults, "Pa! He hit me, Pa!" Then he pointed at the retreating family.

"Vhere do you tink you're going?" the agitated group of grumbling men yelled in broken English as they dashed after the fleeing family. "Tink you can hit my boy and git away with it?" one of the men yelled.

Karl ran between the angry crowd and the black family, waving his hands to stop them, yelling in German. "Whoa! I saw the whole thing. Your son wasn't hit. That family was saving their son from the attack."

"Attack! They were saving that little Neubauer kid from that black boy. That's all. Get out of the way so that we can take care of this. It's no business of yours."

"Wait," Karl insisted, trying to wave Hans back over to us since Hans had fearfully backed away from the crowd.

"I'm right here, honey." I hugged Hans against my skirt as I watched the anger escalate between the men. "Karl won't let anyone hurt you."

I turned Hans around to see Karl try to manage the unfolding crisis.

Karl crouched down to the four-year-old's level. "Hans? Is that what happened?"

Hans buried his face in my skirt again. He had no intention of saying anything in front of the angry mob that gathered around the tall, blond instigator.

Karl tried once again to coax Hans into speaking. "Hans? Tell them what happened, okay? Did you find a new friend to play your game?" Hans nodded an almost imperceptible nod. "Did he hurt you?" This time, Hans shook his head and pointed at the blond offender. "He did. He pushed me."

"Look at them. He is so shook up, he doesn't know what he's saying. Get out of our way and let us deal with this."

"I will not." Karl stood tall again. "No one is hurt here. Go back to enjoying Independence Day with your families."

The group's leader realized the black family had long departed the ruckus, so he turned his ire on Karl. "You can't tell us what to do. You are one of those men who harbor runaway slaves and endanger our families. I'm staying here to celebrate with my family now, but their time will come."

The man turned, put his arm across the shoulder of his unhurt son, and marched him back to his waiting wife.

Herman bent down to talk to the still-shaken Hans. "Hans, you didn't do anything wrong, but next time, you need to ask before grabbing someone to play, okay?"

Hans wiped his nose on my skirt and squeaked, "Okay, Papa."

Herman turned to Karl. "Thanks for taking control of the situation, but I don't think it is a good idea to mix the races here. Look what can happen."

"Nobody was mixing anything, Herman. These people have as much right to be here as anyone else. Too bad, not everybody sees it that way."

"You can't change the world by yourself, Karl. In the meantime, I want my children to be safe and not caught in the middle of a mob."

Herman took Hans' hand to lead him to the food table. "Let's find a piece of rhubarb pie, Hans," he said as they walked away. The little guy perked up and let his father lead.

"Sorry, Lena. I had no idea that would happen. I would do anything for Hans or Hannah. Those two tots tug at my heart, too."

"And I'm sure Herman knows that. He just wants to protect his *kindern*."

"That is all Jasper's dad was doing as well," Karl retorted.

"I hope his little boy is all right. You know who they are, don't you?" I asked as we stood together and watched them walk away.

"Yes. He is a carpenter over there between Upper Alton and Wann. Nice guy. I hope this mob does not cause trouble for him and his family. It will force them to move on." I could see Karl's mental chess pieces reposition to his next move to help the distressed family.

"Maybe I can take them a little something next week and see if their son is okay. After all, if it weren't for Hans, the little guy would not have been put in that situation," I said.

"You'd do that?"

"Why are you so surprised, Karl? I understand how important this is to you, and they didn't do anything wrong. It only seems right to help."

"Lena, I could just kiss you."

"Don't even think such a thing with all these people around!"

I looked over my shoulder to see if any of the town gossips had us in their sights.

Karl straightened his jacket and changed the subject. "I want you to attend the Lincoln-Douglas debate with me. I think you need to understand more about this new country you have adopted."

"I don't think Herman will let me go to something like that."

Karl was standing too close again. All the pent-up feelings after months of not seeing him returned. The late afternoon heat required a shady spot before I swooned like a weak-kneed female awaiting servants delivering libations on the veranda.

"Let's walk over here under the tree," I said, directing Karl to the nearest willow tree.

"Does Herman need to direct your every move, Lena? You are a grown woman."

"His wishes are clear. I am not looking for a suitor here."

He took my hand. "Aren't you lonely, Lena?"

"Actually, I am often with Dagmar. She is a great friend. I came here for Herman, not you," I added in exasperation.

"Can you say you don't think of me?"

I would not lie to him, nor would I encourage him. "Of course, I want to be with you, Karl, but there is no way to do it without breaking my promise to Herman and the family. They must come first." The lump in my throat threatened my eyes.

He whispered, "You give me hope, Lena."

"Don't hope unless it is in the Lord, Karl. He is the only One Who can straighten out this mess."

My eyes searched for an escape and found the *kindern* playing under Dagmar's care. I quickly joined them, pretending to watch them romp as Karl walked toward the back of the church.

I turned to Dagmar. "Do you know anything about American politics?"

"Goodness, Lena. What a question. Why do I need to know anything about politics? Women can't vote, anyway. I let Josef worry about those things."

"Karl wants me to learn more about this country. He thinks that going to that debate in Alton will help me understand more about it."

"It doesn't hurt to be informed, I guess. The Bible does say to seek wisdom and understanding. What do you think Herman will say about your going?"

"I don't think he will like it. 'Politics is no place for a woman,' sounds like something he would say. So many things here are different. Did you have any idea there were so many black people here? Karl said there are five hundred right in Madison County. They must be invisible. We never see them."

"I think they must stay out of sight, so they are not attacked like what happened here today. I am glad your friend Karl stepped in when he did."

"It will be dark soon. The *kindern* are tired. Herman and I must take them home soon."

"You can't go yet. After dark, they fire off some explosions you will not want to miss."

"Explosions? Are you sure we should not be home by then?"

"Just wait. The *kindern* will love them. You will, too. It is an American celebration."

She was right. Dagmar always seemed to be right.

CHAPTER 16

The Visit

"For I was hungry and you gave me food, I was thirsty and you gave me drink, I was a stranger and you welcomed me, I was naked and you clothed me, I was sick and you visited me, I was in prison and you came to me."

Matthew 25:35-36

The following Sunday, our family adorned ourselves in the cool morning. I wanted to arrange them for one of those fancy family photographs and save the image forever. But by the time our wagon bumped along the dusty road to the church and the emboldened sun boasted its strength down on us, the fresh family look had wilted. Pressed shirts and skirts were wrinkled, and the sticky air transformed a fresh family into a disheveled one that drooped into the church and planted themselves into the pew. The sweltering heat pasted our layers of clothing to us like wet rags.

Despite the heat, everyone dressed in their Sunday best, which meant the men wore long-sleeve shirts buttoned to a respectable throat, and their trousers covered their scuffed farm boots. The women folk also covered themselves from head to toe with layers of petticoats under cotton skirts. The fancier dresses sported lace or ruffles about the neck and cuffs that scratched delicate chins and wrists for the sake of fashion. Fancy or plain, no self-respecting woman exposed an ankle, an arm, or a neckline during a Sunday gathering.

Women produced makeshift fans from their purses, pumping the air vigorously as they tried to cool the stagnant heat. Elders propped the widows open, and more prayers were said for a breeze than for any other needs in the congregation—but to no avail. Irritable children poked siblings and clung to mothers who preferred a reprieve from their hot little bodies in their laps.

As I waited for the opening hymn, I saw Karl discreetly seat himself toward the back of the sanctuary. My heart skipped at the mere sight of him. Only a week had passed since the Independence Day celebration, but I thought of him every day. Even though I yearned for him to sit beside me, I loved how considerate he was, since his presence near me made Herman bristle.

The congregation began singing "Was Mein Gott Will."[9] Confident that my younger sister Maria inherited all the singing ability in the family, I belted out my best joyful noise to the Lord, anyway. I sang along as the lyrics started to absorb into my heart by verse three.

> *Temptation's hour shall lose its pow'r,*
>
> *for you shall guard us surely.*
>
> *O God, renew, with heav'nly dew,*
>
> *our body, soul, and spirit,*
>
> *until we stand at your right hand,*
>
> *through Jesus' saving merit.*

---

9   "Who Trusts in God a Strong Abode"

Karl was a temptation for me, but I knew the temptation would lose its power if I gave it all to Jesus.

Lord, fill me with a more worthy pursuit in my life, I prayed. *I don't know if Herman and the children will fill this void left by Karl. Amen.*

By the time the opening litany from Psalm 149 finished, I realized I had only half-listened to the part about singing a new song—not the best metaphor for my life. The reading from Isaiah spoke about a new heaven and earth. Again, not exactly the comfort I looked for. The lesson from 1 Thessalonians reminded me God doesn't want me to be unhappy, or He would have never sent His Son to die for me. I needed to keep busy by helping others and doing the work He has for me.

The congregation rose for the reading from Matthew 25:34-36: "Then the King will say to those on his right, 'Come, you who are blessed by my Father, inherit the kingdom prepared for you from the foundation of the world. For I was hungry and you gave me food, I was thirsty and you gave me drink, I was a stranger and you welcomed me, I was naked and you clothed me, I was sick and you visited me, I was in prison and you came to me.'"

The sermon hymn, "O God of Mercy, God of Light," reinforced these sentiments. Verse five summarized the Gospel reading perfectly.

In sickness, sorrow, want, or care,

May we each other's burdens share;

May we, where help is needed, there

Give help as unto Thee.

The pastor drove the lesson home with illustrations of Judgment Day being so near that we must do all we could for our fellow man. "Whatever you did for one of the least of these brothers and sisters, Christ says you did for him. Compassion for each other is an act of forgiveness and helping others when they need it the most. Do not ignore the needs of others because they are not like you. God does not discriminate based on where you were born, what language you speak, or who your family is. God wants all to obtain salvation, and we can help show others that light of salvation by showing compassion and easing others' burdens when we can."

The image of the boys kicking young Jasper leaped into my mind. What had I done to help this family who was innocently attacked at a holiday picnic? Sure, I had comforted Hans, who was caught up in the turmoil; but he was family, and a brood of older boys had not pounced upon him. So, he was safe while Jasper's family fled— wounded and afraid.

God's Spirit moved me to right that wrong. I must tell Herman that we, or I, should visit that family, offer comfort, and ask forgiveness for what happened.

The closing hymn, "Let Us Ever Walk with Jesus," bolstered my resolve. Jesus would never turn His back on others' suffering, and a child no bigger than Hans should not suffer just because of his skin color.

The congregation disbursed into the aisle, and I felt torn. Should I ask Karl about my plan first? He knew the family and where they lived, and I needed his help to carry out my idea. He would have the answers to all the questions Herman would pose when I approached him about it. Herman would never let me venture out on such a task alone, but I was not sure he would let me go with Karl either.

As our family moved toward the exit door, a long-awaited breeze stirred the air, and we breathed a welcome sigh. Karl cooled himself under a nearby tree, waiting for us to leave the church.

I clasped the pastor's hand and said, "I enjoyed your message, and I have a plan to be a better neighbor."

Herman gave me a sideways look, and the pastor smiled back. "I'm glad some people take the messages to heart, Lena. I am sure the Lord is using you in many glorious ways." He winked at the children, then extended his hand to Herman. "You are fortunate to have such a giving sister."

"She is a wonder. That's for sure." Herman pumped the pastor's hand. As we walked away, he asked me, "What do you have in that head of yours now, Lena?"

Lord, I quickly prayed, *is this how You want me to approach this? Help me say the right things.*

"I was thinking about what the pastor said about helping the least of these, and God brought young Jasper to mind. You know, the little boy who attended on the Fourth of July? I think we should ask how he is doing." I hurried on before Herman could object. "After all, Hans is the one who dragged him into that mess. They are just boys and did not know any better, but we can set a better example, don't you think?"

"Lena," Herman said, wiping his brow, "you don't even know where this Jasper and his family live or if they would take kindly to you coming to visit. You may be walking into a more dangerous situation than what happened at the picnic."

"Karl knows them," I blurted, and I noticed Herman flinch.

"Is this a scheme to spend more time with Karl? I thought we had gone over this before."

"No. It is only that Karl has the connection with this family. He would never let me walk into a dangerous situation."

"Did I hear my name?" Karl asked, walking up to us.

"Lena has a crazy idea about visiting one of the black families who was at the picnic. Was this your idea?" Herman asked, staring at Karl.

"This is the first I've heard of it," Karl said, turning to Lena. "Why do you want to visit any of the black families?"

"I got an idea in church. The pastor said to have compassion for the less-fortunate, and I got to thinking about young Jasper. I think we should check on him and let them know all of us are not like those boys who beat him. It might help to apologize for Hans' involvement, even though he did not know what he was doing."

Karl and Herman looked at each other. Karl spoke first. "They are a nice family. Jasper's father works as a carpenter for the railroad, not too far from here. It might not be a bad idea to meet a friendly face. They don't always get that from the community." He shifted on his feet, not sure he was making any sense to Herman. "If I go, I can introduce you properly and serve as a guide of sorts. What do you think?"

Herman wiped his hand across his face in consideration of this crazy idea. "If the family is to be represented, I should go, too. I think you two need a chaperone, anyway. When were you thinking about going?"

"Sundays are probably the best day to visit people. Other days, they are at work," Karl said.

"You want to go now?" I asked.

I could tell Herman could hardly believe what he had heard.

"How far away did you say they were?" I asked, turning to Karl for the answer and hoping my plan would work.

Karl smirked. "We can stop by your place for lunch and head there afterward, if I can invite myself over." He glanced at Herman for approval. "They are at Wann Junction, just a little southwest of you."

Herman hesitantly agreed to the plan, so we loaded everyone in the wagon and bumped our way home along the dusty road again. With our quick repast at the farm, I gathered extra bread I had baked the day before and some clothes Hans had outgrown that Jasper could probably wear. I fretted that we would not present our best by the time we reached our final destination, but the pastor said nothing about how we must appear when doing God's will. I was happy. I had everyone on board with the plan, even if we had to travel in the heat of the day.

The small houses near Wann Junction were little more than shacks. A few men sat outside playing checkers. Some women stirred a kettle of something that smelled like spicy fish. Children darted in and out of bushes in a game of tag.

Upon seeing our approach, everyone stopped their activities. They interrogated the wagons of white people with their eyes, not believing we dared to interrupt their Sunday solace.

Karl took the lead and greeted a few men by name as we drew closer. "Hi there, Silas. Nice evening, Smitty. Cookie. You aren't cheating, are ya?" I smiled at hearing him speak in English so well.

Karl addressed the checker players with a cheerful, disarming lilt. Each man tipped his hat in response but did not utter a word.

"I told you this wasn't a good idea," Herman said under his breath as he leaned closer to me on the buckboard.

Both Hans and Hannah had dozed off during the ride. Hans used my lap as a pillow while Hannah lay in my arms. I began to rouse Hans from his slumber, but I decided not to be too hasty. However,

Hans instinctually awakened as we entered the gauntlet of people. He yawned and stretched himself alert as we passed the half-dozen homes.

Karl stopped his horse at the last house in the row. Herman pulled our wagon up to the front of the same place and stopped as well. Jasper's father opened the door.

Karl strode up to him, arm outstretched. "Hi, Willie." He grabbed his hand in a handshake. "I hope it is no inconvenience to call on you this Sunday. The Neubauers here want to see that young Jasper is all right after that incident the other day at the picnic."

Willie furrowed his brow but stood squarely in his doorway so no one could pass through if they were so inclined. Herman, the children, and I were off the wagon by this time. I dusted myself and the tots off the best I could and took Hans' hand as we walked to the diminutive porch.

"Willie, this is Herman and Lena Neubauer. They are a brother and sister who farm over by Bethel. These are Herman's kindern, Hans and Hannah. You probably remember young Hans from the other day."

Karl then turned to introduce us to the sentinel in the doorway. "This is Willie Jackson. He and his wife Luella have young Jasper, whom you met at the picnic, and his little sister, Flora." Karl tried to peer past the door, but there were no other family members in our sight.

"I brought a few tings over for you," I said nervously in English. "I made some *brot*, um bread, yesterday, and Hans is outgrowing some tings I tink Jasper might use."

I handed Hannah off to Herman to free my hands so I could offer my bundle to Mr. Jackson. He did not move and eyed me up and down as some oddity that washed up on his front step.

Luella came to the door, wiping the dish soap from her hands, and nudged Willie to the side and made her way through the doorway to meet us. "Willie, don't be so rude. These people have come quite aways on this hot, dusty day. The least we kin do is offer them a drink. Jasper!" The lad appeared beside his commanding mother who stood next to his retreating father. "Find some glasses and get some cool creek water for these nice folks," she said, setting my bundle down on a nearby shelf.

"Dat would be lovely, Mrs. Jackson. Da *kindern* are surely thirsty."

"Call me Lu. Ever-body does. Sorry for our manners. We don't get much Sunday comp'ny."

"Dat's all right. I hope my English ist okay. I am still learning."

"You's doing just fine. I have no book learn'n myself, yet I can understand most anybody."

We both chuckled and chattered about how fast the children were growing, what was available to make favorite cooking recipes, and our respective sewing skills while the children played under our feet and the men gaped at us and shook their heads.

Baffled, Herman said to the men in English, "You'd think dey long-lost friends da way dey are talking."

"My wife cud befriend a panther on the prowl, that she cud. She never met a stranger," Willie responded. "Would you two like somethin' to drink? I have more out back."

A couple of hours later, cooler evening breezes settled over the prairie as we rode home. Karl parted ways with us to return to Alton with a tip of his hat. Herman and I enjoyed the brilliant splashes of peaches and oranges of the sunset in peace while the children slept between us. It had been a good day, for sure.

CHAPTER 17
Breathless Days

*"Behold, you have made my days a few handbreadths, and my lifetime
is as nothing before you. Surely all mankind stands as a mere breath."*

Psalm 39:5

The Southern Illinois heat sweltered into a heavy, damp curtain no one could break through. Herman came in from walking the cornfields each day as wet as if he had jumped into the Mississippi. He wiped his brow with his kerchief and only smeared the grime from one side of his forehead to another.

I learned to rise early to weed and water the garden before the unbearable swamp of a day hit its zenith. The poor laundry seldom dried completely and hung limp on the line. Even the children had less energy, happy to relegate their play to trains and read books in the front room once the sun rose above the barn.

Although both Hans and Hannah were more subdued, they did not nap well. The midday sweat on their precious temples attracted pesky flies that darted to and fro on their small bodies. Hans now protested naps, anyway.

Little Hannah needed her downtime. One day as I watched her fitful sleeping, I realized it was more than flies keeping her from resting well. Her breathing was labored, and occasionally, she gasped to catch a missed rhythm. I stroked her forehead as the breathing became a sing-song wheeze. Something was wrong. I needed Herman, but he was somewhere in the one hundred acres he tended—and he never reported his daily plan to me.

"Hans!" He put his train car down and came to my knee. "Do you know where your *vater* is working today?"

"I dunno." He thought harder. A moment later, he added with a smile, "Papa says he eats lunch by the creek. It is cooler there."

That made sense. I squeezed Hans for being so clever. But how could I get word to Herman? I couldn't leave the children, and Hans was too young to be sent out there on his own.

I put Hannah in my lap and raised her head higher to help her catch what little wayward air visited the room. I rocked her most of the afternoon and left the household chores undone. Dinner could be cool summer sausages, since it was too hot to cook, anyway. I hoped Herman would head home early.

Lord, I prayed, *let Herman know we need him at home. Little Hannah needs a doctor. Help us, Lord. We need Your loving care.*

As I prayed, Hans, hearing a noise, ran to the window. "Papa's here!"

"Go tell him I need him."

Soon, Hans and Herman burst through the door. "What's the matter?" Herman asked. "Hans said Hannah is sick."

"She can't breathe. We need to take her to the doctor now."

One glance at his exhausted Hannah and Herman headed for the door again.

"I'll hitch the horse to the wagon. You keep holding her."

I sent Hans to grab Hannah's favorite doll to take with us. Within minutes, we sat side by side in the midday heat, saying silent prayers for little Hannah.

"I'm so glad you came home. I didn't know what to do."

"My shovel handle broke, and I came back to fix it so I could finish filling some gopher holes." Herman shifted from me to Hannah. "I guess God broke it to send me home for Hannah."

"Yes, He did." The words *Thank You, Jesus* echoed in my heart.

Dr. Howard visited Bethel only several times a week when he made trips to other neighboring villages, so he was not in town when we arrived with our limp Hannah. We rode all the way into Alton to find a doctor. Herman's speed caused me to hang on with one hand while holding Hannah with the other. Hans sat between us and enjoyed the thrill ride—too young to absorb the urgency of the trip.

The small wagon roared into town and stopped in front of Dr. Todd Russell's shingle. Herman scooped Hannah out of my arms and bounded into the small waiting area, startling a woman as she entered the room from the other side.

"Oh my! What do we have here?" The plump woman brushed Hannah's hair from her face and peered down at the distraught child, her sweaty, cherub cheeks puffing for more air.

"Zhe canna breathe." Herman tried not to make it sound like a barking order but did not quite keep his pent-up anxiety in check.

"Wait here. I'll fetch the doctor."

The swirl of her skirts followed her as she stepped into the next room. Herman and I stared helplessly at each other, wishing the agonizing minutes would fade into action. Hans buried his head into my skirt to hide from unfamiliar surroundings and upset adults.

The outside door burst open, and Karl filled the doorway. "I saw the wagon rush in here to the doctor." He surveyed the room with Herman holding his precious daughter. "What's wrong?"

"She can't breathe."

Karl flinched. I knew he had come to care for the children as much as anyone during his winter days with us. "Is there anything I can do to help?"

"Right now, we need the doctor to help her." Herman's frustration needed release. "There is nothing you can do."

I placed my hand on Herman's sleeve. "Maybe Karl can take Hans outside for a while?"

He peered down at his forgotten son and nodded. "*Ja.* He doesn't need to wait here. It may take a while."

Karl reached for Hans' hand. "Maybe I'll show you my favorite fishing hole, Hans. Would you like that?"

Hans took Karl's hand and turned to pull him to the door after Herman nodded permission for him to leave. "I won't be far," Karl said over his shoulder. "Tell Lawrence across the street to send someone if you need us. He knows where we will be."

He hesitated as though he needed to say more but then thought better of it. He turned to the door with Hans, speaking gently to the boy as they walked away.

No sooner had the front door closed than the woman returned. "The doctor can see you now. Follow me."

We followed and answered as best as we could as the robust woman asked questions in rapid-fire secession. "Your name? The girl? How old is she? How long has she been sick?" We turned a corner into an examination room. "Just put her on the table so the doctor can examine her."

Herman leaned over the exam table to release Hannah, but she clung tightly to her papa. Then, seeing a chair, Herman sat and placed Hannah on his lap instead. "I'll just hold her if dat's okay with you," he said a bit defiantly.

A man with round wire spectacles and graying hair at the temples entered the room and faced us.

"Doctor, this is the Neubauer family. Their little girl, Hannah, can't seem to breathe," offered his assistant.

The doctor approached the sick child, but Hannah buried her face into Herman's dirty work shirt.

"It's okay, honey. The doctor wants to help you," I consoled.

Hannah cried and barreled deeper into her father's embrace.

I stepped toward Herman and Hannah. "Let me hold her while you check her, doctor. She is scared." Herman let Hannah practically leap into my arms as we changed places in the chair.

"That's fine. Mommas usually have a calming touch. Let's see what we can do for you. Okay, Hannah?"

Momma? "Oh no, I'm not . . ." I started.

Hannah's big eyes blinked and stared back at the doctor as I held her close. It did not matter if he confused me with her mother. I could explain later.

After listening to her lungs, the doctor said, "Well, this is what I suspected. Your daughter has asthma. It is a disease of the lungs and constricts the airways, making breathing difficult. The hot, humid summers here affect many this way."

"Please, vat can you do for her, Doctor?" Herman did not like being powerless, and I could tell seeing his daughter so weak and vulnerable was undoing him.

"There is a treatment called Fowler's Solution that should help her breathing in no time."

"What is Fowler's Solution?" I asked.

I was certain neither Herman nor myself wanted our little Hannah to be a part of some experiment. Traveling salesmen with their elixirs promising miracles wandered through town from time to time, and we did not want Hannah subjected to such a huckster's concoction.

"It is a pharmaceutical compound of arsenic trioxide."

"Arsenic?" Sounding alarmed, Herman nearly snatched Hannah back. "But dat is poison!"

"It's okay. This is not the kind used for poison. Arsenic is found naturally all around. Like in the soil. The solution they use for treating asthma has been used this way for nearly one hundred years." Herman's alarmed expression remained the same. "Hannah is small. I will not prescribe a very large dose for her, but we should notice a change in her breathing almost immediately."

The doctor sent Mrs. Russell to the back room to mix the medicine. "Don't worry. I have the correct medicines on hand. Mabel is a fine chemist. She can make the solution we need right away."

In no time, Mabel returned with a small, brown bottle and a spoon. The doctor poured a few ounces on the teaspoon for Hannah to drink. "Open up, honey. This medicine will make you better," he said.

Hannah clamped her mouth shut. She looked from Herman to me, her eyes wide. She would have screamed if that did not mean opening her mouth to do so.

"Can you coax her to take the medicine, please? It really will help her breathe," the doctor requested.

I whispered in her ear, "Hannah, the doctor wants to help you feel better, so you can chase Hans again. Let's see what his medicine tastes like, huh?"

I turned back to the doctor. "May I have da spoon? She might take it from me."

With the spoon in my hand, Hannah finally allowed the liquid past her lips. Then, after a quick swallow, she rested her head on my bosom. Her breathing was less labored immediately.

Herman approached the doctor with his hand out. "*Danke*, Doctor. I should have trusted you."

"That's okay, Mr. Neubauer." He handed Herman the remainder of the bottle. "Give her another dose before bed tonight and let me know if she gets any worse. Twice a day as needed should keep her chasing her brother."

"*Danke*, Dr. Russell," I added, and then we walked back to the wagon. I held little Hannah, who drifted to sleep nearly lifelessly in my arms. This must be her first peaceful sleep for some time. Herman went and found Karl and Hans returning from a nearby stream.

Karl stood by as we loaded into the wagon. "If there is anything I can do . . . "

Herman coaxed the horse toward home as Karl's words hung in the humid early evening air. Concern for his daughter erased any manners he may have had to thank Karl for helping with Hans. I waved a half-hearted hand as he disappeared.

We were nearly home when Hannah started crying uncontrollably. She smelled of garlic. Vomiting and diarrhea followed.

"Herman, something's wrong! Let me take her into the house and clean her up."

I rushed Hannah inside and prepared a cool bath, imagining the heat and the long ride were too much for her. She clutched her stomach and howled louder.

"Goodness, little one. I don't think you have eaten anything today either. Hans, get your sister some bread and cheese, please."

Hans hurried to the cellar and brought them quickly. I stripped Hannah and sat her in a bathing basin, but she was still wrecking herself at both ends and had no interest in the edible fare Hans brought her.

"Hans, tell your *vater* to fetch the doctor for Hannah. Hopefully, Dr. Howard is back in Bethel now."

I was drying Hannah when Herman came back inside. "Do we still need a doctor?"

Hannah convulsed in my arms as Herman's answer. "I'll find someone in Bethel to help. I don't think that quack in Alton knew what he was doing." And he was out the door again.

I placed Hannah in her bed and tried comforting her with cool cloths as she whimpered in misery.

Lord, help little Hannah. Don't let her suffer, I prayed.

I sent Hans downstairs to watch for his father as I tried to assist the failing cherub in her room. But when Herman finally arrived with Frau Stolz, it was too late. Hannah's earthly suffering was over, and all we could do was cry.

The world has no solace when you bury a child. Hannah would never fall in love, raise a family of her own, play her imaginary games, or laugh when Hans' tickle monster attacked. The adorable, plump, little girl who cuddled in my arms, giggled when I blew kisses in her face, and chased her brother in her toddler fashion was gone. I wrapped her lifeless body in her favorite blanket and gave her back to God.

People immediately came by the house once word circulated about Hannah's death. The Bruns next door were like an extended family to us and monitored the ever-opening door of sympathies, the food deliveries, and the neglected chores. Yet our broken hearts weighed our bodies down, and our limbs refused to labor.

Pastor Klein visited, but his prayers for dear Hannah fell on deaf ears, since summoning God was pointless for a dead child. Empty arms provide no comfort. Numbly, we moved through the house as disembodied spirits. Little Hans cried for his only playmate. Herman turned into himself, giving only brooding grunts and sighs about the farm while struggling to love a God Who had taken away so much from him—first Katarina and now their beloved Hannah. When Katarina had died, at least he had their children. Now, only Hans remained. What if God snatched him away, too? I sensed he could bear no more.

Pastor Klein tried to console our family during his funeral message. Unfortunately, the typical funeral adages rang hollow. "'Come to me, all who labor and are heavy laden, and I will give you rest. Take my yoke upon you, and learn from me, for I am gentle and lowly in heart, and you will find rest for your souls. For my yoke is easy, and my burden is light.'"[10]

But this burden was too much to bear. It weighed us down to our souls. The depth of our dark sorrow grieved us to despair. Pastor Klein

---

10   Matthew 11:28-30

finished his sermon encouraging our hope in seeing little Hannah again. "'Let not your hearts be troubled. Believe in God; believe also in me. In my Father's house are many rooms. If it were not so, would I have told you that I go to prepare a place for you? And if I go and prepare a place for you, I will come again and will take you to myself, that where I am you may be also.'"[11]

But her room here was vacant, and our arms empty. Seeing her again waved the carrot of hope before us only as a distant promise we might never reach.

The congregation shuffled from the sanctuary to the cemetery. A fresh child-sized grave awaited us next to Katarina's resting place. Her mother's stone stood sentinel to keep her memory alive.

Katarina Neubauer
Loving wife and mother
1834-1856

We would add a smaller stone for little Hannah once the stonecutter finished it. Herman requested a little lamb sit atop the stone for his precious daughter. Her short years filled the dash, 1856-1858. No more birthday celebrations for this child of God.

Through tears, Herman placed wildflowers on the graves of his wife and daughter. Doubled over, he knelt and hid his face in his hands, trying to hide the tears seeping through his fingers. Hans moved next to him, placed a hand on his father's back, and patted him gently. Herman turned and wrapped his son in his arms and sobbed uncontrollably.

---

11   John 14:1-3

I felt Karl watching me from the edge of the mourners, sure he would spring into action if I fell apart in front of everyone, but he kept a respectful distance. He knew Herman did not want me to be around him, and Herman was in no condition to take a stand on social etiquette now. Herman's threshold allowed no more pressure from the world's cruelest blows.

The wagon ride home stretched into a foreboding silence as if the horse realized the unnecessary need to hurry to the daughterless farm. The chores waited as the grief hung in the air—as oppressive as the heat. No birds sang, and no squirrels chattered. All nature sighed for the little girl who had brought life and giggles everywhere she toddled.

A package sat on the front step. "I bet it is more food," I muttered to Herman.

Neighbors had supplied us with a deluge of edibles since Hannah's death. Everything threatened to spoil before we could eat it, and the summer heat did not help. I absentmindedly turned to pick up Hannah from the wagon as I dismounted from the wagon. My arms sought only empty air as I realized she was not there. She would never be there again. I collapsed into a heap of tears.

"Lena, you okay?"

Herman lumbered to my side, lifting me off the dusty ground and urging me to stand. "It is okay. We can always share some of this food with the Bruns or other friends if it is too much."

I wiped my tears and tried to explain. "No, it's not the food. I turned to get Hannah down from the wagon, and she was not there . . ."

"I understand," Herman said as he hugged me a moment more before we walked arm-in-arm to the door.

Hans picked through the bundle lying at the front door.

"*Was haben sie hier?*" Herman asked.

Herman bent over to get a closer look at Hans' find. Inside the brown paper bound with twine was a beautiful wreath woven with pink ribbons and bows. Evergreen vines laced it together; and tiny, bright stones rested in the twisted frame of stripped twigs. The sun caused the stones to sparkle tiny rainbows across the front of the house.

"My, my. It doesn't look like food, does it?" I asked as I touched the enchanting gift.

"It is lovely. Who left it?" Herman asked.

We searched inside the paper for any note, but nothing fell from the wrapping.

"Letters!" Hans said, pointing to the outside of the wrapping.

Printed in block letters were the words, "FOR HANNAH, JACKSONS."

"Jacksons? That family we visited after the picnic? We hardly know them," Herman said, scratching his head.

"It must be. We don't know any other Jacksons. Luella must have worked night and day on this to make it so intricate. I think it is for Hannah's grave," I said.

"We will place it in the church graveyard next Sunday." Herman sighed. "It is a wonderful reminder of Hannah's sparkle, isn't it?"

"Yes, it is. We must be sure to thank them for their kindness."

I took Herman's and Hans' hands as we gathered the cherished gift and walked into the lonely house.

CHAPTER 18
Justice and Mercy

"Therefore, the Lord waits to be gracious to you, and therefore he exalts himself to show mercy to you. For the Lord is a God of justice; blessed are all those who wait for him."

Isaiah 30:18

Dagmar insisted we go through the motions of life. We ate three meals a day. She created tasks for Hans to keep him from being underfoot the barely functioning adults around him. Often, he camped on my lap and enjoyed my squeezing him to within an ounce of his being—in place of the sister who was no longer here to hug. We kept the house in order and the farm running only because Dagmar and Josef came by every day to check on us, regardless of their other obligations.

"I feel so bad for Herman. He has lost so much," I lamented to Dagmar one day.

"He was distraught after Katarina died, too. They were so happy for her to have another child and grow their family. Losing her when Hannah was born took all the wind from Herman's sails."

"At home in Germany, Katarina set her cap for Herman before I think he even noticed her. We girls teased her about it, but she was determined that Herman was the boy for her. We thought that she just wore Herman down until he finally agreed to marry her."

"That's not the way they seemed when we met them. They came the same year as we did, and they were so in love. Katarina was already pregnant with Hans when we arrived, and Herman impatiently waited to be a *vater*. He attended to her throughout the pregnancy."

"I'm glad. Herman was Katarina's everything. I'm sure he must have been a good husband to her. Then her leaving him with two little ones to raise on his own must have not been easy for him either."

"You think he is sad now? It was worse then, I think. When he heard you were coming to help with the *kindern*, his spirits rose considerably. He had hope again. I don't think you know how much you mean to him. I'm not sure he could have continued without you."

"Herman doesn't talk that way."

"Men usually don't tell us their deepest feelings. That's why we women must watch for the signs closely. Maybe Katarina saw that, too, when you girls did not."

I thought about Dagmar's words. Was I watching Karl's signs? The Lord always sent Karl when I needed him the most—the wayward horsewhip, the steamship rescue, the overturned sleigh, the impromptu fishing trip for Hans. Why did God send him so often if I was not supposed to be with him? He was a good man, but how was I supposed to respond to him when Herman needed me for Hans and his spirit, too?

Lord, lead me to do what is right for all concerned. Please.

I was sweeping the front porch when Karl rode out to the farm a couple of weeks after the funeral. Herman offered no greeting but rather harrumphed and headed back to the barn. Karl followed him.

"Herman, can we talk?" Karl asked Herman's retreating back.

"I doubt we have anything to talk about, Karl."

"It's about Hannah." Karl's solid but soft comment stopped Herman where he stood.

"My daughter is dead and buried, Karl." I stopped sweeping and watched as Herman squarely met Karl's gaze as he said those words.

"Yes, Herman. Would you like to go inside while I explain why I came out?"

Reluctantly, Herman turned toward the house and grumbled as Karl dismounted his horse. Looking directly at me, he said to Karl, "This better be worth my time away from things that need tending out here. I don't have time for any foolishness." Side by side, they walked to the kitchen door. Herman stepped in, stared at Karl a moment, and then held the door for him. I followed behind them, leaving my sweeping for later.

Although the windows were open, the curtains barely fluttered as we strode into the kitchen. The oppressive summer humidity still hung in the air but had cooled marginally since Hannah's death, making breathing palatable for everyone. The two men sat at the kitchen table and silently faced one another.

"You want a cool drink? I have some lemonade the Zimmers brought over if you'd like," I asked as I opened the ice box to retrieve the cool jug.

Getting no response, I set two cool glasses on the table before the men, who appeared to be having a staring contest.

"You want me to leave so you two can talk privately?" I asked, untying my apron and preparing to leave the room.

"No." Karl was the first to speak. "I think you might want to hear this, too."

"Hear what?" Herman said. "Get to the point. I have work to do."

"As I said, this is about Hannah." He stopped to judge our reaction before proceeding.

"You said that already. Get on with it."

"I told you the other day the lawyers I work with are right across the street from Doc Russel, who saw Hannah."

Herman rolled his eyes. "You came all this way to say that?"

"No, of course not." He paused and wiped a smudge of grit across his face. "I understand he gave Hannah arsenic for her asthma. I think he killed her."

Wearily, Herman placed his head in his hands. "Don't you think I have thought of that? I didn't think giving her that *concoction* was a good idea when he told us what it was, but I consented." He abruptly stood, knocking his chair over backward. "I let him give it to her!" He paced around the room with nowhere to turn. "I could have stopped him. I could have said, no, but I didn't. It is all my fault. *I* killed her," he whispered and sat down again in the chair he pulled from the floor.

"No, Herman. It wasn't your fault," Karl said, putting a hand on Herman's arm. "It was the doctor's fault. He is the one who is supposed to have knowledge in cases like this. You aren't a doctor."

Herman slapped Karl's hand away. "No. I was her father. I was supposed to protect her, and I let her die!"

I wanted to reach out and comfort Herman but was afraid he would resist my embrace, too. I rounded his end of the table and stroked his back instead. "You were a good father to her, Herman. She knew you loved her."

"*Ja*, like I loved her mother?" Herman glared up at me. "And now they are both gone."

"Herman, do you want the doctor to pay for what he did?" Karl interjected.

"Pay? How do you pay for a sweet, innocent life? No one can bring Hannah back! How can you come here and even suggest that someone can pay for Hannah's life?"

"I am not suggesting anyone can bring her back. I understand how precious she was. I loved that pipsqueak with all my heart, too, and I can't imagine how hard these days are for you as her father."

"Get out!" Herman yelled.

"Herman, let me explain. If the doctor is a danger to his patients, we have a duty to keep him from hurting anyone else. We can make sure he does not practice medicine again."

Herman regained his composure. "Karl, there is no proof. His assistant brought in the medicine. She may have mixed the formula wrong. We may have given her too much—or not enough. That may not have been what even killed her. We just don't know. I have gone over and over this in my mind."

Herman sighed and glared at Karl. "How can you destroy a man's career if he may have been doing everything right, and God just called Hannah home? This is all in God's hands, anyway. Everything. I must lay everything at His feet, and He will judge us all. Doc Russell. Me. Even you, Karl. You cannot fix this any more than I can."

Karl backed his chair away from the table. "I'm sorry. I thought this might be a way I could help. I realize now I was wrong." He looked from Herman to me and back again. "I only wanted to help. I didn't want to cause you any more pain. Honest."

"I'll walk you out," I whispered as Karl opened the door. "You may have wanted to help, but the Bible says not to sue those who hurt you and instead to turn the other cheek. I did not expect Herman to take so much of the blame for what happened to Hannah, but the principle still applies. All is in God's hands."

"Lena, sometimes God uses us as His instruments, and we must measure His justice, but I won't push the issue any further. The wound is too deep, and I don't want to hurt either of you anymore."

Karl peered down into my face. I felt the heat rise in my cheeks—heat that had nothing to do with the noonday sun.

"You'd better go, but I am glad you came."

Karl took my hand before mounting his horse. "I want to take you to a debate in Alton in a couple of months. A whole day with me in Alton. Could Dagmar watch Hans if Herman is busy with the farm?"

"A debate? What sort of debate? Why would I want to go to a debate? I don't know about such things." I stumbled through my questions. A whole day with Karl? Why was he always stirring my heart with hope when I should stay far away from him? What if Herman saw him take my hand?

"My firm helps relocate former slaves who left slave states," he explained in a slow cadence. "A man is running for the senate who may be a champion for our cause. He and his opponent will debate in Alton, and I want you to come listen to it with me. You remember me mentioning this at the picnic? So much has happened since that time, you may have forgotten. But if you are to live in America, you might as well understand what is going on here."

"I don't think Herman will like me becoming political. That is not a woman's place."

"Why does listening make you political? Knowing this country better makes you more aware." Karl glanced back at the house. "It wouldn't hurt Herman to be more aware, too." He backed away a half-step and dropped my hand. "Did he read the book *Uncle Tom's Cabin* that I gave him last winter?"

"I think he did, but he did not talk to me about it. I'll ask about going with you but not for a while yet. I need to give Herman more time to recover before I trouble him with this idea."

As I turned to leave, he called after me, "I think you might like to listen to this Mr. Lincoln, too. He has quite a sense of humor."

"What do I know about debates, politics, or Mr. Lincoln?" I asked more to myself than to Karl as I entered the back door. Though a day with Karl might be the salve I needed to help me overcome my grief.

Lord, help me stay on the path You set out for me. I am not sure I can find my way through the temptations of life without Your guidance.

CHAPTER 19

A Month of Sundays

"And after he had dismissed the crowds, he went up on the mountain
by himself to pray. When evening came, he was there alone."

Matthew 14:23

Karl did not return to the farm for the rest of the summer. The heat and humidity taxed us all. The wash never dried, and I forever chased away the smell of mildew. I enticed breezes through the open windows daily and tried to fight off mosquitoes every evening. The infant trees Katarina and Herman planted when they first arrived remained babes and did not provide the promised shade for the house.

I craved cooler weather, where I could embrace snowy days with a warm fire and hot drinks. There was no relief from the midsummer heat. It was unbearable. Back in Germany, the nearby mountain peaks would break up the heat from the sun and provide cooler climates. Not in Illinois. The rolling hills did not give way to snowcapped mountain peaks. Sometimes, I missed my homeland and family so much that it hurt, especially now that Hannah was gone.

Months languished between letters from *Mutti* and *Vater*, but when they arrived, it soothed me to read that all was well with the family in our homeland. Momma wrote that Heidi started working with Frau Bernhardt as an apprentice dressmaker. Martin would start university in Leipzig soon. Thomas and Eva still drew pleasure from hunting and cooking for the family, whereas the youngest, Maria, continued to provide the family pleasure with her singing.

I longed to be in the middle of all that family activity. Herman and I often sidestepped each other with nary a word. Hannah's death had left a hole in my heart that only more family might fill.

Herman buried himself in farm work from dawn to dusk—and many times beyond. He ate his meals with hardly a grunt, fell into bed exhausted every night, and provided no company—generally ignoring Hans and me as he wallowed in his grief.

Sunday was the only day he socialized and rested from his farm labors. We attended worship services dutifully. He stored up his conversations for men with farming concerns and crop prices but never shared his heart or allowed me to share mine.

I wept that Sundays appeared only once every seven days. Herman was never much of a talker, and the issues he did share with me did nothing to comfort or nourish my soul. Knowing how tall the corn grew, if the fertilizer he was using helped enough, or if he needed to cultivate a field differently held no interest to me.

Nor did Herman take any interest in my domestic matters. So what if I had to substitute wheat flour for potato flour in my favorite dinner dish because it was not in stock at Tryon's market? Who cared if I found a better way to clean the mud out of Hans' trousers, thanks to Dagmar? Everything I did was silly woman's work. Herman had no complaints as long as I graced the table with meals, cleaned and mended the clothes, and did the housework.

Sundays meant belonging to a community beyond the farm. Dagmar still came around now and then, but as the weeks melted into months beyond Hannah's death, she showed up on fewer occasions. But when she did, her presence graced us like a fresh breeze because she never came empty-handed. She either conveniently had too much of something she had baked for Josef, or she had crafted Hans something with excess fabric she spared from another sewing project. As a result, Hans received several new Dagmar shirts, which we welcomed for a growing boy who was excited about getting old enough to start school someday.

The church community also embraced young Hans. He rattled on and on about the lessons he learned at church. He loved the Old Testament stories of Noah's ark and Moses in a basket. Once, he heard about the fiery chariot of Elijah, and I had to keep him from trying to set the wheelbarrow on fire to see if it would fly to heaven.

Keeping up with Hans exhausted me. He needed watching every waking hour as he filled the absence of his little sister. I tried to be available to him as much as possible. He was my little helper when I weeded the garden. He handed me clothes to wash or hang on the line. He helped me make beds and clean the house as much as any four-year-old. I needed to redo almost everything he did, but I loved having my little helper around, even if it created more work for me.

On Sunday, fellow believers greeted us with smiles and handshakes. We adopted our regular pew and sang the familiar hymns of our homeland. The liturgy, the prayers, and the creeds washed over me like a soothing balm, making me feel at home.

After the service one Sunday, the congregation gathered in groups to share the neighborly news.

"Did you hear the Zimmer boy is getting married?"

"Yes, a new family moved in last spring, and I guess he's been courting her since she arrived."

"I'm glad he found someone," I offered, thanking God because I sure didn't want to marry him myself.

"I think he had eyes for you, Lena, when you first came," Frau Schmidt said.

Others chimed in agreement. I blushed a bit and tried to change the subject—then I saw Karl standing near the church entrance. He had not been to church since he had come by the farm after Hannah's death. I had almost given up hope of ever seeing him again. After all, how many times can you tell someone to go away and expect them to keep coming back?

The ladies followed my gaze and read more into my blush than I intended.

"I think you have eyes for somebody else, though. Is that right, Lena?" one lady said. The gathered women giggled.

I turned away. "I am not looking for a beau, ladies. I have my hands full with Hans and the farm."

I walked away from the muffled giggles behind me as I looked for my rambunctious nephew. I found Hans chasing several older school-age boys. Hans was growing tall like his father and matched the height of some of the older boys. With his curiosity and love for books, he would do well in school when the time came. He was well-liked, and the older boys included him in their games of kickball and tag when he was around. I left him for a moment longer before I called him away from his weekly fun.

"He has grown this summer," Karl whispered in my ear.

Shivers ran courses through me as if the cold North touched my temples and traveled to my toes. My involuntary reaction startled me, and Karl chuckled as he reached for my hand.

"Well, well, well, look who turned up. Haven't seen you in a month of Sundays." I pulled myself together, faced him, and pretended he had no hold on me. I knew we must have an audience of churchgoers, too.

"I've been busy and thought you and Herman might need some time to heal without me being around. How have you been?"

"Fine." My comment betrayed me. I lacked conviction, and he cocked his head, waiting for more. "Actually, I've been lonely. Herman works every waking hour, and I am left to chase after Hans, who misses his sister so much."

Why did that pour out of my mouth? Must I blurt out my most private thoughts the minute someone comes along to listen?

He reached over to hug me, but the church ladies kept close tabs on my whereabouts, so I stepped back.

"Did you clear it with Herman to come to Alton with me? The debate is just two weeks away, on the fifteenth."

I did not have an answer—not that I had forgotten. Every moment I had spent with Karl was etched into my soul. How could I forget the invitation?

"I . . . haven't seen you in so long, I wasn't sure it was still a plan."

"Lena, I would put you in every plan I ever make if you let me. We have only one day to attend a debate between two important men. Democracy is key in this country. I want you to understand it better. Please talk to Herman. By the way, are you going to help the church ladies with the Octoberfest and sausage-making next weekend?"

I nodded. My social life was so limited that any activity at church was a welcome distraction from the farm.

"Good. That gives you a week to talk to Herman. I'll stop by the Octoberfest for your answer . . . or I may just kidnap you." He leaned closer, seeming to be only half-joking.

"I don't think kidnapping will be in order, Herr Muller. I will talk to Herman by then. I promise."

"For now, you'd better round up Hans and Herman and head home before your lady friends have more to gossip about," Karl said, tipping his cap and striding away without another word.

Once loaded onto the wagon, I swallowed and began my plea. "Herman, I have something I need to talk to you about."

"*Ja*. What?"

"There is an event in Alton on October 15 that I've been invited to attend. I wonder if you could keep an eye on Hans so I can go?" I crossed my fingers, carefully keeping Karl's name out of it.

"What event?" It was not going to be that easy, and mentioning Karl might send him into a rage. He did like Karl as a person. After all, Herman and Karl had bonded well over Herman's winter accident, but Karl courting me was another situation altogether. I needed to back into this discussion with caution.

"It's a debate. I'll be gone only that Friday. I can fix your meals ahead of time. I'm sure Dagmar would help in a pinch, too."

"Debate? I know who's behind this. Karl." He stared down at me on the seat across from a dozing Hans. I would not lie to him.

"Yes. He will keep me safe, as he did for Hans when we took Hannah to the doctor. You can count on him."

"Count on him? He wants to steal you away from your place at the farm. That is what I can count on. What business do you have going to a political debate? We aren't even American citizens."

"We can become citizens, Herman. Karl says since we plan to make America our home, we should become citizens here."

"He is filling your head, Lena. You can't vote—even if you become a citizen."

"But that doesn't mean I shouldn't be interested in this country. Maybe if I learned more about this country, I wouldn't be so homesick for Germany."

"You just want to learn more about Karl Muller."

"You can't expect me to raise Hans for you forever, Herman. Once he is big enough for school and to take care of himself, you won't need me so much anymore. Maybe then, I will marry and start my own family."

"I didn't think you were so anxious to leave us." Herman sadly bowed his head as the horses followed their own familiar trail home.

"Herman, I'm not talking about running away with Karl. It is only one day. He is excited about this Mr. Lincoln coming to make a speech. That is all. Only one day . . . So, I can see what all the fuss is about."

"I know I haven't been much company, but I don't *want* you to go. There has been too much loss in this family to see you leave. Hans cannot bear another blow like that." He glanced down at the sleeping child. "He has grown very close to you."

"And I him. You aren't getting rid of me that easily. Thank you for letting me go."

"I don't remember saying yes." He wrinkled his brow with a smirky smile. "I guess we can manage one day alone."

"O, *danke, danke.*" I leaned over Hans and placed a quick kiss on Herman's cheek. "You are the best older brother in the world."

"You just be sure to stay in public places with him, since I'm not sending you with a chaperone." He tried to sound gruff again.

"Don't worry. I promise it will all be as proper as church."

Herman whispered, "Don't think we don't need you anymore now that Hannah is gone. If anything, we may need you all the more."

⚜

The true miracle brought about by relentless prayer begged to be told, and each day dragged by like a slug in molasses as I waited to tell Karl about Herman's approval. Karl would be thrilled. It did not matter that I had no interest in politics or long speeches. I was going to have one uninterrupted day with Karl in Alton. The church ladies would not likely be attending such a male-oriented event, which relieved any worry about wagging tongues. I hummed my way through cooking, cleaning, and gardening. No storms could dampen my spirits.

My renewed enthusiasm to attend the sausage-making for the Octoberfest celebration did not translate to Hans and Herman, however. Herman labored twice as long as usual on his morning chores, and Hans took forever dressing and eating breakfast. If he stirred his oatmeal one more time without taking a bite, I planned to feed it to him myself. Why was everyone such slugs when I could have been out the door and gone within twenty minutes of waking? The sun was well above the horizon when we finally mounted the wagon and left the farm for the church event.

When we arrived, the men were already grinding the pork and beef for the sausages. Families from the congregation had donated hogs and cattle. Frau Greta Stolz supervised her husband as the meat crew worked in unison. As an experienced butcher's wife and keeper of the secret sausage recipe, she kept the precise process rolling through its paces. Karl stood amid the hive of activity, offering his strength to the grinding process. I watched his muscles strain beneath his cotton shirt with each turn of the crank.

He caught me staring as he wiped away his perspiration with his forearm. His devilish grin set fire to my crimson cheeks. I stepped away, almost upsetting Dagmar, who passed behind me with a tray of sausage spices. She bore assorted bowls of pungent scents to add to the newly ground meats.

"Lena!" Dagmar caught herself before tumbling into a nearby bench. "You'd better pay more attention to your surroundings than your man."

"My man? Don't know what you are talking about."

Dagmar winked an exclamation point to her knowledge, and my blush deepened. Flustered, I did not know where to turn. Everyone blended themselves into the beehive of activity seamlessly. How did I join this dance?

"You keep telling yourself that, Lena. I don't believe it," Dagmar said, clicking her tongue. "Now, why don't you take these spices over to that table, and I'll go for some more for the next batch?"

She handed me the tray of spices and turned back the way she had come. With hands full and a new directive, I stepped into the sausage-making machine of the congregation. The well-organized, momentous operation continued grinding lean beef and pork.

The Zimmer family oversaw the weighing of bags of salt and pepper. Dagmar oversaw the special secret seasonings that Frau Stolz had entrusted to her. The mixture made its way by several carriers to three sausage-stuffing stations, manned by six-to-eight stuffers. Once stuffed into casings, the sausage links were hung on racks and wheeled to the cool root cellar until the men operating the smoking operation were ready for that batch.

Women scurried with pans, spices, and "beef middle" casings for the soft *Braunschweiger* and different casings for the batches of firmer summer sausage. Even children helped fetch items and keep surfaces clean. All generations worked together. I marveled over the camaraderie of families and friends, and tears threatened my eyes. The last time I had enjoyed such a collaboration was when I was home with Mamma, Papa, and my younger siblings. This was my family now, though, and I rejoined the rhythm of activity, immersing myself in the flurry.

The hours flew by in happy chatter as women, men, and children worked in an organized bustle of activity, resulting in many pounds of sausages for the church community to share, sell, and enjoy. In a moment of rest, I dropped myself on a waiting bench to observe the day's bounty.

Lord, this is Your handiwork. Thank You for Your bounty, I prayed.

"May I join you?" Karl stood above me, waiting for my answer.

"Of course. I'm enjoying the view of a bountiful harvest."

"That it is."

Karl sat beside me, keeping a respectful space between us. I clasped my hands in my lap so I wouldn't wipe the spare strand of hair from his forehead.

"Good news. Herman gave his blessing for me to accompany you to the debate next Friday."

Karl tilted his head. "I must say, I am a bit surprised, though I'm very glad he did. You must be quite a debater yourself."

"Herman is not so bad. He can manage Hans and the farm without me for a day."

I did not want to tell Karl that Herman was starting to realize he could not keep me in servitude forever. It would sound like I expected Karl to marry me or something.

"Where did you go?"

"What?"

"You seem to be daydreaming."

"Oh, sorry. Just looking forward to next Friday, I guess," I lied.

"I'll be there by about daybreak to pick you up. Now, I must return to Alton. There are all sorts of preparations to make for the debate. The railroads are even discounting fares from places like Springfield to entice crowds to come to it. Our law firm is helping set up the Lincoln headquarters at the Franklin Hotel."

Karl's excitement was contagious. He bolted upright, taking my hands and pulling me up with him. After a quick hug, he whispered, "But I'm sure *you* will be the best part of the day."

Before I could react, he was gone, leaving me alone to steady my heart.

CHAPTER 20

A House Divided

"And if a house is divided against itself, that house will not be able to stand."

Mark 3:25

I expected Karl early in the morning, so my fitful sleep kept me listening for his arrival all night to take me to Alton. Before the sun rose, I gave up sleeping and edited my to-do list for Herman and Hans.

> Breakfast: hardboiled eggs (cooked and waiting in icebox), bread, and milk. Choice of jam.
> Lunch: Ham sandwiches in the ice box.
> Dinner: Dagmar to bring over provisions. Dine with Josef.
> Don't let Hans chase the chickens.
> I will be back tonight.
>
> Love,
> Lena

As dawn peeked over the still dark meadow, I heard the sound of hoofbeats before I saw Karl in a small hack he must have rented in Bethel. His silhouette was difficult to distinguish in the shadowy morning glow, but his punctuality betrayed him. He also adjusted his cap to the familiar jaunty angle, which left no question about his identity. I hurried downstairs to greet him before the family awoke.

I wrapped a shawl around me as I quietly closed the front door, not wanting to wake Hans or Herman, although Herman was likely watching us from the confines of his bedroom window. He never slept late, and he would want to be certain Karl kept a respectable distance from his little sister.

Karl tipped his hat and offered his hand as I descended the kitchen steps. I accepted it as if I were a grand lady and he a gentleman caller. Giddy, I sat beside him with an unabashed grin. I felt as if I were playing hooky or getting away with eating the last cookie in the cookie jar. As much as I tried to shake it, the feeling would not dislodge, and I sat there looking like a fool.

"You sure are happy enough. You must have gotten more sleep than I did," Karl said.

"I doubt it." Then I realized how far Karl had to travel to retrieve me. "To be here so early, where did you sleep last night?"

"I stayed with some friends in Bethel last night. They overheard me talking to you about the debate and offered me a bed. I borrowed their conveyance, too. I didn't want to keep you waiting."

We enjoyed a quiet side-by-side ride into town. In Bethel, Karl left the hack at the station as we boarded the train to Alton, which was crowded with passengers from Springfield, Chicago, Peoria, and who-knows-where. Reporters, businessmen, farmers, and the curious left no extra seats available.

Karl swung his arm around me, pulling me close in the aisle as we searched for a place to sit, and said, "Stay close to me. I don't want to lose you in this crowd."

I nodded. I had no intention of losing him, and the warmth of his arm anchored me to his side. In the last car, a young man in a dark, striped suit noticed our predicament and tipped his hat to me.

"Miss? You can sit here if you'd like," he said, rising to offer me the only remaining seat.

I looked back at Karl, who nodded for me to accept.

"Thank you, sir. My fiancée would much rather sit on this swaying rail than be tossed about. I'll stay close and be sure she is okay."

Fiancée? I looked at Karl, and he only shrugged back at me. The young man shifted to let me sit by the window, then stepped aside for Karl to take his vacated seat so we could sit together. Karl may be taking this couple issue a bit too far. Lying to passengers to get a seat on the train? Herman would never approve. On the other hand, Herman would appreciate Karl's attentiveness to my wellbeing.

When the train stopped, the people flooded through the streets of Alton like a swarm of locusts. They swirled around Christian Hill near the river, waiting for the main debate to commence. A steady stream of men courted time from Judge Stephen Douglas at the Alton Hotel, and a different contingency courted Abraham Lincoln at the Franklin Hotel, where the campaigners set up temporary offices.

The two famed men, rumored to have eaten breakfast together, arrived on the same Mississippi steamship and continued their civility toward one another on shore—a civil gesture, I thought, before their seventh debate against each other. I suppose they respected each other after all their political encounters. No reason for them to be enemies.

The thousands of people who arrived by steamship, train, or carriage positioned themselves close enough to the raised platform to listen to the two men. Their differences were startling. Douglas, short and squatty, boasted a rotund middle that jutted forward when he walked. A gold watch chain dangled from his fine three-piece suit, and his shoes were spit polished and shined.

Lincoln, tall and lanky, outpaced Douglas two-to-one with his long legs. His cloth suit hung on his narrow shoulders, and his trousers missed the tops of his boots by an inch. His long arms dangled against his sides when they were not gesturing with purpose, whereas Douglas swung his arms widely as he gestured to emphasize important points.

Lincoln stroked his chin contemplatively, and his eyes wrinkled with humor when he refuted a Douglas claim. Douglas' voice was compact, deep, and booming as the bass drum figure might suggest. Lincoln's high-pitched voice projected over the heads of his listeners well into the crowd. The two men could not be more opposite in stature or demeanor.

The crowd swelled to nearly five thousand, all trying to view these prominent politicians during the final debate of their cross-state docket. Karl had told me their ideological stances were well-established and documented in every newspaper and journal in Illinois and beyond. Douglas relied on Lincoln's previous speeches as his catalyst to begin his own address.

I tried to comprehend his rhetoric as Senator Douglas began the debate.[12] "Lincoln's idea of 'a house divided against itself must fall' is slander upon the immortal framers of the constitution."

"Is he talking about the same thing as the Bible says?" I asked Karl, trying not to disrupt the speech.

"Yes. Lincoln has been using this premise to say we cannot have free states and slave states as part of a *United* States."

"Each state has the right to prohibit, abolish, or sustain slavery just as it pleases," Douglas continued.

"That means those in slave states would never have a chance to become free." Karl clenched his fists and jaw in response as he listened.

"The *union* was established on the right of each state to do as it pleased on the question of slavery and every other question."

"Really?" Karl muttered and shook his head in disgust.

"I hold that there is no power on earth, under our system of government, which has the right to force a constitution upon an unwilling people."

"Do you think slavery is something people willingly commit to?" Karl growled under his breath.

I was beginning to wonder if listening to this man was a good idea for Karl. Every word Douglas spoke agitated him more.

"Under the decision of the Supreme Court, Chief Justice Taney, slaves are property like all other property, and they can be carried into any territory of the United States the same as any other description of property, yet when you get them there, they are subject to local law."

---

12   The full and complete debate between President Abraham Lincoln and Stephen Douglas can be found on the National Park Service website at https://www.nps.gov/liho/learn/historyculture/debate7.htm.

Karl leaned over to explain the complexities of Douglas' words. "That is when our law firm steps in. Illinois is a free state, so we help free escapees when they come here. Douglas is saying the law is not fair, and it stops slave owners from taking their *property* wherever they want to take them."

I nodded, remembering the few black people I had seen since arriving in America, including the Jacksons. Even the free ones were wary of retaliation from whites.

"The Declaration of Independence is speaking of white men. I hold that this government was established on the white basis; established by white men for the benefit of white men," Douglas continued.

Karl shook his head. "The arrogance! In Illinois, we adopted the policy that a black person in this state shall not be a slave and shall not be a citizen."

"Really, Karl? They can't be citizens even when they are free? Herman and I weren't even born here, but we could become citizens in time. Where's the fairness?"

Karl gave me a blank stare, like this information was not new to him, but there was nothing he could do about it.

"Each state needs to mind its own business . . . northern men formed a scheme to excite the North against the South, . . . thinking that the North, being stronger, would outvote the South," Douglas said, wrapping up his speech.

"Good," Karl volunteered. "His hour is up. I've heard good things about this Lincoln. I've read the reports from his previous debates too. I'm anxious for him to speak."

Lincoln stepped up to shouts of "Go get 'em, Long Legs!"

The Douglas supporters laughed, but as Lincoln began his speech, he glanced at Douglas.

"I never declared that a black person should be a citizen or complained especially of the Dred Scott decision because it declared he could not be one," Lincoln began.

"What? I thought he'd want them to be citizens. I guess I'd better read his statements more carefully," Karl lamented.

Karl strained to crowd a little closer to dissect every detail of Lincoln's speech.

"What is a Dread Scott decision?" I ventured.

"A decision the Supreme Court made against the black people a few years ago . . . Shhh. I need to hear."

So, I waited for a better time to ask questions.

"I only mention these things as evidence, tending to prove a combination of conspiracy to make the institution of slavery natural," Lincoln continued.

"I understand. He's appealing to both sides," Karl said, relaxing a bit.

"The founding fathers meant to set up a standard maxim for a free society, deepening its influence and augmenting the happiness and value of life to all people, of all colors, everywhere."

"Here! Here!" Karl shouted, rebuilding his excitement for Lincoln.

"I reassert there never has been a man, as far as I know or believed, in the whole world, who had said the Declaration of Independence did not include black people in the term 'all men.'"

"That's right!" Karl muttered.

"Mr. Clay says, 'I desire no concealment of the opinion in regard to the institution of slavery. I look upon it as a great evil and deeply lament that we have derived it from the parental Government and from our ancestors.'"

Karl leaned over to explain. "You see, the other side used quotes from Henry Clay to support slavery. Lincoln is now turning this against them."

"I'm not sure I know enough English to follow everything he's saying, but the crowd seems to like him."

Another wave erupted in "Hurrah for Lincoln!"

"As for the House Divided . . . either the opponents of slavery will arrest the further spread of it and place it where the public mood shall rest in the belief that it is in the course of ultimate extinction, or its advocates will push it forward till it shall become alike lawful in all States—old as well as new, North as well as South."

"We can't let that happen," Karl spoke softly to himself.

"Three-fifths can be applied to no other class among us than the black people."

"Three-fifths? What does he mean? How can a person count as only three-fifths?" I wondered aloud.

I might not have understood what Lincoln was saying. My English skills did not venture far from their beginning infant stage, generally surrounded by German-speaking people. Karl shushed my question away and said he would explain later.

Lincoln continued. "The purpose was that in the constitution, after the institution of slavery had passed among us, there should be nothing in the face of the great chamber of liberty suggesting that such a thing as slavery had ever existed among us."

Enthusiastic applause erupted, and Karl said, "That is what I came for!"

"Here, men can settle upon new soil and better their condition in life as an outlet for free white people everywhere the world over—in which Hans, Baptiste, and Patrick may find new homes and better their conditions in life."

"That's like us!" I exclaimed.

Excited, I understood Lincoln's meaning clearly and joined the crowd's reaction. The multitude roared while Karl squeezed my hand.

"If there be a man amongst us who does not think that the institution of slavery is wrong in any one of the aspects of which I have spoken, he is misplaced and ought not to be with us. What has ever threatened our liberty and prosperity save and except the institution of slavery?"

"He makes a strong case," Karl said, pulling me closer. "This is why I thought bringing you with me was important; I wanted you to understand the important work I do against the institution of slavery."

"He contends that whatever community wants slaves has the right to have them. So, they have if it is not wrong. But if it is a wrong, he cannot say people have a right to do a wrong That is the real issue— the struggle between right and wrong!"

Lincoln's time lapsed. Why it seemed shorter even though it was longer than Douglas' was a mystery to me. Douglas refuted Lincoln's claims in a rebuttal but said nothing new from his previous speech. Lincoln's words about what was right and wrong rang in my ears as Karl led me back through the crowds toward his law offices.

I was happy we were moving again. My feet had cramped from standing in one place for so long. Karl gently guided me through the crowd until we reached his workplace, a modest office facing the Franklin Hotel, the temporary debate headquarters for Lincoln.

Karl chattered on like a schoolgirl as we traveled home in the small buggy he had hired for our trip home. Rather than take the Alton-Terre Haute train full of debate travelers, he secured transportation from an attorney friend to avoid the masses. He was excited that a like-minded man was running for such a high office.

"Just think, Lena, if we elect him to Congress, all the influence he can have on the nation. This could be the turn of events this country needs."

Much of what he said I didn't understand. I still did not understand the finer points of the Dred Scott decision Karl and his colleagues debated in their office after the speeches. A spread of sandwiches and fruit graced the tables while men imbibed in various drinks supplied by the office. Both intellect and stomachs were nourished in the aftermath of the debate. I rested in the comfort that Karl kept me close, and he openly held my hand in front of his Alton friends, warming me against the October chill that enlivened the air. It bred a familiarity we did not share in public anywhere else.

Multitudes of people filled the streets and offices throughout the town, although the world held only us. I wanted to kiss Karl, and I wondered what a life with him could be like as I watched him expound on his political theories that meant nothing to me other than that it made him happy.

The sun set in rapid degrees as we approached the farm, the descending glow wrapping the remaining fall leaves in a mysterious aura, dropping each wistful autumn fairy gently to the ground. The windows became reflective beacons for our arrival. What a perfect exclamation point to the wonders of the day.

Wrapped in the enchantment of the evening, Karl drew me close on the buggy. He cupped his hand behind my head and pressed his rugged lips against mine. I pulled slowly away and rested my head on his shoulder, savoring his smell and strength. He kept his arms around me as if I belonged to him.

"This can't be the last time we do this, Lena."

Do this? Do what? Go to Alton? Enjoy a sweet kiss? It was true I wanted more, but more what?

"Herman was kind enough to let me go for a day, but I don't think I can make this a habit," I solemnly said.

I decided Alton was a safer topic than the kiss.

Karl grinned down at me in his devilish way. "You are my world, Lena. I can't let you go, no matter what your brother says. You are never far from my thoughts, and I want to share so much more of my world with you."

"I can't leave. Hans needs me now more than ever now that Hannah is gone. I don't know what Herman would have done if someone didn't keep things going around here as he worked through more grief."

"You are not his wife, Lena. He cannot expect you to give up your entire life for him—or Hans."

Karl's earnestness fluttered my heart. I wanted him to win this debate, but I had to keep my head. My family needed me. I looked away. This conversation was similar to the one I'd had with Herman. I agreed with Karl, but I did not have a way to leave Herman when he still needed me so desperately.

"I'd better go," I said. I leaned away from him and his warmth. I straightened my skirt and tried to compose myself for Herman's scrutiny inside.

"When will I see you again?"

"Will you be at church?" I hoped my voice had returned to a steady tremor again.

"I can be anywhere if you are there." He pulled me in for another kiss. "Can you promise me another of these?"

"No promises." I blushed and turned to dismount the carriage, but Karl was quick to jump down ahead of me for assistance. Back on the ground, I looked up at him again.

"But who can resist such a gallant suitor?" I asked before giving him a peck on the cheek before I hurried into the house while I still had the resolve.

CHAPTER 21

What Dreams May Come

"Like a dream when one awakes, O Lord, when you rouse yourself,
you despise them as phantoms."

Psalm 73:20

The house was dark. The earlier sunset reflection was an illusion. No lamps or fires stemmed the chilling autumn night. The house was still. Even if Hans had gone to bed, Herman should be up reading or pacing while waiting for my return.

"Herman?"

I called, at first tentatively, in case Hans was sleeping, then more urgently as I checked the rooms of the house. No one was home. I ran to the front door and yelled for Karl, but he was already out of the yard and headed toward Alton. I was not sure if my shouting reached him.

"Karl! Karl! Stop!"

Finally, I saw his head lift and the horse turn toward me as he gained speed in my direction.

He reined the horse to a halt. "What's wrong?" He was off the buggy and by my side instantly.

"I don't know. No one is here. Maybe Hans got sick. Where do I go to find out where they are?" Panic rose as all the horrible reasons why my family was not home mounted in me.

"Don't panic. Let's think. Didn't you say Herman might ask Dagmar to help out today?"

"Yes. She was to bring over dinner, and the two families were to eat together."

My mind raced to other disastrous thoughts instead of more probable ones without peril. I should be checking with the doctor or someone. Karl jogged over to peek in the barn.

"Herman's horse is gone. Maybe they went to the Bruns' because Dagmar probably invited them for dinner over there or something, and they lost track of time. They will likely be home any minute."

"You don't know that. They might not be coming home at all."

Where had my alarmist thinking come from? *Lord, tell me what to do. All things are in Your hands,* I desperately prayed.

Karl took my hand to calm me. "I'll tell you what. Let me take you to the neighbors', and we can find out. If they are not there, Dagmar might be able to tell us where they went. Did you look for a note or anything Herman may have left for you?"

"A note? No. I only saw that all the rooms were empty, and no one answered when I called."

"Why don't you double-check for a note or other sign that might help us? If you don't find anything, I'll take you over to the Bruns'."

"How do you stay so calm? Would you come inside and help me?"

Karl put his arm around my shoulders and led me back into the house.

"Sure. Anything for you. I'm sure things are just fine."

"The kitchen table would likely be the place for Herman to leave a note."

But the kitchen was the way I had left it that morning, including the note I had left the family. No more notes or other clues surfaced after a quick investigation of the house. So, I got in Karl's buggy next to him, and we headed to the next farm over the hill.

The flurry of activity around the Bruns' farm was unusual for so late in the evening. The wagons and horses filling their yard gave the impression of a party; but no laughter filled the air, and soon, muffled crying and murmurs floated to us on the autumn breeze.

I grabbed Karl's hand. "Something's wrong," I whispered. "Hurry."

"Don't jump to conclusions, Lena. We'll find out what's going on in a minute."

His reassuring words rang hollow because he sensed I was right. I wanted to run in and scream at the gathered crowd, "Where's my family?" Instead, Karl slowed my pace by firmly taking my arm and walking with me more respectably as we reached the front door.

Herr Zimmer opened the door before we knocked. "So, you heard, too?" he asked as we entered.

"No. Heard what?" Karl asked.

"What's happened?" I blurted.

I pushed past him and was relieved to find Herman and Hans sitting in the parlor unharmed. I rushed to Hans and gave him a giant hug. Then, I saw the tears in Herman's eyes.

"What happened?" I asked again.

"Josef was killed trying to disc the field. Something must have spooked the horse, and somehow the plow blade got him." Herman paused. "The doctor worked on him most of the afternoon, but he had lost too much blood before Dagmar found him." Herman buried his head in his hands and fought back more tears.

Josef was Herman's best friend. They often worked side by side on each other's farms, lending a hand when one of them needed more manpower. How could God deal Herman yet another fatal blow like this? A wife. A child. Now, a good friend. Surely the man could not take much more.

Hans was sleepily fading into the divan next to his father. "Tell me, was Hans there?" I quietly asked Herman over the boy's head.

"I planned on clearing the south field today and thought Hans might be in the way, so I asked Dagmar to watch him. While he ate one of the sandwiches you left, Dagmar took some food out to Josef. That's when she found him hurt and bleeding. She fetched me while Hans was still in the house. I got Josef out of the field while Dagmar ran for the doctor, but we were too late to save him." His head was in his hands again.

I found the women in the kitchen with Dagmar, preparing Josef's body for burial. I was told the minister had arrived shortly before us, led the women in prayer, and tried to comfort the grieving widow. One glance at Dagmar's ashen face, and I knew she had not heard a single prayerful word he had muttered. I wrapped my arms around her and led her to an empty chair.

"You need to sit down before you fall down," I said.

"What am I to do now? I can't run this farm by myself. Josef was my life."

She dropped her head into her hands, and her sobs erupted into convulsive shakes. I held her tightly until her body eased into gentle whimpers.

"You don't need to worry about that now. We will help you with everything. Right now, you need rest. Let's move all these people out of your house."

Dagmar raised her head, appearing to notice for the first time that her neighbors surrounded her.

"Oh, I'm a terrible host. I should offer them something for their trouble." Dagmar started to rise, but I gently kept her in her place.

"You don't need to do anything. These people are here to help you. I'll stay with you tonight. Herman can get Hans into bed, and we can sort out things in the morning."

I led Dagmar to her bedchamber. "Do you need help getting into your night things?"

"I'll manage," she muttered as she pulled a sleeping gown from her dresser.

"I'll be right outside here if you need me." I quietly shut the door and turned to the house full of guests.

"Dagmar appreciates all your concern, but she needs some sleep right now. You can help her with Josef's death, farm operations, and such tomorrow."

The men retrieved their hats and escorted the women through the front door like orderly geese.

I caught Herman's arm as he jostled his sleeping son in his arms. "I told Dagmar I'd stay the night here. I didn't think you'd mind. I don't think she should be alone right now."

Herman nodded and headed through the door with Hans. Karl stood near the door, awaiting further instructions.

"You want me to stay, too?"

"Dagmar and I will be fine. Herman is just over the ridge and will be back in the morning. So, you can head back to Alton. Sorry I kept you so late."

"That doesn't matter. You and your family mean more to me than sleep. If you need me, send for me."

The bond we had shared that day in Alton and the kiss at the house lingered in his eyes.

"I will. I promise," I whispered.

I gave Karl a quick kiss on the cheek, and he was gone. Dagmar was sprawled on her bed when I checked on her. I brushed back her tangled hair and tucked her under the covers before saying a prayer for her to get some rest.

I made myself comfortable for the night on the divan. My head swirled with all the events of the day: Karl, Lincoln, Josef.

Everything melded into a crazy, incongruent dream.

Lincoln delivered Josef's obituary, while Karl cheered for the good man. It was hard to tell if he were celebrating Lincoln or Josef. The deep hole in the cemetery opened up to receive the plain, wood coffin. The first shovel of dirt hit the coffin . . .

I awoke with a start. I waited and listened to an owl hoot for its mate before drifting under the covers again.

Karl's warmth threatened my chill away as I snuggled up to him on the carriage ride. He draped his arm around my shoulder, and he squeezed me closer. I dropped my head to his shoulder as the steady rhythm of the horse's hooves lulled my evening thoughts. The stars blinked like jewels, winking blessings to my newfound earthly joy.

Had this joy been here for the taking all along? Why was it masked behind the toils of each day? Surely, God would pull the blanket of deceit away, so the softness of peace and grace could bloom freely. Ah, what bliss to be wrapped in the one you love.

A tightening pressure circled my wrists beneath the cozy blanket. "That hurts. Let go!"

Karl's protection no longer surrounded me. His warmth vanished into the bitterness of the night by an unseen force. I tensed. A man? A spirit?

"Wait. Where are you taking me? Karl! Help me, Karl!"

But Karl disappeared into the darkness. The clouds obscured the once-starry night and veiled the once-bright moon. Karl's closeness was exchanged for Herman, who held my arms and dragged me away toward the farm. His worn farm hands became shackles around my wrists, and the loud, clanging chains rattled as he sought to imprison me.

"No! No! No!" I sobbed with less effort with each protesting word. "You can't keep me forever." But no one came to my rescue as I huddled there in the cold.

Suddenly, with a jolt, I sat straight up on Dagmar's divan. The protesting in my dream gave way to Dagmar's screaming in hers. I shook off the remnants of my own horror and rushed to Dagmar's side to wake her from her nightmare of no's.

"Dagmar." I shook her gently. "Dagmar, wake up. You're dreaming."

She came around slowly, trying to focus on this strange person in her chamber. She looked to the empty side of her bed, and the previous day's events seemed to rush back to her.

"He's gone." She exhaled the words.

"I know."

I pulled her into my arms to let her cry. The clanging shackle chains in my dream drifted back to my awake ears.

"Do you hear that?"

Dagmar shook off her dreadful night and claimed, "Oh, that's Bossy. Time for her morning milking."

The morning sun filtered through Dagmar's window as she pushed her bedclothes aside to rejoin the world. "I overslept."

She rose to dress and wiped her hand over her face to clear her thoughts. She opened drawers for fresh clothes and then she noticed the discarded dirty and bloodied garments from the previous day draped over a stool. She trembled at the sight and almost dropped the fresh chemise she had chosen from her dresser. I gathered the bloodied skirt and blouse to remove them from her sight.

"Let me take those. I can soak them for you. And I'll get some coffee going, too, while you dress. I'm sure we'll have company before too long."

Dagmar did not respond to my offers of help, but I collected the soiled remnants of her current horror and left her alone to dress in a clean frock. Thankfully, Herman arrived to milk the bellowing cow before Dagmar emerged from her room.

The following two days were blurred with funeral preparations. A coffin? A burial plot? Desires for Josef's service? Too many decisions.

Pastor Klein spoke in his most somber tones whenever he came around. At the funeral, he said words that might have been mistaken as the beginning of a wedding instead: "Dearly beloved, we are gathered here . . . "

Then his words fell, entombed by a bereaved darkness. The clouds gathered in threatening silence and leaned in to listen to the congregation gathered between the tombstones for the interment.

The pastor recited John 11:25-26: "*I am the resurrection and the life. Whoever believes in me, though he die, yet shall he live, and everyone who lives and believes in me shall never die. Do you believe this?*" But I was fixated on a nearby small grave—Hannah's.

Hannah's burial had been only three months ago, but the prairie grasses sprung upon her grave like evil, tormenting weeds. They crept upon her carefully carved headstone in hopes of obscuring it.

I'm sorry, Hannah. I have not tended your burial spot as I should.

Even though the church doors stood a mere few yards away, I never glanced at Hannah's resting place when we attended services. It was too painful. I wanted to remember a lively, little tot chasing after her big brother with squeals of delight. Instead, my mind could not grasp the lifeless child we had laid to rest with her favorite doll.

Do all the dreams here become nightmares? Hannah's grave lay next to her mother's. Where were Katarina's dreams? Her dreams of a life with Herman and her children had died with her. The last time I had seen her, she was leaving on a grand adventure of hope and love. But God did not let her live out those dreams.

And what about Herman's dreams? He buried a wife, a daughter, and now a dear friend in the land of his dreams. Did he still have the same dreams for his life in America? I had arrived only a year ago, and the names I knew in the cemetery were multiplying beyond measure. Did we belong here in America?

Lost in my dreary thoughts, I did not notice the funeral had lapsed into hugs and well-wishes for Dagmar.

"If there is anything we can do, dear . . . "

"We will look in on you to see how you are doing next week."

"We are so sorry . . . "

Sorry? Sorry another widow or widower dwelt among the congregation? Sorry? I was sorry, too.

"What are you sorry for?"

Karl's rich voice soothed and startled me at the same time. His hand touched my back, and I leaned into it. Part of my dream came back to me, and I wanted more of his warmth. I looked up, and his quizzical expression reminded me he had asked me a question.

Had I spoken my thoughts aloud?

"What's that?" I asked.

I must have imagined he read my thoughts.

"You said you were sorry—low and under your breath, for sure, but you did say it."

"Oh, I was looking at little Hannah's grave. I have not tended it as I should, and I told her I was sorry. I need to take better care . . ."

"You've had it rough since coming here," Karl said, drawing me into a hug. "Let's follow the others indoors before those clouds break loose. The wind is coming up."

The clouds lost their silent patience and moaned through the trees, whisking away the last few stubborn leaves that remained on the oaks. The breeze danced around my skirt folds, and I held them at bay as I pulled my cloak about me and headed indoors with all the others.

The congregation hovered around Dagmar as she grieved. I stood by her side to help answer for her and wave off overzealous offers of help. Dagmar had done much the same for us when Hannah died because we had no wits about us for pleasantries. I could do no less for her. Karl kept a polite distance while the townspeople tarried longer to avoid heading out into the sudden cloudburst.

After the crowd thinned, Herman offered to take Dagmar home, since we lived the closest to her.

Karl pulled me aside for a final farewell. "I've been watching you." I blushed. "I know. I bet everyone knows." I glanced around to see who remained in the room.

"You are unhappy. I want you to smile as you did when we went to Alton together."

"I *am* happy with you," I confessed to Karl. "It's just . . ." I flung my hand across the room. "I have been here only one year, and see how many I know in the church graveyard in such a short time. Who knew there would be so much sorrow here in America?"

"It is not because you are in America, Lena. There is sorrow everywhere in the world. You were fortunate, indeed, if tragedy never touched you before coming here. Had you not experienced death before this?"

"I'm not that sheltered, Karl. I have seen death before. Little ones on the *Olbers* even died on the voyage here. Is this the promised land? If it is God's will that we come here, why so much suffering?"

"No one goes through this life without suffering, Lena. Remember the Old Testament reading last Sunday? 'And he became their Savior. In all their affliction he was afflicted, and the angel of his presence saved them; in his love and in his pity he redeemed them; he lifted them up and carried them all the days of old.'[13] God feels all our afflictions, but He also came to redeem us from all our troubles."

"You do surprise me, Karl Muller. You certainly have a mind for memorization. My God is always there, but sometimes, I'm not sure I listen to His voice clearly."

---

13   Isaiah 63:8-9

I pecked his cheek and left to join Dagmar, Herman, and Hans. Dagmar had settled in close to Herman, clasping her hands tightly in her lap. She had no one to contact now. All their family was still in Germany. How could she run a farm all on her own? Would she search for a new husband?

Many men came to the New World without wives and now wished for companionship and families to help them settle here. She and Josef had presented a well-suited couple. They complemented each other in their rhythm of life. There was an ease between them, and the only thing they lacked to complete their happiness was children in their quiver.

Dagmar and Josef had married a couple of years before leaving Germany. I could tell she envied Katarina and Herman for their blossoming, young family—until Katarina's death. She mentioned once that she almost felt guilty, as if being jealous of her life somehow caused Katarina to die in childbirth. In turn, she showered as much attention on her neighbor's children as was proper, although it did not take long for her Christian duty to turn into an act of love for Hans and Hannah. She grieved for Hannah as much as we did.

Poor Dagmar. But she would not want anyone to call her poor. She was a strong woman. Not subject to vapers or fits of fancy, she insisted on managing her household and accepted help only as a courtesy to those wishing to assist her in her time of trouble. She would never take advantage of those offers or make charity a habit following Josef's death.

The congregation regularly visited in those early weeks to milk her cows and feed her chickens, she mentioned one day. They put away the farm equipment and tended the horse that was left in the field where Josef had died. For a week, no one knocked. They came into her home at will, delivering food and condolences. Neighbors poured to the Bruns' farm to offer assistance for more than a week. Then, suddenly, they vanished almost as quickly as they appeared.

Once the flurry of immediate needs stemmed, so did the well-wishers. With winter approaching, Herman, Hans, and I continued to attend to Dagmar's needs. Herman supplied chopped wood for warmth and cooking. Dagmar and I walked the path between our two places—swapping recipes, quilting winter coverlets, and sharing embroidery patterns. We also created schemes to keep Hans busy with books and building blocks. Sometimes, Herman worked in his shop, and sometimes, he looked after Josef's tools. The Bruns' and Neubauer's farms almost operated as one unit by the time Christmas neared.

CHAPTER 22

Filling the Void

*"And amazement seized them all, and they glorified God and were
filled with awe, saying, 'We have seen extraordinary things today.'"*

Luke 5:26

We settled into our new routine of traipsing back and forth between our place and Dagmar's, giving life a sense of purpose as the winter weather approached. We no longer rattled around the house, looking for projects to occupy our time. Rather than mending and pressing the bedroom curtains myself, we became a sisterhood of redecorating each room. Herman helped move larger pieces of furniture, and soon everything took on a fresher spit-and-polished appeal indoors that offset the overcast gloom outdoors. Herman and Katarina had built this house five years ago, and it was time to refresh some of the linens and update Hans' room to accommodate a growing boy.

"Dagmar, instead of tossing out some of the things we replaced around here, what do you think about sending some of the items over to the Jacksons and their friends? With winter setting in, I'm sure they could use a few things," I commented one day.

"A splendid idea. I can take some of these scrap pieces and make a crazy quilt for the children. It won't take long, since Josef bought me that fancy pedal Singer machine last year."

Dagmar gathered the box of discarded pieces and turned toward home, humming to herself with purpose.

A few days later, she reappeared, holding a small quilt for the two Jackson children to cuddle, along with a few other scrap quilts.

"My, Dagmar. You are a wonder. You must have done nothing else but sew since I saw you on Monday." I ran my hand over her haphazard layout of intersecting angles and mismatched patten—a design the children would love. "How about we deliver them tomorrow? That will give me time to bake something delicious today to take along. We can make it an early Christmas gift."

Dagmar folded the quilts and placed them into a box. Before she could leave, Herman met her in the doorway.

"What do we have here?" he asked, nodding toward the box.

"It is not for us," I answered. "Dagmar made some scrap quilts for the Jacksons, and we thought we'd deliver them tomorrow, if that is okay."

Herman scratched his head. "I'd better go along. Two ladies should not travel to Wann Junction without some protection."

"It is not far," Dagmar answered. "We won't get lost, if that's what you are worried about."

"I bet both of you have a better sense of direction than that, but I still think I should go since that area is not always safe."

"The Jacksons would never hurt us," I retorted.

Who did Herman think he was protecting us from?

"The Jacksons are not the only ones out there, Lena. It amazes me how little you seem to know about mankind. I am surprised you made it all the way here from Germany without an escort."

I hadn't. I'd had Karl, but I knew better than to voice that thought aloud. I was not as naïve as Herman seemed to think, but if he wanted to escort us, I had no problem with that. So, Dagmar agreed to return in the morning for the ride over to Wann Junction.

*T*he wind howled on the ride to the Jacksons' with its early warnings that winter approached. Dagmar and I cuddled with Hans in the shawls and blankets, while Herman managed the wagon. I was glad he was there to drive the wagon while we warmed ourselves. Big brothers had their uses.

Smoke billowed from the chimney of the Jacksons' makeshift home. Luella appeared in the doorway as our wagon pulled up to the front porch as if she were expecting visitors.

"Mercy. Why yo travelin' in dis windstorm? Scoot yo'selves in here, ret now."

Everyone followed orders as we scrambled off the wagon trying to keep hats, shawls, and hair from flying away.

Herman grabbed the closed box from the wagon, and I retrieved the freshly baked bread I had made for the occasion. As we walked inside their one-room home, I noticed the room was arranged as we had found it before—a bed on one side for the parents and a bed for the children on the other. A rough-hewn common table sat between them. On the opposite wall was a fireplace next to a shelf for meal preparation supplies and food bins of dried beans and lentils.

Hans plopped down beside Jasper and his sister, who sat on the floor near the fire, moving dust on the floor around with a stick.

"Hi! What ya doin'?" Hans asked.

"I'm writin'," Jasper offered, pointing to the squiggles on the floor by his sister.

"Dat's not writin'. Dat's just scribbles. Here, let me show you."

Hans reached to take the stick, but Jasper pulled it away.

"Is too writin'. You think I don't see writin' b'fore?"

"Aunt Lena taught me to write my name. Let me show you. You have to use letters to write."

Jasper slowly relinquished to see what Hans would show him with it. Hans snatched it from him before he could change his mind and started to draw shapes next to Jasper's designs in all capital letters.

"Look. Dis is an *H*, den an *A* and *N* and an *S*. Dat spells my name—Hans."

Jasper studied the letters that did not resemble his scribbling.

"Kin yo spell my name?"

Hans shook his head. "I don't know. I started to learn only my letters. Do you know what it starts with?"

Jasper shook his head but still wanted to be a member of this writing society. "Don't worry. We can ask my aunt Lena. I am sure she will know."

As the boys talked, Luella gingerly opened the box Herman set on the table before the ladies even offered it to her and started touching the brightly stitched fabric.

"My, what you bring wif you? Dese are so pretty."

"Dagmar made dem for da *kindern*. We had some spare material, and we tought dey might enjoy dem for vinter."

Luella hesitated to take the quilts out of the box as she pinched her nose to fight back tears. I quickly added, "You can consider dem an early Christmas present. I also did some baking before we left. So, here is some fresh bread for you."

"Now, you ain't lookin' on us as some charity case, are you?" Luella asked, stepping back and crossing her arms.

"Of course not. We're just trying to use some of our unused things. I never had a chance to say *danke* for da lovely wreath you left for Hannah. It was so kind of you, and I wanted to say *danke*."

"I was heartbroken when I heard what happened to your Hannah. It was the only thing I could think to do to ease your pain. I'm glad you liked it." She stepped forward again. "The young'ns will love dese. I might tuck 'em away for Christmas. It will be nice to have a surprise for 'em."

Hans tapped me on the elbow. "Aunt Lena? Can you help Jasper spell his name?"

Dagmar interrupted. "Hans. Why don't you let your aunt visit with Mrs. Jackson for a bit? I can help you and Jasper with your letters."

Until then, I had not noticed how Dagmar had watched the boys' writing exchange while I spoke with Luella about the quilts. Dagmar was more than anxious to interact with the children. She placed Jasper's sister, Flora, on her lap and played teacher while Herman and I visited with Luella a while longer.

"Is Willie around?" Herman asked, searching the room empty of male companionship.

"Sorry, he's workin' at the railyard today. Yous just got me and the young'ns."

Luella shrugged, and Herman resigned himself to one of the few chairs in the room to listen to the chatter of children and women until we headed home. Thankfully, the winds subsided by the time the sun sank low in the sky for the late afternoon ride back to the farm. The warmth of friendly fellowship and gift-giving sparked more holiday spirit in the whole family as Hans broke out singing "Jingle Bells," a new song he had heard in town. The catchy tune had us all joining him, which increased the merriment all the way home.

※

A few mornings later, Dagmar appeared at our door with boxes of extra Christmas decorations she and Josef had brought from Germany when they had first arrived.

"Most of these were wedding gifts," she said, as she placed the armload of boxes in the front room.

Each box held many seasonal wonders. She lifted out a rough-hewn stable with a partially thatched roof that left areas open to the sky. Years of use had worn some of the small compartments bare. Although only fifteen inches wide, the creche filled the room with Christmas hope. It needed to be displayed in a special place.

Dagmar positioned it on a side table Herman had created the previous winter. In the spring and summer, this spot held fresh-cut flowers; but the vase was tucked away for the winter, and it sat empty now. The side table welcomed the handsome creche as if it were made for this occasion, and the tough edges offset the high gloss-polished stand Herman had made for that place in the room.

Next, Dagmar retrieved an embroidered cigar box lined with a soft cloth from her treasures. In it lay wood-carved Nativity figures. Dagmar gingerly took out each one and held it a moment before placing each piece in and around the stable. Joseph stood five inches tall over a kneeling Mary.

A couple of camels accompanied the three regal magi, who bore their gifts of gold, frankincense, and myrrh for Baby Jesus. Dagmar placed the donkey near the demure Mary as his reward for carrying her to Bethlehem. On the other side of the creche, she placed shepherds, staffs in hand, to guard the few sheep that accompanied them. Dagmar left the tiny figure of Baby Jesus in the cloth-lined box instead of placing it in the small manger.

Hans, eyeing each piece and itching to touch them, knew better than to disturb the carefully laid-out scene. Puzzled, he asked the most obvious question. "Where is Baby Jesus?"

"We do not put Baby Jesus in the manger until Christmas Eve, Hans. We must wait for Him to arrive as the shepherds and wise men did."

Hans began to understand the arrangement's significance and continued examining the characters Dagmar had shared with our family.

"Now, Hans. You must remember. These are not toys. Even though they are wooden, they will break, and we are only to look at them to remind us what Christmas is all about."

Hans watched Dagmar with wide eyes and nodded. There were more items in the larger box, and we awaited the other wonders Dagmar would share. The next box she extracted from her wares held a three-tiered, wooden carousel-like pyramid. She assembled the topside capstan with many small, wood slats, replicating the angel's wings or propellers circling above the structure. At the base, four planks jetted out with small, concave bowls, where Dagmar placed small candles in each.

The main floor displayed Mary, Joseph, and Baby Jesus. On the other side of the same level, the wise men carried their gifts. The second tier held shepherds, watching their sheep by night. The top level held three angels blowing trumpets to Heaven. The ornately carved figures with brightly painted robes and faces were framed by the bare oak pyramid.

"Oh, Dagmar, I've never seen anything like this."

"I grew up outside Seiffen by the Ore Mountains. After my father left the mine because of his health, my family began carving wooden toys for a living. I helped make these," she said, pointing to both the creche and pyramid. "My father did all the finishing work, though. He was quite skilled. In the winter months when the snow was high, we all sat around, carving toy figures to pass the time."

Dagmar's voice trailed off with thoughts of her homeland so far away.

"Are you sure you want to leave these here? Wouldn't you like to have them at your place?"

"I am here all the time, anyway. We can enjoy them together." Dagmar turned to Hans. "I want to show you something about this *Weihnachtspyramide* that is like magic."

Dagmar struck a match and lit each candle around the three-tiered pyramid. The candles' heat rose, causing the wings above it to move in a circle around the top. The entire carousel of characters traveled around their spheres. Hans' eyes grew wider, and his mouth dropped open. Soon, the characters sped so fast that the images became a blur.

"How did you do that?" Hans finally exhaled.

"The heat creates wind energy that moves the wings above here. They are attached to a spindle that moves all the tiers on the pyramid when you light the candles."

"Someday, I can imagine you making machines like that, Hans," Herman said.

Hans spent so much time with his blocks, building castles and bridges, I knew Herman recognized his engineering heart. I imagine Hans had plans in his head to make a Christmas pyramid of his own before the day was done.

"Dagmar, speaking of wood, do you need me to check your firewood supply for the house?"

"Herman, you know I am capable of chopping my own wood. So, there is no need for you to keep such a close eye on me. I am a healthy woman and won't faint away after a little hard work."

Herman blushed. "I did not mean you are not a capable woman, Dagmar. It would not be right for me not to see after your welfare. Josef would want it that way."

"I appreciate your taking good care of me, but you should not have to tend to two whole farms. I have to decide what I will do before planting season. I'm not sure I can till and plant enough acres to make a go of it on my own. I can't expect you, or anyone else, to do that for me. You have your own place to mind."

Dagmar stared more poignantly at Herman. "I'm sorry. These are some of the things that keep me up at night. I don't want to go back to Germany because we failed here. Yet I'm not sure what God has in store for me." She shifted her focus to the window. "It is not your problem. You and Lena have been more than gracious to me. You have been like family."

"We love having you here," I said, giving Dagmar a quick hug. "You *are* family. We don't want you to go anywhere. I'd be so lonely for female company without you."

"Me, too." Herman blushed before he realized his statement said more than he intended. "I meant we love having you here. But you don't need to rush into any decisions right now. Winter is only beginning, and God has plenty of time to give you an answer to your dilemma before spring."

Abruptly, he turned and walked out of the room.

CHAPTER 23

Tis the Season

"Glory to God in the highest, and on earth peace among those with whom he is pleased."

Luke 2:14

Karl became a faithful churchgoer. I saw him every Sunday, which gave me another reason to relish worship besides the sermon message and reconnecting with the townspeople. Josef and Dagmar had always shared our pew before his death, so Dagmar continued sitting with our family. The makeshift remnant of Dagmar, Herman, Hans, Karl, and me birthed a new church family. For over a month after Josef's death, we sat in the same order, Dagmar and Karl becoming bookends for the Neubauer family.

The Christmas season had arrived, and the church was again decorated with evergreen boughs, helping to cheer our souls from the bleak outdoors. No snow had fallen yet, but the brisk winds and dark clouds threatened a storm at any time. A white coating for Christmas always provided the symbol of purity as we celebrated the arrival of the Christ Child, reminding us that He came to rid us of our sins. The Bible said it best: "Though your sins are like scarlet, they shall be as white as snow."[14]

Seeing Karl dismount his horse before services always caused my heart to flutter. Tall and strong. Wavy, blond hair escaped the jaunt of his cap, and alert and intelligent eyes searched for justice and meaning in the world. This man cared for me, but how long would he wait? How long would merely a Sunday morning rendezvous satisfy him?

Lord, I want a relationship with Karl, but I want to know that it's Your will for us to be together, I prayed one Sunday.

"Goodness knows where your mind is, girl."

Karl interrupted my silent prayer as he bound up the three steps to the church doors and gave me a quick peck on the cheek.

"What?"

I pretended not to be caught in a daydream I could not possibly share with him.

"You were looking right through me." He gave me a tug to urge me inside.

I ignored his observation and led the family to our preordained pew. Today, I was happy he did not seem to read my thoughts.

With just two weeks until Christmas, the congregation fell deeply into Advent. We sang one of my favorite hymns, "O Come, O Come Emmanuel," which soothed the aching souls that had gathered in God's house.

O come, Thou Dayspring, from on high,

And cheer us by Thy drawing nigh;

---

14   Isaiah 1:18

Disperse the gloomy clouds of night,

And death's dark shadows put to flight.

Rejoice! Rejoice! Emmanuel

We approached the end of a cruel year with the deaths of both Hannah and Josef. Gloomy clouds reinforced the sense of doom shadowing thoughts of the loved ones no longer with us. We all needed some celebration, laughter, and rejoicing.

As we wrapped our winter garments closer around ourselves and prepared to leave the church, I grabbed Herman's hand. "Herman. I have an idea. Why don't we invite Karl and Dagmar for Christmas dinner this year?"

Herman looked from Dagmar to Karl. "I suppose if they want to join us. Dagmar, does that sound like a plan for you?"

"I'm at your place daily, anyway," Dagmar said with a little wink. "I'd love to be with your family for Christmas."

I turned to Karl. "And you?"

"You don't have to ask me twice where there is abundant food and gracious company." He squeezed my hand, leaned closer, and whispered, "I'd like nothing more."

The two weeks flew by. Dagmar and I coordinated holiday dishes to cook. We pulled out favorite recipes for sweet ham glaze, a hot potato dish called *Himmel und Erde,* and stuffed cabbage rolls. I found the recipe I had brought with me from home for Eva's famous butter cake, and Dagmar created the best Spritz cookies. These aromas, along with fresh baked rye bread, filled the house. Herman kept busy in his workshop—a place forbidden to everyone else. Hans secretly

"The mare—I've been working on it for some time for you. I thought you might like it."

"Oh, I do." Hans took the cow and placed it near the Nativity donkey. "I think the cow should go right here. The two of them can be friends."

Hans had chosen the perfect place for the new animal. I gave each person a set of crocheted mittens and a scarf for the predicted cold weather. Herman made a shelf for Hans' room where his new horse and books could reside. Karl added to Hans' book collection by bringing him volumes of local Native American stories that could be read to him until he could master reading them himself. Dagmar had carved Herman and me lovely wood boxes in which to put small treasures or coins. Karl had brought chocolate treats from Alton for us all to share. The holiday was a joyous affair of mutual giving.

Karl followed me to the kitchen after we finished with the gift exchange and dinner. "There is one more present I neglected to put under the tree." He turned to take a small box out of his jacket pocket. "This is for you."

"You brought chocolates for everyone. I thought that was your gift."

I stared at the box for a moment. I almost did not want to open it since turning him away every time was too difficult. What if the box's contents symbolized a stronger bond between us—like marriage?

"Maybe I shouldn't . . . "

"Shouldn't what? Open a Christmas gift? The family has been opening them all morning. Nothing in there is going to bite you."

I released the green ribbon around the red box and found a jeweled hair comb. The dying light in the kitchen reflected the sparkle of precious gemstones arranged in a stained-glass cross pattern.

"Oh, Karl. It is magnificent. I don't know where I'd ever wear anything so glorious."

"I'm sure we can find somewhere to wear this pretty bauble. It belongs on you," he said before embracing me and then kissing me lightly on the lips. "You served a delicious meal today, Lena. I think playing hostess serves you well."

He pulled me to him again for another kiss, but I turned my head away in time for him to peck my cheek. "I don't think you know how much I want you as mine," he said as he pressed my shoulders back to take in a final look before grabbing his coat and leaving.

The Christmas glow on our celebration soon faded. The winter storms blew in with a vengeance, howling and blowing new snow into drifts against the barn and the house. After last year's disaster that had kept Herman off his feet most of the season, we did not risk any foolish trips to church or the market in the severe weather. Content to stay home and entertain each other, a well-worn path stretched between our place and Dagmar's. Herman cleared it often and constructed rope courses that led us from one home to the other if conditions soured.

Each week, the question that hung over us dampened our joy in each other's company: Would Dagmar sell the farm and move away? She tutored me like an older sister on matters of sewing, cleaning, and cooking. My mother never spent that much time fine-tuning the art of housekeeping. Hans listened to her like another mother figure, and Herman loved her masterful meals.

Lord, is it selfish to keep Dagmar here for my sake? What is best for her?

One bright Sunday in late January, the weather heralded deceptively spring-like conditions. The sun beat the drifts back, and the skies returned to a happy blue. We headed to church while the heavens welcomed us there.

Dagmar, Herman, and I rode on the wagon seat, while Hans lounged in the back. Herman handled the reins while we enjoyed the close company. Our breaths circled us in the brisk air, but because we were bundled tightly in our wraps and muffs, the ride charmed our senses. We arrived at church, where other congregants welcomed the weather outing as much as we did. The sanctuary filled with exuberant singing voices.

My heart leaped when it saw the only person I hoped to find in worship. Karl sat in our family pew, waiting. I steadied my gait, denying the run my heart urged after weeks of absence. I neared the pew, one measured step at a time, as he stood to greet me.

Karl had stayed away from the farm since Christmas, and I saw a stubble beard covering his face below his piercing blue eyes. Sadness crept into his smile, and I wanted to ask the cause; but the opening hymn began, and the question went unasked.

Karl did not look my way the entire service. He sang the hymns while facing the altar, recited the litanies and prayers to himself, and sank into his thought during the sermon. My worry mounted.

I anxiously finished singing the closing hymn, "Now Thank We All Our God," as I waited to learn of Karl's distress. When I placed my hand on his sleeve, he leaned toward me and whispered, "I need to talk to you privately for a few minutes."

Privately? At church? Where could we go for privacy here? More churchgoers attended church today than on an average winter Sunday because of the break in the weather, and groups formed around us to catch up on the latest happenings. The gathering blustery winter winds made the outside an undesirable option. My mind raced for a solution.

"I'm sure the Stolzes would allow us to use their shop for a few minutes."

"They are nice people, but we must be careful that this does not turn into a Sunday dinner invitation." Karl chuckled. "I guess it doesn't hurt to ask."

"Give me a minute, and I'll be right back."

I shuffled through the congregating ladies to Frau Stolz. She and Frau Zimmer were exchanging ideas for the best sauerbraten recipes.

"*Guten tag*, ladies."

"*Guten tag*, Lena. How are things at the Neubauer stead?"

"We are fine, *danke*. Greta, I have a favor to ask."

I paused to allow Frau Zimmer to finish her discussion and walk away, but she lingered to hear my request.

"Anything, my dear. What do you need?"

"Karl." I paused again. Did I need to mention Karl in this request? I could have asked to use her shop for a minute without bringing his name into the discussion, but his name had escaped me before I realized it, and it now hung between us. I looked back at the puzzled ladies, realizing I had answered her "What do you need?" question with "Karl." How embarrassing.

"Yes? Karl what, dear?"

"Karl and I need a place to talk for a few minutes. I wondered if you'd allow us to use your shop. We won't be long."

Greta Stolz winked. "Private time, huh? Of course. Take all the time you need. I'll tell Helmut to let you in."

I predicted she would read more into my question than I intended. Frau Zimmer would likely have me married to Karl by the end of the day after she overheard my request. No time to worry about that now. I weaved my way through the dwindling parishioners back to my family and Karl.

Herman and Dagmar had visited with the Bartels in the pew behind us while I searched for Frau Stolz.

"Herman," I said, "Karl and I need to talk a minute. We will be over at the Stolzes for a little while."

Herman scowled, but Dagmar touched his shirt sleeve, nodded at him, and mouthed, "Let it go" before he could utter his disapproval.

Hans braved the wind with other boys and practiced hurling snowballs at them beside the church. Karl and I ducked one missile as we rushed over to our private shelter.

Helmut unlocked the door, and once inside, he left so we could have the privacy we had requested.

"Now, will you tell me why you would not look at me in church? What is going on?"

"I have some bad news." Karl hesitated to continue.

"Out with it. What news?"

Arranging for the clandestine meeting had left me breathless and impatient for whatever Karl intended to tell me.

"I am being relocated to Springfield. Some of the documents our office sends to the state capital are not being filed properly. It may be that some are not arriving there at all, and we need someone at that end to assure all we do here is legally represented at the statehouse."

"Can't someone else do it?"

"Not at this time. The other men have families, and I may be there for some time before I come back here."

"Some time? How long do you think?"

I shuffled my feet and tried not to look devastated about his departure. There had been times in the past year when I had not seen him for months at a time, but I looked forward to our Sunday greetings, even if that was all we had between us.

"It may take months to straighten this out. I leave Tuesday. I'd hoped you'd be at church today, but if you were not here, I had planned to come out to the farm to tell you I was leaving."

"Leaving? You make it sound so permanent."

"I think we should think of it as permanent. If Herman ever lets you leave his farm, find a nice young man around here to marry and settle down with him. I cannot keep coming to see you when there is no immediate future for us."

"You can't mean that."

I leaned into his chest, and Karl stroked my hair.

"Lena, I don't think you know how difficult it is for me to be with you and not make plans for us. We cannot stay in limbo forever. I think we should break things off and go our separate ways. Me being sent to Springfield is probably a blessing. I need distance from you to keep my sanity."

"I knew it wasn't fair to ask you to wait for me. I never thought you'd go away, though." My unwarranted tears trailed down my cheek. "I don't want to say goodbye."

"It is time." Karl pushed me away from his familiar green jacket. "Please tell Hans and Herman goodbye for me. I'm sure Herman will be relieved."

Before I knew it, Karl had disappeared through the door before the wind closed it behind him again. I stood alone in the room, stunned. What had happened? I stepped outside, and the invigorating morning chill now froze my soul. My cloak felt paper thin, and my muff itched like straw. I almost dared the boys to hit me with a fresh snowball to shake me from my despair. A blast of snow might revive my senses. But the youths threw clear of the adults as singularly their parents called the lads to return home with them.

I followed their lead and called Hans to climb into the wagon. "I'll get your papa and Dagmar from the church so we can go."

I entered the sanctuary and gestured for Herman.

"Hans is in the wagon, and we are ready to go." They said their farewells and followed my urging so we could plod our way home.

As we traveled in silence, Herman and Dagmar shrugged and shook their heads when they thought I did not notice. Dagmar finally braved the question.

"What did Karl want to talk to you about?"

"He is leaving. Moving to Springfield. I will never see him again."

"Springfield? That's not the other side of the world. There is a train to Springfield, making it less than a day's journey," she said.

"No. He told me it was over. I can settle down and marry someone else when Herman doesn't need me anymore."

Dagmar sank further into her seat. "I'm so sorry." She placed a sympathetic hand on my arm, but I kept my hands in my muff, staring ahead.

The ride home was eerily silent.

CHAPTER 24

New Horizons

"Through him we have also obtained access by faith into this grace in which we stand, and we rejoice in hope of the glory of God. Not only that, but we rejoice in our sufferings, knowing that suffering produces endurance, and endurance produces character, and character produces hope."

Romans 5:2-4

Hans galloped his Christmas horse up and down the stairs until he collapsed on the couch. His joy did not transfer to me, however. Instead, I stewed in my juices for days as Dagmar took charge around the kitchen during my emotional absence. One day, she hung the dish towel to dry and slid her arm into one coat sleeve, preparing to leave when Herman cut her off at the door.

"Dagmar, I want to show you something in the barn if you please."

I wondered what this was all about. Herman had not let anyone in the barn since before Christmas. But Josef was gone, and I was not much company. He might as well take Dagmar to the barn for a secret rendezvous. Secret rendezvous? That made it sound like they were out there holding hands in a love match.

Could they be? How had that thought crept into my h. The image of them together came into focus. Dagmar was a great ͡n, and she was so congenial and helpful. They would make a great m͡.

Thankfully, Hans bounded onto the couch next to me, and shook the silly ideas from my head.

"Hans! You know better than to jump on the couch. Calm down."

I peered through the frosty window to see if I could see Dagmar and Herman. Nothing stirred outdoors except dancing snow flurries gathering on the porch. I retrieved a book on the side table to distract me. It was one of Herman's farming books, and it held no interest for me, so I tossed it back on the table.

Voices outside drew my attention back to the window. The breeze swirled around Dagmar's skirts. Herman helped reposition her scarf more tightly around her. She clutched an ornately carved wooden cross to her breast. Herman assisted her into the carriage and took her home.

Why do they look like a married couple going for an evening ride? What had Herman given Dagmar that was so precious she had not come in to show me before they left?

Lord, why doesn't the world make sense anymore?

The weather turned nasty again. One Sunday ran into two, and the storms shrouded us in another heavy blanket of white. Herman suggested that Dagmar bring her livestock to bed with ours and stay with us for a time so she would not be alone. I rejoiced in having a woman companion, but I also watched the interactions between Dagmar and Herman more closely after my head filled with a potential love story between them.

...ey never touched, but Herman smiled more than he had the ...ious winter. Granted, he was laid up last year with an injured leg, ...it Dagmar brightened up the weary doldrums of the season. She brought colorful fabric with her, and even though it was the dead of winter, the house seemed to come alive with new pillows and stitchery. She loved to mend and clean so much. It became infectious. Hans and I joined in her endeavors, and chores became a game.

Herman tended the stock in the barn every day, but he spent far less time there than he had before the holiday. Suddenly, he was content to sit inside and read, plan for next year's crops, and instruct Hans about building more elaborate block structures. This must be the definition of domestic tranquility.

A month elapsed before we returned to the church. Herman, the faithful head of the household, had read Scripture each week to his family but had not attempted to give a pastoral message. We also missed singing with the congregation. Dagmar had a lovely voice, although she could not overpower the sour notes the rest of us offered. We sounded best when the congregation drowned out our group.

What I missed most was a handsome young man from Alton who had once attended church with us. I had not seen Karl since he said goodbye after church that day. Even though nasty weather cut us off from town for weeks, I half-expected him to appear at my door anytime. When he did not appear, I tried to hide my disappointment. Did I think he had lied to me, saying he was leaving as only a trick so he could surprise me later? How foolish to think crazy thoughts like that.

Although happy to be in the house of the Lord after so many weeks away, my mind still wandered, and I did not concentrate on the sermon. Finally, the closing hymn, "Sing Praise to God, the Highest Good," soothed my solemn days. The third verse especially lifted my spirits with godly praises.

Herman touched my arm as each row filed out of their pew and headed into the cold again after their socially obliging gossip.

"Wait." I turned and caught Herman give Dagmar a side glance. "Could you keep an eye on Hans for a minute? We need to talk to the pastor about something." He paused. "It won't take long."

Herman gave me Hans' hand, and he walked with Dagmar and Pastor Klein back toward the altar.

"What do you think that is all about?" I asked Hans.

He shrugged, and I searched for a distraction for us.

"Aunt Lena, can I play outside?"

I had almost forgotten I held his hand.

"Honey, it's cold out there. Don't you want to stay here where it is warmer?"

But for a youngster to sit in church for over an hour, Hans had reached his limit of stillness. He was eager to escape.

"He can come with me for a minute," Frau Greta said. "I might find a treat at the shop for a fine boy like you." She looked back at me and added, "The boy needs to stretch his legs, and I haven't seen you folks for a month of Sundays."

"Thank you. We'll be over to get him shortly."

"No hurry. We will be fine."

Hans was immediately out the door and ten paces ahead of the grandmotherly figure. I turned toward the front of the church where Herman and Dagmar talked in near whispers to the pastor. With heads together in serious conversation, their voices did not carry to me; but within moments, all three walked toward me. Herman clasped Dagmar's hand, and his face flushed.

"Something wrong?"

I was alarmed. Why did they need to consult the pastor in private like that? The look on Herman's face concerned me. Herman did not fluster easily, and he was clearly flustered now.

"No," Herman assured me. "We just wanted to check with the pastor about something before telling you." He shuffled his feet, looked at Dagmar. "Dagmar and I want to get married."

"What? Married!" I leaped into Herman's arms, shook him vigorously, and then turned to Dagmar. "When did this all happen? You two hardly left my sight these last months. How did you manage an engagement?"

"When I helped Herman in the barn sometimes with the animals and when he escorted me home in the evenings . . . Well, we've been talking. We didn't want to say anything in front of Hans."

"Hans? What about me? Did anyone think to tell me?" I did not know who to yell at first.

"It didn't seem fair when we knew you and Karl wanted to get married, but Herman never gave you consent. We didn't want to throw salt in your wound."

Dagmar stepped forward to calm me with another hug.

"I would like to be informed, too. I'm not a child like Hans."

I couldn't believe they had left me out of such an important event that affected me as much as anyone.

"Where is Hans?" Herman asked, when he realized his son was missing from our gathering. "I asked you to watch him."

"He's fine. Frau Greta took him to their place. He was too antsy to stand here and wait with me."

I dismissed the subject of Hans and continued with their news.

"Since we are on the topic of marriage . . . when is this happening?"

"The pastor said next Sunday after church would be fine."

"Next Sunday? But there are no flowers for a bouquet this time of year. And what about a dress?" Next Sunday meant I had no time to plan an elaborate celebration for them properly.

Herman answered, "We wanted to marry and have some time as husband and wife before spring planting. If I am to take on Josef's share, I will have to work harder than before." He blanched at his mention of Josef's name.

"Don't worry. I don't need flowers and frills. This is not the first wedding for either of us. We will keep it simple," Dagmar added. "We thought we might spend a couple of days in St. Louis afterward, if you will keep an eye on Hans for us."

"Of course. Hans and I will be fine without you for a few days. I am glad you can have some time together before planting season."

I secretly wished the wedding celebration included my nuptials. Imagine if Karl had stayed only a month longer to hear this announcement. Things could have been so different for us.

After this, I shifted all my thoughts and energy away from Karl to Dagmar and Herman. I conspired with Greta Stolz to create a celebratory meal of *sauerbraten*, potatoes, pickled beets, and carrots the following week. Frau Zimmer offered to bake them a cake from apples she had stored in their cellar. She had also kept a few decorative dried flowers from her son's wedding the previous fall, so we placed them around the altar, which we laced with red ribbons held over from Christmas.

Dagmar had purchased a new Brandenburg lace collar from Mape's Store to add to her best burgundy holiday dress. I wove a scrap of velvet ribbon through her long, blonde braid that swung down her back as she walked. During the ceremony, she held the ornate wooden cross Herman had crafted for her instead of a flower bouquet. My heart ached with joy and longing.

Will I ever marry, Lord?

After the wedding celebration in Bethel, Herman and Dagmar boarded the train to Alton to head for the short paddle-wheeler ride to cross the Mississippi River to St. Louis. Dagmar was giddy with plans to attend a concert and eat at a fancy restaurant one evening. They splurged on the extravagant fare for only one night since they saved their pennies, which they needed to join their two farms when they returned.

I was certain Dagmar would delight in experiencing the sights and smells of St. Louis and marvel at the thought of the melting pot of faces, fashions, and festivities that rural Illinois' vanilla landscape denied. But she later confided in me that a taste of city life was all she needed before the farm and the quiet life she craved beckoned them both back home.

I busied myself in the hum-drum, day-to-day farm chores in their absence. I fed the stock, kept the house tidy, cooked simple meals for Hans and myself, and tried to keep boredom at bay by reading Scripture and writing in my nightly journal.

Lord, I must keep my mind busy, I prayed one day, *or I will fall into wallowing over my plight. Will I end up an old maid in my brother's house without a man for myself? The only man I ever wanted left me, and I am alone.*

Hans' boredom evidenced itself, too. His Christmas toys lost their luster, and playing card games with Aunt Lena held no more enthusiasm than playing with rocks. I resolved that all the joy had entered the house with Dagmar these last few months. Without her, a cloud hung over our moods.

Thankful that the new Mrs. Neubauer would return with Herman in only a few days, I urged Hans to help me make a sign welcoming them home as a surprise. A few neighbors had sent wedding gifts home with us, and we organized them in the front room as a display. The project gave our minds something new to settle on, and we felt a small sense of purpose return to our dreary existence.

Dagmar and Herman reappeared as scheduled on Friday. Herman stopped in the doorway and dropped their bags to turn and carry Dagmar inside.

She gasped. "What are you doing? I walk through this door all the time. You do not need to carry me."

"You have never been through this door as Mrs. Herman Charles Neubauer before. Today, I carry my bride into her new home."

Herman slid his arm under her legs, lifted her close to his chest, and stepped inside with a single stride. Dagmar giggled as he set her back on her feet. Hans and I applauded the frivolity, and life returned to the farm.

⚜

The camaraderie Dagmar and I had established since Josef's death was different now. She and Herman became a team. They planned their future together and decided on improvements to the farm. She was more involved with the farm operation than Herman had allowed me to be. Still, I was satisfied filling in as a glorified babysitter and relegating my time to Hans.

Herman and Dagmar found a young couple new to the area, the Holztens, to rent the place that Dagmar now left vacant. The new neighbor was willing to be hired as a farm hand when Herman needed extra help. Young Daniel Holtzen apprenticed with Helmut Stolz when Herman did not need him, since Helmut Stolz had eyes on the young man to take over the butcher shop in the future.

Helmut's health and eyesight weakened more each month, which caused Frau Greta to excessively fret over him as he puttered around the shop. "You need to take a break, Helmut. Give me that order to read, so you don't ruin your eyes. That's not the right weight on the scale. Let me measure that roast," she would say.

Greta was forever at his elbow, and his patience would wear thin with her. "Get out of my way so I can do my job," he would say. He then would resign himself to rest in the back a few minutes before resuming his place at the counter. Directing Daniel Holtzen to fill orders and move sides of meat to be cut became a much-needed blessing.

At home, Dagmar was more than capable of running the Neubauer household without me around. We fell into a routine of preparing meals together and other household chores, but she managed without me well enough. Sometimes, I thought she and Herman would appreciate some privacy, so I would take a walk down by the thawing creek at the edge of the property.

One day, as Dagmar and I hung fresh linens on the line, she said, "You have been rather quiet lately. Is something wrong?"

"No. Nothing is wrong, but you and Herman don't need me here anymore, and I feel as if I am in the way."

"In the way? We love having you here. You are family."

"You can run this farm with your eyes closed. Herman is so happy to be with you, and I am sure you two would like more privacy. Maybe I should move to town and ask if Mape's needs some help or something."

"I don't think being a shopkeeper will make you happy, Lena. What you need to do is find Karl. I think your happiness lies in being with him. Did anyone tell him that Herman and I got married?"

"I doubt it. He left before you two announced your intentions, and I don't think he's been back as far as I know."

"I must tell you something. Herman and I stopped in Alton on the way back from St. Louis. I had Herman stop by Karl's law office."

"Why?"

"I didn't think it was right that we got married and you did not get the chance with Karl. I wanted Herman to check on Karl's whereabouts so you could contact him if you wanted to."

"He told me where he went, Dagmar. He went to Springfield."

"Lena, Springfield is a sizable place as the state capital. Do you know where he lives or what office he works in? If you went there, where would you look?"

"Go there? Why would I go there when he told me we would never be together again? He told me to find someone else to marry if Herman ever no longer needed me."

"That's because he thought you two could not be together. He had to move on and live his life. A man like that is a man of action and not built to wait in the background forever. I am sure Herman would give you his blessing now." Dagmar reached into her apron pocket. "This is the office where Karl works in Springfield. The firm is associated with that Mr. Lincoln you saw last fall. I am sure they will help you find him if you go there." She placed the slip of paper from her pocket in my hand. "The train runs from Bethel to Springfield. We can pay your way, and you can find him. If he is the man I think he is, he will be overjoyed that you came. You must try, Lena."

"It almost sounds like you are trying to get rid of me." I stared at the paper until tears made it impossible to read. "I have been trying to forget him since he left, but his memory invades everything I do. He may not want me to follow him to Springfield."

"Listen to your heart, Lena. If this is God's will, reconnect with Karl. If not, you always have a home here." Dagmar pulled me in for a sisterly hug.

※

I packed my carpetbag the next day, and Herman transported me to the train station while Dagmar stayed home with Hans.

"Sister, I hope you knock some sense into that man. I did not think I'd actually drive him away from you, and I am sorry for that. But remember, we love you, no matter what happens." Herman embraced me in his strong arms for a farewell hug, and I boarded the train.

The train ride left me four or five hours to stew about Karl and my destination. Would Karl be happy to discover me at his workplace? Would anyone be at the address in my hand? Where would I stay? I did not know anyone besides Karl in Springfield, and I could not stay with him, even if I did find him.

I had brought along my Bible for something to read, so I opened it to the book of Ruth—the story of a woman who lost the people she loved and followed her mother-in-law to a foreign land. Her mother-in-law sent her to seek a man to marry. Ruth had to go out of her way to get Boaz's attention to broker their marriage.

I guess this was my journey—to go out of my way to seek Karl's attention to broker my marriage with a man I deeply loved. The rhythm of the train eventually swayed me into a fitful slumber.

"Miss? Miss? Didn't you say Springfield was your stop? We are pulling into the station now." The porter startled me awake.

I had slept most of the trip. My Bible still lay in my lap, mixing the stories of Boaz and Karl in my head. With address and bag in my hand, I disembarked at the Illinois state capital.

A train porter loaded steamer trunks on a cart near the railroad platform. I approached him with my slip of paper. He paid me no attention, so I ventured to interrupt his work.

"Pardon me? Do you know where I can find this address?"

He almost ignored the query until he noticed that a lost creature stood before him. He held out his hand for my offered address and gave it a perfunctory glance.

"Certainly, ma'am. It is about only four blocks. Turn right and pass the capital building looming over there." The capitol dome rose on the horizon as the porter pointed at it, southeast of the station. "The office is a tall, brick building on your left. You can't miss it."

"Thank you."

I felt emboldened with the end of my journey in sight, so I hastened my pace and allowed the spring breeze to whip me back to life after my extended nap. The capitol building stood grand and dwarfed the three-story brick façade facing it. The Lincoln lettering marked it as the proper place to enter, and I boldly stepped through the door.

A clerk peered over his glasses from the document he hovered over. Many other papers scattered across a long table where he sat perched on a wooden stool.

"Can I help you, miss?"

He did not look at me but kept his finger on the file before him, not wishing to lose his place.

"Yes, sir. I am here to find Karl Muller."

The address paper crumpled in my hand as I tightly held my carpetbag in front of me with both fists, holding my chin high as I awaited a response.

"Do you have an appointment?" he asked, without yet giving me his full attention.

I hesitated and the owl-eyed glasses finally landed on me in full assessment. He pushed them back up his nose, and he leaned back on his stool.

"No, but I am a friend."

I shifted, uncertain what I should divulge about my visit to this stranger.

"I think he is working on the second floor, room 205. Would you like to leave your bag here, so you do not have to drag it up the stairs?"

"No, I am fine. *Danke*," I said, turning to mount the indicated stairs before I lost my courage.

When I arrived at room 205, I saw the door was ajar. I rapped three times before I let myself into the room. Karl sat at a long table similar to one the downstairs clerk occupied. His chair was turned to file a folder in the cabinet behind him, and he called over his shoulder, "Be with you in a minute."

I held my breath, bag in hand, as I waited for him to turn back around and discover me.

"Lena!" He dropped the file in his hands and stood and crossed the room in two giant steps to take me in his arms.

"What are you doing here?" he asked in our native language Then he pushed me away and asked, "Is something wrong?" He looked from me to the bag I had dropped at my side. "You came to stay? You have your bag."

"I came to find you. I brought news."

I tried to take in the man before me. His familiar green jacket was replaced by a gray topcoat over a paisley ascot, tied at the neck of a silk shirt. His rugged, handsome nature in rural Illinois had evolved into a polished businessman here at the capital city.

"What news? Lena, you are scaring me. I don't think you came all this way to say hello."

"Of course not. My news is that Herman and Dagmar married three weeks ago."

"They . . . what? Are they kicking you out?"

He furrowed his brow as if he could not comprehend such behavior in a family.

"Really, Karl? You think I came here because they kicked me out? My brother would not be so heartless, but maybe I should not be here."

I stooped to retrieve my bag and turned to leave, but Karl touched my arm to stop me. Against my resolve, tears leaked down my cheeks. Karl obviously did not want me here. What a fool I was. "I thought you left because Herman did not want us to be together. Now, he gives us his blessing, but I realize that was not the only reason you left me. You have built yourself another life here. I will catch the next train back home."

"Lena, you misunderstand. I do want to marry you. You just caught me by surprise showing up in the doorway with a bag. I didn't know what to think. I love you with all my soul. You are the only one I think about day and night, and if you will have me, I will marry you as soon as we can arrange it."

"Are you going to stay here in Springfield much longer?" I looked around the room to see if there were any signs of permanence for Karl in this place, but there was nothing of his in the room but himself.

I had difficulty meeting his gaze, and my cheeks burned red under his scrutiny.

"That's another great piece of news. I will be able to return to Alton next month. What do you think about an April wedding?"

I melted against him as his words sunk in.

"April is perfect. I love April. The flowers will start blooming, and it gives Dagmar time to create a beautiful dress and—"

"So, is that a yes?"

"Oh, Karl, I was so afraid I was being too bold coming here and that you would have found someone new or would not want me anymore. Yes, Karl, I will marry you in April."

Karl gathered me in his arms tenderly. "I will never find anyone to replace you, Lena."

Warmth flowed through me, starting in my head and rushing down to my toes as he leaned down to kiss me. His lips pressed against mine—this time with promises of a future together.

CHAPTER 25

Choice Fruits

"The mandrakes give forth fragrance, and beside our doors are all choice fruits, new as well as old, which I have laid up for you, O my beloved."

Song of Solomon 7:1

We sent a telegram of our wedding intentions to Dagmar so she could begin plotting the making of a dress. I lodged a couple days at Karl's employer's home so he could show me around the capital, and we dined at some fine restaurants. Then Karl sent me back home to make all the wedding preparations for us.

Frau Greta donated lace for my wedding dress, which Dagmar swept around the collar and the sleeves of the pale blue cotton bolt she had chosen to accent my blue-gray eyes. She tightly pulled the stays around my waist, and I suddenly had an hourglass figure like the fine ladies on the streets of New Orleans or Bremen. The only thing that mattered to me was impressing my groom when he returned and becoming Frau Lena Muller this spring.

Dagmar helped style my hair with ribbons that matched the dress. Frau Greta came through again when she arranged some early blooms from her garden and fashioned them into a petite bridal

275

bouquet. Greta also arranged for her baker friend, Gisela, to bake apple cake for the wedding and frost it with creamy white icing.

Word of our upcoming marriage spread quickly—so much so that we needed no invitations. The entire congregation attended our wedding. Hans carried the rings for the wedding, and the reception followed at the Stolzes' place. Thankfully, the spring rains evaporated that day, and much of the festivities overflowed into the garden surrounded by Frau Greta's prized multicolored irises.

Karl brought an Alton photographer to Bethel. Dagmar, Herman, Karl, and I had daguerreotypes made for our respective marriages. We posed like statues while he caught our images to keep forever. I was so excited to send Momma and Papa pictures of us. The Neubauer and Muller marriages filled our homes with such joy, especially after so much sadness last year.

Karl whisked me away to a fancy hotel in St. Louis for a few days, and we attended a concert by a beautiful soprano singer before returning to Alton, where Karl resumed his work. Karl relinquished his bachelor lodgings above a downtown storefront and acquired a home on Christian Hill, a thriving new neighborhood where many affluent citizens built homes so different from the clapboard houses found at most farms. This one boasted a brick front and a sitting veranda, facing west to watch the sunsets over the Mississippi.

"How can you afford such a nice place?" I marveled at his generosity.

"I've not had anyone so precious to spend my money on, Frau Muller, until now. I've been saving for it."

I loved being called Frau Muller. Although it was foreign to me, it sounded so perfect. Karl pulled me close for another long embrace.

The Alton home needed some feminine touches that I would happily apply after Dagmar tutored me.

By summer, Dagmar and I both carried future cousin playmates to be born in the new year.

I wrote Momma regularly about our new life in Illinois. She wrote back about Martin's studies at university, how Heidi blossomed as an apprentice seamstress, and how Thomas grew so strong that he was often hired out as labor on neighboring farms. Eva did most of the cooking for the family these days because Momma's eyesight was failing. Momma even admitted she dictated many of her letters through Martin when he was home from school. Maria, the songbird of the family, continued to be the pampered baby of the family by all accounts.

When I had set sail for America on my own, I had been fearful of my future. Yes, there had been a lot of sadness in that future—Katarina, Hannah, Josef. But all along, God had a perfect plan for all of us and had formed families through that loss and given us more love than we could ever have imagined.

Coming Soon

FOR *Love* OF HONOR
IN A LAND SO STRANGE, BOOK TWO

PROLOGUE
Headline News

NOVEMBER 1860

"Lena! Lena! You won't believe this!" The door swung open in a gust as Karl blew in, waving the *Daily Alton Telegraph* newspaper over his head.

Alarmed, Lena dashed out of the kitchen into the parlor to address her husband. "What happened? Is the town on fire? Goodness, Karl! You'll wake Johanna."

The tot, snuggled against her favorite blanket, continued sleeping on the nearby couch without a stir.

"He won, Lena! Lincoln won!"

Relieved that Karl's news did not require her immediate attention, Lena turned back to chopping carrots for dinner.

"Oh, Lena, did you ever think that the man we saw debate here in Alton a few years ago would end up being president of the United States of America?" Karl's excitement thwarted his breathing. "We have our own man . . . in the White House . . . a man who honors free men of all colors . . . not at all like Douglas . . . I was so upset when he wasn't elected to the state house after those thoughtful debates, but God must have saved him for this particular time."

Lena only half-listened to her overexcited husband, so Karl reached out and spun her around in the kitchen. "Lena, do you realize how wonderful this is?"

Caught up in the moment, Lena felt the baby gently kick; and she held her hand over her bulging stomach. Smiling up at her husband, she said, "Karl, you know I don't follow all this political news like you. But I can tell you think this is very important for us, so I am happy."

He pulled her forward, arching beyond the swell of the babe, and drank in a kiss. "Oh, Lena, I couldn't be happier. I have you, the children, and now a president that will put all this slavery oppression to rest. God is so good."

Johanna stirred from her sleep and rubbed the back of her fists into her half-opened eyes. Karl scooped her up, and she giggled and came to life at her father's notice.

"We have only great days ahead, my ladies." He spun both Lena and Johanna around in an impromptu dance. "We'll be able to raise our family here in peace and safety, Lena. Goodness, they even moved the prison to Joliet this year. What more can go right?"

December 1860

Karl pushed open the front door as Johanna ran to her daddy on chubby toddler legs. However, Karl's eyes remained on the newspaper he had brought in with him.

"Daddy! Daddy!"

Karl, pulled from his newspaper momentarily, lifted the child with one arm without missing a paragraph of reading from the treasure in his other hand.

Johanna cupped his face with her two small hands and turned him to her. "Daddy?"

Karl's gaze landed on his cherub's rosy cheeks and sapphire eyes. Her blonde ringlets mimicked her father's, although his were shorn close to his ears and hers framed her impish face. She was her father's daughter; a keen observer of her world, she absorbed the adult energy around her.

She peered into his face for a moment. "Daddy sad?"

Realizing how his mood affected his little daughter, Karl pinched her cheeks and tickled her. "Nothing to worry your pretty little head about." Starting to put her down, he asked, "And how was your day, princess?"

Johanna resisted his release and held tightly to her father with a pleading grip. "No, Daddy. I gots to tell you 'bout Cwis-mas."

"Christmas, heh? What do you know about Christmas?" He put the paper down and let Johanna chatter on about all the wonders of the season she had learned.

"Mommy said it's Jesus' birf-day."

Chuckling at her pronunciations, Karl sat her on his lap and confirmed, "That's right! And we will celebrate by singing Christmas songs at church, too."

How could anyone remain downcast when greeted at the door by this whimsical creature? He leaned close and whispered in the tot's ear, "If you are a good girl, you might get a new dolly, too."

Johanna squealed and hugged her daddy tightly.

Lena left her kitchen duties for a moment to enjoy father and daughter huddled together in the parlor. Karl was right. Life could not be any better than this. Their darling little girl would soon have a baby sibling to accompany her. Karl was a doting father and husband. The Lord showered His blessings on them every day.

Over dinner, while Johanna was busy building castles in her mashed potatoes, Karl shook his head at Lena. "The world is about to explode, Lena. *The Telegraph* says South Carolina seceded from the Union."

Puzzled, Lena replied, "I don't know what that means."

"It means that those traitors are furious that Lincoln was elected president, and they want to leave the United States and become their own country."

"Can they do that?"

"Not if Lincoln can stop them."

"Isn't South Carolina far from us? I'm not sure why you should be so upset. Surely, we won't need to worry about something happening so far away."

"I don't want to worry you, Lena. I hope you are right. But if other states decide to follow their lead, this may turn into an awful problem—for everyone."

"I'll pray that doesn't happen, then."

Lena cleared the dishes before cleaning up their potato-caked daughter.

April 1861

The rain blew in with the swing of the door, and Karl swiftly rushed in, slamming the door behind him. He held a damp edition of *The Telegraph* in his hand.

"Lena! They did it. Those scum did it. South Carolina attacked Fort Sumter, and now we'll have war!" Spitting words in contempt, he stormed into the kitchen to show Lena the headlines that turned him into a charging bull in his own household.

Lena gave the paper a cursory glance as she nudged past her raging husband to the now-squalling babe he had awakened from a fitful nap. "Karl, really. I've been trying to lull her to sleep all afternoon. And just when I finally put her down so I can get something else done, you come storming into the house like a mad man."

Jostling the three-month-old to her shoulder, Lena cooed and hummed a soothing tune to her fussy infant daughter, Dora. This baby always had some disagreement with the world. She nursed fitfully, slept restlessly, and screamed often. Dora only settled somewhat when she was held, but keeping her bundled to her mother was wearisome and restrictive while completing daily housekeeping chores. Lena's home collected uninvited spring mud, and meals became a basic fare because of the demands of the newest family member. It seemed nothing was getting done at home.

"And look . . . you scared Johanna, too." Clutching her Christmas doll on the couch, Johanna sucked her thumb.

Karl softened at the sight of his cowering princess. "Oh, honey, I'm so sorry. Daddy's not mad at you. Come here." Lifting her, Karl tossed her in the air as she squealed in delight. "That's my girl. I knew you had a smile in there somewhere."

Nestling Johanna on his lap, Karl spoke in softer tones over her head to Lena. "Six more states have joined South Carolina in leaving the Union. Lincoln is calling for seventy-five thousand volunteers to join the Northern army."

Alarmed, Lena quit stirring the pot of stew on the stove. "You aren't thinking of joining the army, are you?"

"No. I think I can help from here. There are rumblings about them opening the Alton prison again for the war effort. Plenty of legal work will be created right here, and I can contract with the military to do that without leaving you."

"Thank goodness. I was afraid you were going to leave me here with the girls." As she eased into the rocker, trying to rock Dora back to sleep, she added, "I couldn't bear that."

Placing Johanna down to scamper off with her doll, Karl kissed Lena on the forehead before she handed the dozing child to her father and turned back to slicing some bread for dinner. Karl dutifully received the child and assured Lena, "Don't worry. I plan to stay right here. This war shouldn't last long at all."

About the Author

Terri writes for church programs and events for all ages. Since retiring from teaching Language Arts, writing has been her full-time passion. She resides with her husband and two dogs in the Idaho mountains north of Boise.

Terri's German background prompted her interest in writing a story concerning the German immigrants in Southern Illinois, where she was born. Further research into the German-American culture prompted her weekly blog, Germanschatzblog.com.

You can follow Lena's family through the *In a Land So Strange* series as more of them follow their hearts to America and contribute to the growth of a nation.

Many of Terri's published Bible studies, devotions, and women's retreats can be found through the resources of the Lutheran Women Missionary League (LWML.org). One of her guiding Bible verses is, "And we know that for those who love God, all things work together for good for those who are called according to his purpose" (Rom. 8:28).

Ambassador International's mission is to magnify the Lord Jesus Christ and promote His Gospel through the written word.

We believe through the publication of Christian literature, Jesus Christ and His Word will be exalted, believers will be strengthened in their walk with Him, and the lost will be directed to Jesus Christ as the only way of salvation.

For more information about
AMBASSADOR INTERNATIONAL
please visit:

www.ambassador-international.com

Thank you for reading this book!

You make it possible for us to fulfill our mission,
and we are grateful for your partnership.

To help further our mission, please consider leaving us a review on your social media,
favorite retailer's website, Goodreads or Bookbub, or our website.

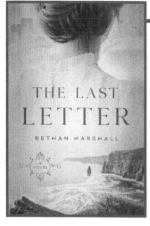

Niamh is a devout Catholic in Ireland in 1908. She has never doubted her faith, but when she joins a suffragist movement, Niamh suddenly finds herself being introduced to women from who all believe that women deserve to be treated as well as men. As Niamh begins to imagine a world where women and men are equal, she meets Fred, the brother of one of her sister suffragists. Based on a true story, *The Last Letter* is a tale of overcoming prejudice and finding love against all odds.

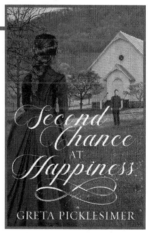

After Catherine Reed's husband dies, she moves back home in order to accept a new position as the teacher for the town's one-room schoolhouse. Samuel Harris has suffered his own loss and guilt has burdened him ever since. When his old flame comes back to town, he wonders if they can find healing together . . .

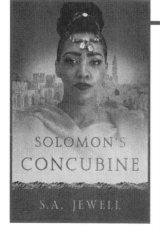

King Solomon is well-known as a wise man and the wealthiest king to have ever lived. But with great power often comes great corruption, and Solomon was no exception—including his collection of wives and concubines. But who were these women? What was life like for them in Solomon's harem? S.A. Jewell dives into a deeper part of Solomon's kingdom and shows how God is always faithful, even when we may doubt His plan.

Made in the USA
Middletown, DE
29 August 2024

59674052R00175